JARROD BLACK

GUILTY PARTY

JARROD BLACK

GUILTY PARTY

Another Unashamed Football Novel

TEXI SMITH

P POPCORN
P R E S S

First published in 2020 by Popcorn Press, a division of Fair Play Publishing
PO Box 4101, Balgowlah Heights NSW 2093 Australia

www.popcornpress.com.au
sales@fairplaypublishing.com.au

ISBN: 978-0-6481333-6-0
ISBN: 978-0-6484073-5-5 (ePUB)

Cover design and page layout by Leslie Priestley.

Front cover photograph: wilpunt (Getty)

All inquiries should be made to the Publisher via sales@fairplaypublishing.com.au

NATIONAL
LIBRARY
OF AUSTRALIA

A catalogue record of this book is available from the National Library of Australia.

Contents

CONTENTS

Chapter

To my son Zach,
one day you'll read this book.
I know you'll like it.

Chapter 1

WHISKED

The players had been given specific instructions to be at the Rosco Pronto restaurant for a 6pm sitting, no partners, no driving, no curfews and smart casual attire. Any potential fines for being late would be administered by goalkeeper Wes, although now the season was over the fines might be over too. The threat of a fine was enough to make everyone arrive in good time, and as Jarrod pulled up in his Uber, there was a throng of players at the door waiting to gain entry.

The weekend had been huge and Jarrod was still on a high. The unbelievable scenes at full time in the play off final had still not sunk in. The night in London, and the day out with the family yesterday were an absolute whirlwind. The news he had received that afternoon had knocked him sideways - he had made the Socceroos squad for the upcoming international weekend. That was followed by an emotional call from Dad to announce interest from Newcastle United in his signature.

Seeing his beautiful wife Marianne arrive back from the hairdressers in a headscarf covering a buzz cut had refocused him on what really matters. Seeing the kids' astonished reactions after coming in from school to see their Mum's new look had been priceless. This was a day that just kept on giving. Now he was out on the town, sampling his first end of season get-together with Darlington FC.

Jarrod thanked his driver Mick, one of only a handful of regular drivers in the town, and made his way over to the door. There was no big greeting when he sidled up. Those outside were impatiently jostling to get past the security on the door and into the venue. This was a modern Italian restaurant, more fine dining than pizza and pasta, and somewhere Jarrod had been keen to try since its opening last month.

The club had clearly booked out the whole venue. It was all hands on deck, the crowd having arrived seemingly all at once. The maître d' was trying his best to courteously greet them and quickly get them seated. There were round tables of six throughout the spacious restaurant. The tables looked to have been pushed close together to give a feeling of togetherness and intimacy. There was a makeshift stage with a microphone for speeches from the owner and management team.

Jarrod walked over to an empty table and took a seat. He often did that just to see how the seating arrangements worked out around him, who would be the first to join him, who would be the ones that didn't dare be on the captain's table. It was an interesting experiment in social behaviour. He liked to think that's what it was, but in reality it was subconsciously so he could sit with people who wanted to sit with him.

All the staff were there, and Pauline was first to come up. She put her hands on his shoulders and started to give him a massage. Jarrod did not put up a fight, instantly relaxing to take advantage of the soothing hands.

"Keep doing that," said Jarrod.

"It starts to cost after the first minute," quipped Pauline, moving to the seat next to Jarrod with a smile, "although you should be able to afford it after the weekend you've had."

She was alluding to the bonus payments that had been put on the table by owner Gerry Lincoln as a carrot for promotion.

"Two kids, a wife and a mortgage," said Jarrod chuckling. "Not much left after that."

They had a great working relationship, Jarrod and Pauline, and there was mutual respect. Jarrod could honestly say that he had a great relationship with the majority of the people in the room. Some of the characters were slightly over the top and Jarrod had learned to limit exposure to those players, but in the main he felt that after the crazy season they had just been through, he could not be tighter with this group of people.

The table was quick to fill up, centre forward Ghali Barbera joining the table, club photographer and all round legend Caroline Streener, coach Des Davis and finally the young superstar Connor Naughton, a player who had broken through towards the end of the season and had played a big part in the promotion push at the end. A great cross-section of the club, the conversation flowed from the beginning, right up to the point when manager Gary Hollister got to his feet and walked over to the microphone with a piece of paper.

"Ladies and gentlemen," he started with a hint of a smile, "fellow League One players and distinguished members of the club, welcome to our end of season event."

Jarrod had just been served his main, and had only taken one mouthful of his gnocchi to savour the light garlic tang of the sauce. He would do the honourable thing and leave his meal until after the speeches. That opening address had brought the room to a crescendo. The evening was off to a great start.

"Tonight is a night for celebration," continued Gary once the room had calmed down. "Please make the most of the hospitality on offer, enjoy your main course, enjoy the delightful wines on offer and our fabulous owner Gerry will address a well-fed audience later in the evening. Thank you."

This was a very short speech and Jarrod was relieved, tucking into his delicately constructed meal, trying to avoid demolishing it in five mouthfuls. He had chosen a Chianti from the wine list and wasn't quite sure what he was going to get, but the smooth flavour that washed across his tongue as he took his first sip made him sure that the table would enjoy it with him. He leaned back and intentionally bumped seats with right-back Mitch Short, who leaned back too and reached across with his arm to give Jarrod a hug.

"Hey Mitch," said Jarrod, "when are we doing our end of season awards?"

It was assumed that there would be a 'Mad Monday' affair at some stage, the players getting together out of the jurisdiction of their club officials, but no one had mentioned anything.

"Hey, could be tonight," said Mitch with an air of mystery, "we've got everything we need with us. If the timing's right …"

"Cool," said Jarrod, not having his question answered at all, "I'll be expecting to sweep the board."

Mitch let go and pushed Jarrod away playfully. Jarrod did have a good season, but it was more about consistency than flair and exuberance, the end of season awards typically reflected that.

Mains were over, glasses were charged and Gerry finally appeared at the microphone. The lights dimmed and a spotlight trained on him as he adjusted the microphone downwards to cater for the difference in size between himself and the towering

Gary Hollister. He stood at the microphone, his mere presence enough to bring the room to a respectful silence in a matter of moments. He seemed a little edgy, but started in his familiar broad and loud voice.

"This club is bigger than any of us," he started, "it will be around when I'm dead and buried, it will be around when you've all retired, it will be gone when Eleanor has served her final cup of Bovril."

There was a snigger, eyes turning to the evergreen head of catering, Eleanor, who was smiling broadly and was being embraced by Will Telfer.

"Our objective this season has been achieved. We did it the hard way, but by getting the right people in at the start of the season, thanks to the experience of Gary and the guidance of Des and the coaching team, we have been able to propel this club up the league and clinch our place in League One."

Gerry was simply stating facts here, there was no cheering or applause. He had everyone listening.

"We celebrated in style on Saturday," he continued, "and quite rightly. It was a wonderful occasion."

There was a murmur as though everyone was being coy about letting out a whoop or a holler.

"It won't be long before we're back on the training field and plotting our assault on this new division. That means we have to take full advantage of the situation we have created for ourselves."

There was a flashing of headlights in the window as night began to fall. There seemed to be a lot of movement outside with cars parking in formation out the front. Eyes wandered and the murmur grew louder.

"That's why," shouted Gerry, "that's why, we're going to take this evening and we're going to transport it back to my house and we're going to have a party."

The players and staff all looked at each other with puzzled looks, eyes widened and eyebrows raised.

"Listen up!" cried Gerry, "We have cars for everyone. Rendezvous at the Lincoln residence in 15 minutes."

Gerry stepped down from the podium and walked briskly out of the door, signalling to everyone that he was not kidding. Jarrod had been looking forward to dessert – he didn't often get dessert and this would be one of the rare times he would indulge – but he was going to be denied it this time. No time for anything in fact. There were half-full bottles of wine on the tables and glasses still charged awaiting a toast, but this was really happening, a mass exit into the warm summer night.

Each car was taking four passengers, one in the front and three in the back. All cars were the same, large black sedans with tinted windows. The drivers and some extra helping hands were making sure everyone was assigned a car. Before they even knew what was happening, the players and staff were loaded up. The cars were leaving in quick succession and at a great speed.

Jarrod's driver was smartly dressed in corporate uniform. The sleeve of his black jacket was embossed with a logo, also in black. Jarrod couldn't make it out and found himself staring at it until the light flashed on it and Jarrod could see it read 'Viktor A'. He followed the car in front, doing well over the speed limit but keeping a respectable distance. The last three corners of the ten minute journey were taken at quite a pace causing the three in the back, Jarrod in the middle, to be squashed up together. Jarrod could see ahead. The cars arrived quickly, depositing their passengers and then speeding off to be replaced by the next car.

This was a part of suburban Darlington that seemed to have a little bit of exclusivity, one road in and out, backing onto the River Tees, sort of on the way out of town, towards Jarrod's home. There seemed to be very little happening in the street, perhaps Gerry had pre-warned the neighbours that he was having a party. There was a buzz coming from the house where everyone was heading. Jarrod walked over alongside Dec Hines, both of them puzzled by what was happening, but both a little fidgety through excitement at what was ahead of them.

Chapter 2

FLYING

The party invitees were greeted at the front door by two well-dressed ladies with clipboards. The players were invited to come through the entrance, whereas the staff were ushered around the corner and into the back garden. Jarrod and Dec walked in and it was clear that they were to follow a velvet rope into the next section of what seemed to be a very grand house. There was quite a hum as they walked into the adjoining room and out into a marquee, in what would normally be a garden area.

The majority of the players were already there, though some were getting undressed. It was a most peculiar scene and Jarrod felt a tinge of unease. What the hell was happening?

"Hello there," came a friendly voice. It was another clipboard-wielding person, a middle aged man that you would expect to be taking your measurements when buying a suit. "Welcome to Gerry's house. There is one condition of entry to the party. There is only one way in and one way out, and that is through the sky."

Jarrod and Dec had been joined by a few others in listening to the instructions. That last sentence had thrown them all.

"We have sky-suits for you to wear," he continued, "so when you are ready, grab one of the blue suits and undress down to your underwear and put on the suit. We'll take your clothes and valuables and put them aside until the end of the night."

The group listening seemed to have frozen, so Jarrod, two glasses of red to the good, took the first step towards the rack of blue boiler suits and made his way over to a bench to start getting undressed. There were five or six staff on hand to assist with clothes. They were courteous when asking for earrings to be removed and mobile phones to be placed in the trays provided. It was a little like the security gate at the airport and also a little bit like the entrance to a prison, but it was the blue suits that intrigued Jarrod the most.

The suit was like an overall from the hardware shop and it was fairly loose. Jarrod handed his neatly folded pile of clothes to one of the staff members, his phone, wallet and keys in the tray on the top of the pile. This was carefully taken away, the clothes put into a plastic bag with his name written on. The bundle was placed in a big cupboard at the back of the marquee. The players who were ready were invited over to a doorway to wait their turn.

Jarrod was still unsure as to what this was, but with the whoosh of air that rushed into the room every time the door was opened, it would have to be an indoor skydiving arena. Jarrod was next and he immediately felt anxious. No time to let the anxiety get to him though. An orange-suited man came and grabbed his arm to lead the way. The noise immediately filled the hallway, making conversation impossible. The hallway opened up into a room with a glass cage, where the whistling of wind and the grinding of the generator gave it a sense of danger.

Jarrod's orange-clad chaperone walked to the edge of the glass cage and simply launched himself into the middle of the cage, as if meeting a cross with a diving header. He immediately fell to within a few inches of the ground before steadying himself and was propelled upwards into the centre of the glass cage. He was flying, as if he had just jumped out of a plane. He took a moment to turn around to face Jarrod and beckoned him to do the same.

Jarrod took one step and launched himself into the air, as if he was jumping on to a big bed. The powerful jet of wind caught him and threatened to upend him, but his orange friend grabbed his arm, keeping him horizontal as the wind pushed him up to the right height. Jarrod could feel his face flapping around, his cheeks filling with air, and his eyes drying out. It was quite a sensation, and took a good ten seconds to be able to breathe properly. Once he overcame the initial shock, Jarrod relaxed, and was invited to look out the side of the cage where club photographer Caroline was snapping away.

A big thumbs up and it was time to dismount, this time his orange friend demonstrating by stretching out his arms in front of him to head for the exit, then pulling his knees to his chest to flip vertically and simply stepping onto the floor. It looked easy. He wouldn't need to do this himself though, as he was pushed forward by the next orange-suited superhero and was caught by his friend at the door who helped him stand upright and graciously leave the arena.

He clasped hands with his instructor and they embraced. Jarrod was then instructed to follow the hallway down to the next doorway, where the noise started to subside and he could hear again once the door was closed behind him.

This was a small room, still part of the first marquee he guessed, with a doorway to a real building. He was in there with another female staff member dressed in plain black who said a cheery 'hello' before inviting him to sit down in a big barber's chair in front of a mirror, as if he was getting make up done. And it turned out that he was.

The make-up artist fixed up his hair a little after it had been blown around before applying some thick combat-style paint to his face. He had one stripe of thick black paint across his nose and two smaller stripes underneath his eyes. He looked like an NFL player. The make-up artist had clearly done all she was going to do and invited him to stand up and make his way through the door into the next building.

The change in temperature from warm to chilly suggested that he was back in the main house. When he got in there, there was a warm greeting from Gav Selley and Raynor Gunn, who had both been given the face paint treatment and were full of life after their own sky diving experience.

"Oh my god," said Jarrod, "what is this?"

"Ha ha, I have no idea, Jay," said Gavin, coining a rarely used nickname, "but after Saturday night in London, I didn't think Gerry could up his game any further. What a man!"

Jarrod surveyed the surrounds, his eyes were immediately drawn to an impressive ice sculpture. Raynor grabbed his arm and pulled him over, like a young child keen to show his favourite uncle something new.

"You have to see this!" he said.

Chapter 3

EXHIBIT

This was effectively a working bar, and there was a menu with only two drinks, a bramble martini or an elderflower gin fizz. The three of them huddled around before Raynor asked for the elderflower drink.

The barman poured a shot of gin into a small glass, not much bigger than a shot glass, and invited the big central defender to pour the liquid into a trough that had been carved in the slightly blue ice. The gin trickled down the ice and into a longer trough next to the words 'League Two' carved meticulously into the ice. Small blasts of air from the sides of the trough then propelled the liquid up the long channel and through the 'O' of 'League One', where it cascaded through three levels of waterfall and into a large cocktail tumbler.

A second barman was then on hand with a ready mix of cocktail and poured the remaining mixture of ingredients over the gin. He invited Raynor to pick up his drink after it was adorned with a slice of lime and a splash of champagne. The glass was frosted up, ice-cold and the rim was coated with small crystals of crushed ice. This was living!

Jarrod moved in next and, just for the hell of it, ordered the other drink. After a similarly grand experience, the barman completed the drink and Jarrod took his glass, savouring the icy rim and the delicious blackberry flavour. They had been joined by more players in their blue suits and warpaint and they were fascinated by this spectacle. Jarrod slipped away to see what else was going on, Dec catching up with him.

"What *is* this?" he exclaimed.

"This," Jarrod replied, "is pretty cool."

They walked over to the corner of an immense room. Probably a living room, he thought, with all the usual furniture removed. More staff were circulating with trays of exotic finger food - oyster shots and sushi rolls - Jarrod couldn't help himself from trying some of the fluffy white rice rolls. A tuna and cucumber filling transported him back in time to grocery expeditions to the local shopping centre, back in the cultural melting pot that he still called home back in Sydney. Jarrod moved on, unable to stop himself after catching a glimpse of the next artiste.

Jarrod had been to a party years ago, where businessmen ate delicacies from the near-naked body of a model. He thought at the time it was odd, but it was definitely a conversation starter. This time though, he could only think that this was a personal touch by Gerry – this was a model, a plus-sized model, lying on a table with her arms above her head in a Picasso-like pose. She appeared to be naked, but covered with patisseries in all the right places, exquisite chocolate torte slices, petit-fours and meringues lined up on her midriff.

The temptation was definitely there to press his ice-cold glass against her thigh, but he'd rather leave it to one of the younger guys to make that comedic move and deal with the aftermath and embarrassment of potential spillages. Instead he settled for a cheeky 'Hi' and a wink as he wandered past.

Connor bumped into Jarrod, craning his neck as he walked past the pastry queen, and didn't feel the need to apologise, such was the peculiar mood – it really felt like a place where anything goes.

What appeared to be the other main spectacle on show in the room was a large tank with fish in it. Jarrod and Connor stood there for a moment working out what this was. The attendant spoke up, handing Connor a fishing rod, the hook already laden with bait so that there would be no unwanted fish hands.

"You get one chance," said the attendant. He turned and flicked a switch which opened a plug on the side of the tank, causing water to rush out and into an adjoining swimming channel. The surge of water created a force and sucked out one of the unsuspecting fish into the swimming channel, where it was clear that there was a current. The fish was propelled along the channel and into a wide tank where it swam around confused for a moment.

"Here's your chance," said the attendant, giving Connor a suggestive raise of the eyebrow. Connor was straight in with the hook and the fish sensed it, flapping around furiously and taking a chunk of the bait.

"C'mon, c'mon," pleaded Connor as Jarrod looked on, other players coming over to see what the commotion was. By the time the fish had been pushed further along the channel by a rush of water and into a second tank at the end, Connor had turned the room blue with his Irish cursing, the crowd roaring with laughter as Connor's face turned red with a mix of frustration and embarrassment. He had to admit it was funny though, this looked like a great game.

"No points," said the attendant calmly.

"Come on," said Connor, "give us another go."

"Get out of it," said Sam Basaan, lifting the rod carefully out of his hand, making sure not to fling the bait and the hook around the room, "England against the rest of the World – come on England!"

A surge of water from the tank caught another fish in the flow and it was game on. Sam danced the bait around frantically and dragged it right in front of the fish's mouth. The attendant busied himself transferring the other fish back into the big tank and found himself staring at the stand-off. There was a sudden snap of the rod and out came the line, fish and all to an almighty cheer. One-nil to England.

The players looked around for the next non-Englishman in the group as Caroline appeared with her camera and snapped Sam with his prize catch. Jarrod finally reminded everyone that Sydney was not a suburb of Birmingham and snatched the rod playfully from Sam, the attendant removing the fish carefully from the hook and adding another piece of bait to the hook. The whole squad was now engrossed.

Jarrod had no luck, the fish ignoring his gallant effort, England maintaining their one point advantage as Mitch took the spotlight to press home the advantage. Jarrod loved the fact that you could put his teammates in any situation and they could find something to have a competition over.

The lack of club staff in the room they were in started to raise a few questions. Jarrod and Gav chatted as they marvelled at the making of their second cocktail, affirming with each other that there was something even bigger coming tonight. Caroline was the only member of staff to have been in the room, and now even she was gone.

The cocktails continued to flow, and even the teetotal Ghali

Barbera was joining in, studying with fascination the jets of air as the vodka was blown up the ice channel. Roni Verelo and the rest of the guys were conversing with the patisserie model they had dubbed 'Greggsy'.

One of the barmen had left his post and walked over to the centre of the room wheeling a large gong. This was probably one of Gerry's artefacts from his travels in some far Eastern land. He gave an almighty bash on the gong which made a deep rumbling sound that sent vibrations around the room. It definitely got their attention.

"Gentlemen, thank you for visiting our playground," he said. "At the second and final beat on the gong, the door through which you entered the room will open."

All eyes turned to the doorway over near the ice sculpture.

"You will all move through into that room where the club has arranged some new clothing for you all. Thank you, we'll see you all again very soon."

The second beat indeed heralded the opening of the door and the players cautiously made their way through into the small room where they had received their face paint. The make-up artist had gone, and in its place was a clothes rack of dinner suits, white shirts, bow ties and cummerbunds, each one with a leather name tag with a player's name.

This was no cheap tat either, Gibson & Brookes the name on the coat-hangers which Jarrod instantly recognised from his time at Gateshead. Underneath were shoe boxes, again all named with a pair of black socks attached to the lid. There were three male staff members, all in black, and all keen to get the players ready and into their attire for the next part of the evening.

"This is amazing," said Wes, flicking through the rack until he found his name.

"I can't quite believe this," said Freddie Asquith as he opened the shoe box to discover a pair of silver cufflinks in one of the hand-stitched leather brogues.

"Don't forget to thank Gerry," said Jarrod in a quiet moment, "he's gone to town on us."

The intimate space was like a changing room at one of the smaller grounds they had visited this season. Jarrod was impressed to see the now famous photo of the fans celebrating the win at Luton Town had been hung on the wall above the row of mirrors.

The players checked each other over, Roni brushing off some stray strands of thread from Connor's collar and straightening his bow tie. There was even a small table of hair products available, although only a couple of the players indulged, Jarrod having opted for a quick spray of a communal deodorant before putting on his shirt.

They all still had their warpaint on too, the staff explained that it would take a little bit of getting off at the end of the night so better wait until then. The room finally had a bit of order, a bin in the corner was full of paper from the folded shirts and empty shoe boxes, while a laundry basket was now full of blue boiler suits.

The last of the players preened themselves in front of the mirror, a quiet began to descend on the room. There was a murmur coming from behind the door they had come through, lots of chatter and some jazzy music starting up. The staff members arranged the players in two lines as if they were going into the tunnel for a game. One of them reached for the door much like the introduction of a contestant on *The Voice*. The noise hit them. The sound of a trumpet heralded the entrance of the main guests. The door was opened fully to amazed looks from the players.

Chapter 4

PARTY

The door was open. There was no referee to lead the players out, so the two at the front looked at each other and, with a nod of the head, Will Telfer and Gav Selley led the two lines out with a beaming smile into the dimly lit area near the ice sculpture.

"Welcome the players of Darlington FC!" came the voice of the Matchday announcer who had a small pedestal in the corner of the room. It was lit with a beam of white light from above. He was going to be the MC for the evening and was dressed for the big occasion.

There was a huge cheer as the players made their way out, all looking absolutely magnificent in their brand new tailored dinner suits. The facepaint accentuated the look, they looked like the tightest bunch of players you could ever meet. They were met by a staff member with a headset. As the applause rang around the room, the players were directed over to four huge tables in the middle of the room.

The area had undergone the quickest makeover in the twenty minutes since the players had been in there enjoying fishing, cocktails and pies. All the 'performers' had gone, the fish tank had gone, only the ice sculpture remained. It had been carved up into two pieces containing the logos of League One and League Two, the former now with the words 'Play Off Winners' underneath and the latter with 'Welcome to' above it. The two pieces were at either end of a full bar that had either been assembled in record time, or had been wheeled in. The bar had a crowd of thirsty party-goers around it, including Darlington staff members. Everyone had turned around and were enjoying watching as the snappily dressed players found their seats to light-hearted heckles and cajoling.

Jarrod found his seat on one of the four tables, all of which were at right angles to an ever-so-slightly raised stage, craftily positioned so that no-one would have their backs to the action. The bar area was at the other side of the room, again no one with their backs to it, and the conversation restarted at the bar as some light Ibiza-style jazz music kicked in.

Once all the players had found their allotted seats, it was obvious that they were only half of the guests, and that the room would be seated alternately with a player then a guest. Three members of staff began to approach partygoers to direct them to their seats, and Jarrod was keen to find out who they were. There were spaces for about fifteen, filling in the gaps, and Jarrod recognised a few faces.

Female boxing champ Nicole Madejski, a local legend in these parts, was the first person that registered, although it took him a moment as she wasn't in boxing gear. Then his eyes trained on Andoni from light entertainment TV duo Murat and Andoni. Former TV star and Geordie crooner James Tack was guided to the tables, looking delighted to be sitting between larrikins Wes and Dec. Former Newcastle United star Alfonso Barolo, the saxophone-playing Chilean midfield maestro, was next to take his seat, as former Belgium playmaker and ex-Boro player Giuseppe

Rolando was also walked over to his place.

Jarrod secretly hoped that Sherri Schoular, a girl band member and an absolute stunner, would be seated next to him. He was disappointed to see her get a spot next to Gav, with actor and local star Jackie Tuppens sitting opposite her. There were lots of people left at the bar, journalists from the local media, and all the staff from the club. It was clear that they were going to remain at the bar as there were only four or five seats remaining. Jarrod was on a seat at the end of the row and had a spare seat next to him, with Raynor next seat over. Opposite there was another empty seat next to Ghali. They looked at each other with shrugs and puzzled looks.

Jarrod took a peek at the menu. It was all sweets. He could feel the saliva forming in his mouth as he read down the list of items that would make up a dessert tasting plate. This was pure decadence, but first he thought he'd better grab a drink of water and made sure he gulped down a glass before refilling from the jug and skulling half again.

There was slight confusion as the players gingerly thought about starting conversation. There was barely a moment before the lights went down and a beam of light trained on the entrance where the players had just come through moments before.

"Players and staff from Darlington," started the MC, "we are joined this evening by the most ardent fans who have been specially selected to join us for our celebrations."

"Fans who you may know," he continued with gusto, "supporters who cheer you on week in, week out, win, lose or draw. Please make each one of these people welcome as we introduce you to individuals who devote their time and hard-earned dollar to follow the Darlington cause."

There was a sense of anticipation, and all eyes turned to the entrance.

"Marcus Tanninstall," announced the MC as if he was reading the team sheet at the start of the game, and the partygoers responded with a loud cheer as a youthful but very well-dressed Marcus stepped into the light. "Marcus has been to every first team game home and away this season, including all of our friendlies. Welcome to the party, Marcus."

The fan was invited to the table but via a long winding route to shake all the hands of his idols, and some of the celebrities he recognised. He took his seat next to Freddie. Freddie reached across and put his arm around him to welcome him to the table.

"Erwin Foster," came the next name, again to a big cheer as he stepped out into the spotlight. "Erwin is an expat living in Tokyo, a former season ticket holder through the darkest of days. This season he has flown back to the UK to attend eight games, including the final just a few days ago."

There were nods of approval from players and staff alike, and he got a lot of love as he circumnavigated the tables to find his seat.

"Miriam Kennedy!" was the third name, and the middle-aged woman stepped into the light looking a little coy, but looking very happy to be at the party. "Some of you will know Miriam as the unofficial supporter of our Under 18s team. Since her son played in the Under 18s nearly ten years ago, she has been hooked and travels to all the games, sometimes on the team bus, and helps give the boys guidance in a volunteer capacity."

Miriam made her way straight to the space next to Connor, who would have been playing in that team earlier in the season and gave him a big hug from behind. Connor got to his feet to turn and continue the embrace.

"Two more empty seats to fill. We have a superfan next. Alex Horsley!" Again, a loud cheer, but that increased as Alex stepped into the light. The majority of players recognised him as the guy who was always there to greet them off the bus at away games. "Alex has not missed an away game in eight seasons, and that was only when he broke his leg in a completely non-alcoholic injury on the way to a game in Swindon."

Alex punched the air and gave a shout of his own as the party welcomed him to the room. He found his seat next to Jarrod. Jarrod was compelled to put his arm around his shoulder, but stopped short of a hug. The sixty-something-year-old Alex seemed to appreciate the restraint.

"And finally," said the MC, "I'm sure that most of the players and staff who have been with the club for a few years will know this fan … Jill Skene." The biggest roar was saved for Jill. She was a forty-something lady and Jarrod did know her, simply because someone pointed her out one week, saying that she was at every home game – never sat down, always stood up. "Jill has been at every home game, league, cup, friendly, since the club reformed all those years back, and she is a club legend. Welcome Jill, we hope you enjoy the hospitality of the players and this fine venue this evening."

As Jill finally got to her seat behind Jarrod, the lights slowly brightened. Gerry appeared and took the seat opposite to no fanfare whatsoever. A sea of waiters then pounced on the tables as the jazz grew a little louder and dessert wines were placed at every setting. A tasting plate of dessert classics was served. Jarrod didn't hesitate to grab one of the crème brûlées, totally non-negotiable, before offering the plate to those around him and starting conversation.

The waiters then produced a big round glass for each place, pouring in a generous shot of an apple-smelling liquor that reminded Jarrod of a trip to Normandie he'd had with Marianne a few years ago. The conversation flowed. Jarrod was fascinated with superfan Alex, and he seemed to have a photographic memory of events that he had forgotten himself.

"You were lucky to stay on the field," said Alex, referring to a rainy Friday night game at Colchester early in the season when Jarrod managed to slide for over 20 metres in the damp conditions, collecting the last man with his leg and nudging the ball away inadvertently with his hand when the striker would have had a clear run at goal.

"Wow," said Jarrod, "I'd forgotten about that."

"And Ghali," he said turning to face the Darlington striker, "how did you squeeze in that goal at Oxford?" This was reference to a mazy dribble that took Ghali to the byline before realising he had no support and firing off a shot from a ridiculous angle that took a deflection, hit the post and then cannoned in off the goalkeeper's knee.

"That was on target and I'm claiming it," laughed Ghali and they all had a good chuckle.

The evening was going so well, the guests at the bar were loving it, the guests at the tables were being treated to some amazing food and drink and there was a real buzz about the place. And Jarrod was worried that he hadn't got his dessert back at the restaurant in town.

Chapter 5

MOVIES

The waiters appeared and cleared away the dessert plates, replacing them with platters of individual chocolates, all spaced out for effect. Jarrod noticed the name 'Viktor A' embroidered in white into the white lapel of the waiter. Must be some big corporate event company, Jarrod thought.

The division between bar-goers and sit-downers was getting rather blurred as conversations grew rowdier, the staff members eventually doing the rounds to send people gently back to the bar area as the lights brightened slightly but noticeably. The wait staff began to clear away the last of the food, leaving only their drinks and water on each table.

The dimming of the lights again signalled the next part of the party, and a huge projected screen flickered to life behind the stage. There was clearly going to be some sort of presentation. Jarrod could feel a breath of fresh air as a gentle hum brought oxygen into the room via some sort of electric fan.

A movie burst onto the screen. The title sequence started with 'A Day To Remember' with the subtitles 'All footage in this movie was taken by real fans on mobile devices. Editing by Darlington FC. Enjoy.' The music started low but slowly built up as the movie started with a young boy in his bathroom in the dark brushing his teeth. His Dad asked him where he was going today.

"We're going to Wembley," said the boy, before the movie then cut to the fans assembling at the ground. A further scene cut to the station where Jarrod caught a sight of Marianne and the kids waiting for their early train to London.

The music then kicked in and the movie went through a series of shots of people leaving, driving with their scarves out the window, stopping at the motorway services amongst crowds of fellow Darlington fans, then into the pubs around the Wembley area, fans singing together with the Chesterfield supporters. The editing was outstanding, the music was thumping by the time the footage came around to the players coming on to the field, the National Anthem, the coin toss and the kick-off.

Jarrod could feel his skin tingling all over. This was quite possibly the best footage he had ever seen, and all of it had come from Darlington fans mobile phones. He looked around the room and all eyes were fixated. This was serious viewing – after all it had only been two days since it happened, and memories were still fresh. There was joy on the faces of the fans as they celebrated the goals and then the final whistle, and all the footage of the players coming over to celebrate with the fans.

Jarrod felt his eyes well up and he was happy to let a tear roll down his cheek as he broke into a smile. The chants of 'We are going up' were raucous, as was the dancing and jigging of the players as they lifted the play off trophy to massive roars from the crowd. The wobbly mobile phone footage simply enhanced the viewing.

There was a shot of the players in the change rooms after the game, Jarrod trying to work out who had the phone from the angle, but unable to place it. There was hugging and bouncing and shouting in the changing room, champagne bottles out, smiles and high fives.

The final footage showed a train leaving Kings Cross station then passing the Emirates stadium, happy Darlington fans in their cars on the M1, and one of the coaches still singing away. The fan who started the day off brushing his teeth was shown being carried from the car, then being tucked up in bed; his dad asked whether he'd had a good day.

"Best day ever," he croaked before snuggling into his pillow. There was anticipation in the room, the players unsure as to whether it was the end of the movie until the titles rolled on to the screen. The room erupted.

"Oh my God!" shouted Wes, "How good was that?"

An impromptu round of applause rang around the room, the titles were interrupted by some out-takes, much to the delight of everyone. There was a fan tumbling on the escalators at the Tube station, a guy celebrating a goal with a full pint in his hand and not dropping any of it. There were shots of the players' kids giving thumbs up, before a quick out-take of Connor stumbling along the corridor in the hotel and Freddie Asquith catching him before he fell over into a doorway, Freddie turning round to the camera shouting 'Wahey!'

Jarrod wondered how on earth someone would have had the time to collect all that footage, let alone put it all together in such a fantastic movie like that. He suspected that Pauline and her journalist connections would have had something to do with it, but it was truly a masterpiece.

The room was pretty rowdy by now, the oxygen being pumped into the room had given everyone a bit of an edge. Wes then sprung to his feet and quickly made his way over to the stage where he grabbed the microphone out of its stand and beckoned Mitch up to the stage. It was obviously time for the end of season awards! At midnight on a school night, the timing could not have been any better.

Chapter 6

CHAMPAGNE

The Darlington players had taken it upon themselves to implement a fine system during the season, from the very outset. No one remembered where it came from and who instigated it. Perhaps it was simply someone shouting 'Shot out for a throw-in. That's a fine!' in an early training session, but it was well and truly embraced and snowballed into an institution.

Wes would be the bank, keeping meticulous records of the misdemeanours. He and Mitch would put out suggestions to a vote in the changing rooms if a player had done something worthy of a fine. There were the obvious ones for football related incidents – giving away a penalty, foul throws, booked for diving, dissent, sending off with a straight red, missing a sitter, missing the target from a penalty and so on.

There were also fines for being late, which had instilled great discipline in the players, but also those more frivolous and debatable penalties, such as forgetting a key piece of clothing for an away game, forgetting a senior player's name, regardless of the squad they were in. Even being late paying a fine incurred a fine.

Jarrod had been a little taken aback by this self-governance at the start, and some of the players had struggled, especially with punctuality. What it did do though was force the players to conform, and it made the management team's job a lot easier knowing that everyone would be where they were meant to be in good time.

A great moment during the season that everyone remembered was at Rochdale, with the game sewn up and Sam Basaan sitting on a proud zero fines. He went to throw the ball in and the ball slipped out of his hands. All the Darlington players shouted 'Foul throw ref!' in unison, much to the bemusement of the Rochdale players. The referee blew for the foul throw, which sent the players racing over and jumping on Sam as if he'd scored a goal.

Sam was laughing at the spontaneous 'celebration', but Gary wasn't laughing as the home side played on with five Darlo players out of the game and contrived to miss a golden opportunity to pull a goal back. Jarrod remembered Raynor Gunn roaring at his teammates in anger, but it was all smiles at the end, the three goal victory richly deserved.

Wes had been shopping with the proceeds and produced a case of Mumm champagne and a series of trophies. He set them up on a small table next to the microphone stand, each champagne bottle in its individual box sitting proudly behind equal sized trophies. Caroline was straight on the scene, taking photos after lining up the bottles in a perfect arc, while Wes started the presentations.

"Ladies and gentlemen!" he exclaimed excitedly, "The moment that you've not been waiting for at all has arrived."

Wes was as self-deprecating as they come, he was a funny guy to be around.

"Our end of season presentations have been and gone," he continued, referring to the official club awards night that took place rather awkwardly before the last league game of the season and all the drama that followed, "but we now give to you our own Darlington FC players awards. Voted by the players, for the players, and ultimately paid for by the players."

There was a murmur that took over the room, as some players shifted in their chairs and the rest of the gathering waited in anticipation. Wes handed the microphone over to Mitch. His unmistakably thespian voice, in the style of commentating legend Stuart Hall, filled the room.

"The first award is for the Foul of the Season," he started. There were oohs from the room and players began pointing, most of them in the direction of Gav Selley, who shielded his face as if trying not to be seen. "The nominations are ..."

Unbelievably, Mitch and Wes had gone to the trouble of trawling through the club video archives to get the footage they needed. This was just like the Oscars. The screen flicked into action and the music burst into life – the Tom Hark ska number "... you'll have to laugh or else you'll cry ...", the one played at 95 per cent of football grounds and darts tournaments across the years, filled the room. Jarrod felt like dancing as the familiar beat introduced the first nominee, the voiceover of Mitch at its most theatric as he introduced the clip : "Dean Minto – Cambridge United Home".

The clip was of a moment when the Cambridge right winger tricked Dean and left him in his wake. Dean raced back, almost caught up with his opponent, and then launched into a scything challenge that sent the winger off the field and into the advertising hoardings. The room filled with gasps and roars of equal measure. Will reached over to Dean and patted him on the back, as the footage showed the referee finally catching up with play and producing an instant red card.

Next up was "Raynor Gunn – Mansfield Town Away". This showed a long ball up the middle of the park that seemed to catch the wind and hold up; Raynor had already made his leap to win the header, but the ball was nowhere near, and the striker had not jumped. That left the Darlington central defender hanging in mid-air, catching the home striker in the back with his knee, an elbow in the back of the head for good measure. The referee raced on the scene as Raynor retreated as if nothing had happened. The room erupted in laughter after the footage focused on the perpetrator, some slow motion of Raynor mouthing obscenities as the referee reached for a yellow card.

This was awesome, Jarrod had never seen anything like this at a club presentation night, official or otherwise. This was an absolute marvel. He had remembered filling in the questionnaire before and during the flight to London for the play off final, and had remarked at the time how detailed the questions were, giving examples if there was not a stand out for each award.

The final nominee was announced.

"Gavin Selley – Rochdale home," came the smooth voice over, and the footage rolled, the bouncy music still playing. This would surely be the winner. The wobbly footage showed Gav racing to close down a defender, who got the ball stuck between his legs as Gav steamed in. Just as he homed in, the defender managed to get the ball away, Gav stretching out his leg to try and block it. This led to him simply flying into the defender at full speed with his legs wide apart, wrapping them around his midriff and bringing him to the ground in a move that would not have been out of place in an 80s karate arcade game.

It was purely unintentional, and the video showed Gav apologising to his hurt opponent as the referee pulled out the red card. Again the footage slowed as Gav closed his eyes, dropped his shoulders and mouthed 'f--k' just as the footage cut out. The room was roaring, and Gav sat with his head on his hands as his teammates shouted their approval. Gav was a fairly quiet guy, and this was totally out of character, but it definitely was a worthy winner.

"And the winner is," said Mitch, as Wes held an oversized spangly gold envelope and the players banged on the tables. "The winner is ... Gav Selley!"

Gav leapt to his feet and made his way to the stage to collect his award, Caroline snapping furiously away as he accepted his trophy and champagne. The whole room was applauding, mainly because it was a bloody fantastic bit of editing, and everyone knew they were witnessing something very special.

Mitch quickly moved on to the second award, which was for the Messiest Player. Jarrod thought that surely there would be no footage for this one, but he was wrong. The footage started as more football-themed music, *Seven Nation Army*, accompanied the grainy mobile phone footage of Freddie Asquith's side of a shared hotel room on an away trip, his bag simply tipped all over the floor as if he'd been searching for something in a hurry.

There was also footage of a player's car strewn with rubbish and half-eaten sandwiches, and another player after eating his pre-match bolognese in a white shirt where there was a minimal success rate in hitting his mouth. Freddie Asquith took that one out to great applause.

After Connor had taken out the 'Worst Haircut' award, a controversial award followed, and that was for the 'Fittest Missus'. Gerry was shaking his head at this one as *Go West* by the Pet Shop Boys accompanied shots of some of the wives and girlfriends. A shot of a slinky looking Marianne, pre-cancer and totally carefree, caused Jarrod to miss a heartbeat. Wes sensed the unease in the room, so quickly raced through it. Ghali Barberi took out the award though and seemed pretty happy to be accepting it. His Iranian girlfriend was, to be fair, incredibly pretty.

"The nominations for 'Dive of the Season'", said Mitch, before his voice over self took over to an old Italian version of *Volare*, perhaps unintentionally suggesting some sort of connection to diving.

"Will Telfer – Exeter City away" – the footage showed Jarrod racing through the midfield to draw the last defender and slip in Will for a run on goal. His touch was heavy though and the goalkeeper looked odds-on to win the race for the ball. Will did get there first though and pushed the ball again a little too far, realising that the ball would roll out for a goal kick. His attempt to con the referee was outrageous as he flopped artistically to the floor. The referee eventually entered the frame and pulled out the yellow card, Will smiling as he accepted his punishment. The room was again engrossed by the footage and the players were hollering at the screen.

"Roni Verelo – Hereford United Away". This was a cup game, and Darlington had a difficult time overcoming their lower league opponents. With the score locked at 0-0, and maybe fifteen minutes left on the clock, Dec Hines played a one-two with Roni on the edge of the box and the wily midfielder danced into the area onto his weaker left foot. As he shaped to shoot, a challenge came in from a defender and the Darlington man skipped over it and simply fell to his knees, sprawling his arms out like Jurgen Klinsmann. The referee waved play on, and Roni peeled himself off the floor, suggesting that he had been poleaxed. This brought the room to a crescendo, Roni laughing and doing a jig to the music.

"Will Telfer – Luton Town away." A second nomination for Will, and all eyes turned on him. He didn't flinch and kept watching the screen. This was a slightly different scenario. Will had gone into a challenge with the Luton defender, both players going in hard to win the ball. The Luton player sprung to his feet in anger, and Will slowly got up to confront him, both players used to being the tallest on the field but finding themselves staring eye to eye. The defender feigned to cock his fist ready to land a punch and Will took that as a cue to take a backwards step but simply stumbled and fell to the ground. Both players were laughing and it all ended in an embrace.

"And the winner is …" said Mitch. "Oh wait, there's another late nominee for Gary Hollister for Notts County away." There was a collective sharp intake of breath, Mitch evoking memories of Gary collapsing to the ground when he was struck by food poisoning before the game in the changing room.

"Oh no, that's a typo," said Mitch with a chuckle, laughing at his own totally inappropriate interjection, "The winner is Roni Verelo!" The popular pint-sized midfielder bounded to the stage to get his award, shouting something in Spanish into the microphone before running off giggling with his goods.

Jarrod was still amazed at how the footage had been put together in record time. Someone must have helped out – these two clowns would never have been able to pull this off on their own.

"And now for the main awards of the night," said Mitch, with pomp and ceremony, "Goal of the Season." This had been a quick-fire presentation, but was done so professionally, and there was genuine anticipation in the room for who would be selected by their peers as the scorer of the goal of the season. Jarrod felt that he had at least one goal worthy of nomination but he couldn't be sure if he had made the top three.

"Jarrod Black – Northampton Town, home". Question answered. Elvis Presley's *Falling in Love* anthem started up, a staple tune of Sunderland fans, as the footage popped up of Jarrod going in for a crunching tackle and emerging with the ball in the centre circle. Advancing quickly, he drew an opponent and played the one-two with Ghali. The obvious move was to push the ball past the last defender and run in on goal, but Jarrod simply clipped the ball nonchalantly over the keeper from fully 30 yards out, not breaking stride and continuing his run into the corner to celebrate with the fans.

The cheer in the room as the goal went in on the screen was huge. Jarrod got to his feet and punched the air. He did enjoy that one. That was echoes of Glenn Hoddle and Matt Le Tissier.

The other two nominees were Raynor Gunn with his Exocet of a piledriver against Crewe in the play off semi-final – he couldn't have hit the ball any sweeter – and Sam Basaan who lined up a shot from way out and managed to beat the keeper's despairing dive with an absolute screamer. Jarrod was feeling nervous, he was in the running. It would be great to win it.

"And the trophy goes to …" Mitch was loving this role, and it wouldn't have been a surprise if he somehow cut to a commercial break to keep the suspense going.

"The Goal of the Season goes to our captain Jarrod Black!" The room erupted again, and Jarrod made his way to the stage, jostled along the way by his raucous teammates. It was quite warm under the lights. Jarrod turned to get his photo taken as Wes handed him the trophy. He noticed that whole room, including everyone camped in the bar area, were completely caught up in this.

"Our final award of the night," said Mitch, flagrantly ignoring the fact that he had two trophies left on the table, "is the much coveted Player of the Season award."

This would be an interesting one. The voting had been done using five questions, ranging from 'which player has made the biggest impact on the team this year' to 'who has been the best representative of the club.' Voting could be all over the place.

Wes and Mitch kept the pace of the presentation running and the screen flicked through the player photos of each player, speeding up as it went, scrolling through the whole squad before slowing down like a roulette wheel. The clicks slowed down, each one maybe the last, and anticipation was growing. A roar was building, just like a goalkeeper taking a goal kick, and it kept going until the screen went black and flashed up a picture of central defender Freddie Asquith.

The tune *Guantanamera* started up, the winner's name fitting beautifully into the song. Soon the room was singing 'there's only one Freddie Asquith.' Everyone was on their feet, the chant went on until Freddie appeared at the front and continued as he headed back to his seat with a wide smile across his face. A worthy recipient, solid as a rock, and a player who had been with the club for a few seasons.

"You might …" said Wes, who had taken the microphone in an attempt to quell the crowd. "You might be wondering why we have one more trophy."

"Let me tell you," he said, "we have collected a good kitty this season and okay, we've lashed out on a bit of champers, but we have a solid five hundred pounds left over. This is going to be presented to a champion of the club, someone who serves the club and who has gone above and beyond the call of duty this season. Ladies and gentlemen, to announce the worthy recipient, Mr Gary Hollister!"

"Yes," said Gary after he reached the stage and accepted the microphone, "Wes and Mitch asked me to nominate a worthy recipient of Darlington FC's inaugural Club Champion award, and there were a lot of people who came to mind. There is a whole army of people who make your football a reality every week, and without their unwavering support and assistance, we would not be able to host football games or travel the length and breadth of the country to fulfil our fixtures."

Everyone was looking around the room, puzzled as to who it would go to.

"The award this season goes to not one, but two people. Our very own coach drivers Mal and Tony!" The tables erupted again as two of the most unassuming and nicest guys you could meet made their way from the bar area, Mal with his arm around Tony. They entered the stage to great applause.

The envelope was handed over and Mal, the rounder of the two, picked up the trophy and champagne and held them aloft.

"No coach driving for these two in the morning I hope, " quipped Wes, both men shaking their heads, Tony making the international drinking gesture with his hand as he walked off to re-join the throng.

"Ladies and gentlemen," said Wes, "thank you for your attention, and thanks to all the players for their efforts this season. League One, here we come!"

The applause, hollers and whistles rang out as the lights dimmed, some colourful lights came on and the beat started. A hasty removal of the microphone stand and tables from the stage followed as the music thumped into life.

A selection of the waiters and waitresses then put everything down and moved in unison into the stage area, the sole male removing his top and the four girls removing their clothes to reveal skimpy outfits. As the beat kicked in, it was clear that they were a dance troupe and they put on a fantastic show in a high energy routine set to some thumping techno hits from twenty years back.

Everyone was up out of their seats, and the area in front of the stage became an impromptu dance floor. This gave the remaining waiters and staff a chance to clear and remove the heavy tables from the area and make the dancefloor much bigger. The end of the show brought huge cheers and the music stopped. The stadium announcer was back in position and his beam of light turned on. He announced the arrival on stage of the next guest.

"Ladies and gentlemen!" he cried, "Your favourite football club owner, Mr Gerry Lincoln!"

The table and microphone stand was back in place, the crowd turned around to see the tables gone, and replaced by the majority of the people from the bar area, signalling the move into the next part of the evening. This was so cleverly done, moving from one part of the evening to the next with such precision. Gerry appeared on stage and took the microphone, the host of the venue ready for another speech after his short one in the restaurant earlier in the night. There was a little bit of bustle in the dark as instruments were moved in behind Gerry, but this was the club owner's moment.

Chapter 7

SAX

"My goodness!" exclaimed Gerry, "We certainly know how to party, don't we?"

The room was his, he could say anything at this moment. He stepped back from the microphone and waited until the eager crowd calmed down. He was used to commanding the room, but the audience was a little more charged than usual. He said only a few inclusive words of congratulations to everyone at the club before signing off.

"Enjoy the night!" yelled Gerry. That was the cue for a 1-2-3-4 from the drummer, and some funky R&B started up. Gerry took a step down on to the floor to be joined by several partygoers who were ready to let go and shake their thing. After a few bars of the first tune, local celebrity James Tack appeared on stage and grabbed the mic, giving it some 'ugh' and 'right on' as the music suddenly stopped and launched into the classic intro of James Brown's *Sex Machine*.

The funky bass got even more people up to dance. Jarrod was never the first on to the dancefloor, but was confident that he could shake it like any other. Everyone around him was dancing and it just felt right that he should be moving to the beat. This was some party, and everyone was still going despite it being well after midnight.

The live music was a masterstroke, and young and old were lapping it up, youthful striker Jason Glenn giving some moves straight out of the seventies, and family man Martin Howard bringing out Michael Jackson moves that he hadn't dared show off for years. As the tune entered the rambling solo bit, up popped Alfonso Barolo with a glistening saxophone to take the tune to new heights and lead it back into the finale. A couple of breaths to reset and the band then moved straight on to a sax version of Cat Empire's *Hello* that got the room bouncing again.

The wait staff produced trays of oversized syringes, obviously filled with some sort of red jelly and started handing them out to the hyped-up crowd. Jarrod noticed straight away that more people seemed to have arrived, a few more familiar faces from the world of entertainment, some shady-looking underworld types, and some very suave-looking ladies in revealing ball gowns. The area by the bar had acquired some lounges all of a sudden, and the live music was seamlessly replaced by a DJ.

Jarrod was handed one of the syringes, and it seemed like the right thing to do was to squirt the thick liquid into his mouth. It was a super-strong vodka taste with a hint of raspberry, but when he swallowed, the raspberry took over his mouth and made him go for another squirt.

This truly was the most surreal party he had ever been to, and it was probably still not over. The music was amped up gradually and everyone was dancing, at least those who had not taken to the couches after realising how tired they were. Even the lighting was superb, as if it was a show to go with every song that was played by the DJ, and dancing seemed like the only option.

Chapter 8

POCKET

The atmosphere was more like a pub now. There were twice as many people in the room, and there were conversations going on over the music. Jarrod remarked to himself that the music seemed to be on its way down, either that or every throat in the room had been well and truly lubricated by the raspberry vodka shots. Jarrod had been in conversation with Jack Thomas, a fellow midfielder who had been in and out of the team all year. His view on not getting that much game time was an incredibly mature one, especially as Jarrod was one of players who kept him out of the team.

They both had their war paint still on, the thick black paint having dried much in the way that wax cools when dripped from a candle, and it had resisted all manner of stray hands, wiping of faces, kisses and hugs. Jarrod touched Jack's and remarked that it didn't even come off on his hands. They both thought they might have trouble getting the stuff off when the time came.

As the music really started to die down and the voices grew louder in volume, the two players found themselves stumbling into conversation with two of the new arrivals, a pair of likely lads who wouldn't have been out of place as extras in *Lock Stock and Two Smoking Barrels*. They seemed to be in good spirits, but had the unhinged look of someone whose mood could change at the drop of a hat. They introduced themselves as Ivan and Dimitri. Jarrod could detect a definite Eastern European accent.

"I hear Newcastle are interested in signing you," said Ivan, the taller of the two, turning his body to face Jarrod. Jarrod looked at Jack and raised his eyebrows. *This would not be common knowledge* he thought.

"I wouldn't rely on the newspapers to give you reliable news at this time of the pre-season," retorted Jarrod, making out that he was a little annoyed at the question.

"No, no," continued Ivan, "I am hearing from a very reliable source that you are a wanted man."

Jack looked a little uneasy and Jarrod continued the resistance.

"I think they've got their eye on plenty of more talented young players than a creaking old man like me," he said, knowing very well that he would be able to match any player from the Premier League with his pace and fitness.

Dimitri got out a small bag, much like the kind Jarrod would use in the kids' packed lunches for snacks. It contained a white powder. He opened the bag and tapped some of the powder out on to the back of his hand and offered the bag to Jack, who immediately recoiled.

"Oh, I'm sorry," said Dimitri, genuinely apologetic. "Of course you don't want any, you're a footballer! We are not footballers so we can do as we please."

The Russian-like accent and slightly broken English didn't mask that these were actually very friendly and likeable guys. Ivan took the bag as Dimitri licked the powder from the back of his hand and quickly did the same thing before putting the bag nonchalantly in Dimitri's back pocket.

"Please forgive us," said Dimitri, sucking in his cheeks as though he had eaten a slice of lemon, "We don't get out to party very often."

"But trust me, Jarrod," interjected Ivan, "You will be getting the call from Newcastle very soon. Good luck with your endeavours."

That was quite a tricky word for someone with such patchwork English, and was used in a really English context. It wasn't lost on Jarrod as he shook hands with Ivan, then with Dimitri as they both stumbled off and started dancing.

"My God!" said Jack, "That's proper loose. What would Gary think?"

"I know!" said Jarrod, "Are these guys trying to catch us out?"

That unwanted brush with a career-ending substance didn't faze Jarrod, and he was keen to work the room and meet some of the stars in the crowd. He made a bee-line for Jackie Tuppens when he saw her over by the bar area. He bided his time to check if she was in fact in a deep conversation or not with the two ladies and the enormous frame of Premier League super-agent Duddy Freiberg standing opposite them. His booming Scottish accent was holding court. Jarrod gave him a tip of an imaginary hat as he moved in.

"Jackie," said Jarrod, with little forethought as to what was to come next, simply letting his thoughts convert to words. "I just had to come over and say hello."

It sounded like a little bit 'chat up line' and a little bit 'deranged stalker' but he persisted.

"We used to be next door neighbours back in Gateshead," he said, holding out his hand to shake.

"Really?" smiled the sultry actress, her eyebrows raised in the manner she would raise them on her early evening soap opera slot on ITV. "Well hello neighbour. Tell me, where was this?"

"We lived on the top floor of the new apartment block on Hawks Road," Jarrod stated. "Well, it was new at the time, are you still there?"

"Yes, we live on the second floor," Jackie replied, "we've been in there since they were built. Say, that wasn't you who moved in and had the big party on the day you moved in?"

Jarrod was instantly mortified, remembering the time when his best mate Reggie organised a housewarming while Jarrod was away playing in the first team down South.

"Er, what's the right answer to that question?" asked Jarrod jokingly.

"It was a great party!" she shrieked, holding on to his forearm to steady herself. "I hadn't been out in ages after we'd had our first, and I'd been down with a cold, but the young man, very tall he was, who was moving in came and knocked on every door and introduced himself. He invited all the neighbours to the party. Well, I wasn't going to turn down that invitation, and I left our Dean back at the flat with the baby and came up for a while."

Jarrod's mouth was agape.

"You were there?" he finally blurted out. "That is seriously freaky. I had no idea!"

Jarrod had his hand on hers now and they were both laughing.

"I'd seen you on TV a few times, and we'd bumped in to each other maybe once or twice at events. Reggie told me you lived downstairs, but I'd never actually seen you there. Oh my god, wait until I tell Reggie, I thought he was pulling my leg."

Another lady then joined the conversation, and she was striking, clearly an athlete. It was Nicole Madejski. She had a presence and piercing eyes. She had caught Jarrod's eye a few years ago at the North East Sports Personality of the Year awards in Newcastle, and they had enjoyed a quick chat before it was abruptly curtailed as she was called up to accept her award.

There was no question of anything other than friendship as he had convinced himself that she wasn't in to men. The tabloid press had then given that impression when she finally hit the international stage in a world championship bout on prime time TV. Nevertheless, he couldn't help admiring her figure that night and she was looking equally toned tonight.

"Nicole," he said softly, leaning in for a kiss, "how good do you look?"

"Thank you," came the response and they exchanged ambiguous smiles, "Say, Jarrod, do you know *everyone*?"

"Ha!" snorted Jarrod, "The Jarrod of ten years ago might have given it a good nudge, but these days I don't get around as much. How could I steal the limelight from someone like you?" He was referring to the fact that Nicole took out the Sports Personality Award that time by twice as many votes as Jarrod received in second place.

"Oh Jarrod," pouted Nicole, "how can you forgive me? Now run along …"

Jarrod left the girls, laughing as he went. He really did feel an inferiority complex when he was around Nicole, and besides he may have been interrupting a bit of chemistry there between the two local stars. As he moved away, he edged past Giuseppe, the former Middlesbrough star, and put his hands on his shoulders.

"Sepp!" he offered, squeezing past him, "How the hell are you?"

"Jarrod!" cried Giuseppe, flinging his arms in the air. "*Ça va, toi?*"

Giuseppe Rolando was a player that Jarrod had admired so much in the past, so much so that he'd happily travelled down three or four times to the Riverside to see him play whenever their games didn't clash and the circumstances were favourable. This was just as Jarrod was making a name for himself at Gateshead, and Giuseppe's own career was entering the end zone after a glittering career in Europe and with Belgium. He was still as fit as a fiddle, and Jarrod squeezed his biceps to suggest that he looked as though he'd been working out.

Giuseppe had always tried to coax Jarrod into speaking French once he'd learned that he was married to a French lady, and Jarrod had never taken the bait.

"*Ça va bien, mon gars*!" said Jarrod, reaching in for a 'bise'. That took Giuseppe by surprise and he was clearly impressed as they completed the three kisses on the cheek, Jarrod remembering how many he had to do without any hesitation.

"Are you well, Seppe?" he asked, coining another derivation of his name.

"I'm feeling quite relaxed," said Giuseppe, "this has to be the best party I have ever been to."

"You're not wrong there my friend," stated Jarrod. "Say, where are you living these days?"

"I'm up in Newcastle," said Giuseppe, "living in Gosforth. You were just on the other side of the river right? United have me coaching the youngsters and doing some scouting. It's kind of fun, keeps me young."

"And you're looking good too," said Jarrod. "Say, is everything all good at the Toon? You know, there's not much love from the fans."

"It's a tough gig," said Jarrod, "I feel sorry for all the full time staff. They have to deal with so much abuse from the fans, even if it's not directed at them."

"We might be playing them in a couple of years' time too," said Jarrod, referring to the fact that Newcastle were perennial strugglers in the Premier League and Darlo were on the up. "Say, do you know the time?"

"Yes," said Giuseppe rustling in his pocket before remembering that he had a watch on. "Oh my goodness, it's way past your bed time, you *petit-joueur*!"

Jarrod grabbed his arm and bent it around so he could see the time, accidentally on purpose twisting as went, causing Giuseppe to flinch, and laughing as he did it. Before he got a playful twist of the ear in return, he saw that it was just before two-thirty. Wow, this had been some epic night. The two friends clasped hands in an embrace before heading in their separate directions. The lights started to brighten and the music quickly gave way to the MC, whose voice filled the room.

Chapter 9

WRAP

"Ladies and gentlemen," said the MC, "this evening has been a very special one for all of us. As you make your way home, please acknowledge the generosity and dedication shown by your host Gerry Lincoln."

There was a huge roar, feet stamping on the ground, tables and chair backs being slapped. It went on for twenty seconds, the roar morphing into a chant as someone started shouting 'Way hey hey Gerry Lincoln, na na nah na …' and everyone joined in. It was a lovely moment. As it subsided, the MC spoke again.

"Would all players and staff please make their way over to the door where you first came in," he said. "Caroline will be taking a team shot to capture this moment for us all. Everyone else, if you could let the players through and then come closer, we'll all get in the photo."

The music had completely stopped by now, there was a lot of chatter and shuffling as people moved and party-goers realised that they were in fact really tired. The last of the players came, Ghali having been in the bathroom when the call went out and he joined the throng a minute after everyone else. Caroline had taken a position standing on a chair next to the MC's position and beckoned the players into a team shot, much like the one they had done as a whole squad at the beginning of the season.

Once she was happy that everyone was there and in position, she urged Gary and Des to squash in from the sides, and then asked all the rest of the people in the room to come a little closer. The MC asked Caroline if she wanted to put her chair on his raised platform, and she jumped at the chance for a bit more elevation.

She cajoled the crowd into a few serious shots and then some fun shots and then, just as she was getting down off her chair, she shrieked and turned to organise them one more time. This time she whipped out her mobile phone, turned her back and took a selfie, much to the amusement of the crowd, who hammed it up for this cheeky final photo of the shoot. She really was a great girl, Caroline, thought Jarrod.

That signalled the end of the party, and all of a sudden there were a lot of staff again. The players, easily recognisable by their face paint and sharp suits, were ushered out. Jarrod was secretly hoping for another go at the skydiving, but that had been dismantled. They simply made their way across the courtyard and in to where they got changed previously. Their belongings were all neatly packaged up in a travel bag, each with a name and their squad number, their valuables and mobile phones sitting on top of the bags.

There wasn't enough space for everyone, so the staff brought out the bags to some of those waiting to enter the room. These were really good quality bags. Jarrod remarked that he needed one of these after surviving the last four years with a classic tattered and worn bag for hand luggage whenever he flew. Being reunited with their mobile phones was a moment of relief for some, and the first instinct was to check for missed calls or at least check the time. Jarrod noticed that a lot of players were checking their phones and were no longer concentrating on anything else. He reached for his and flicked it on.

The first item in a long list of missed calls and messages was an image, sent by Darlington FC. He anticipated that it would be the team photo that they had just taken – but no, it was a match programme. Its headline: 'Al-Wasl v Darlington FC, Zabeel Stadium, Dubai.'

"Holy shit!" said Jarrod as he looked around to see most of his teammates reacting in much the same way. The date was this Friday at 8pm local time.

"Jesus, have you seen this?" said Raynor, turning with his mobile phone to face Jarrod.

"The Darlo boys are going to Dubai!"

This evening could not possibly have gone any better, a great party followed by finding out that the whole team was going on tour. Jarrod was quickly doing some calculations in his head, hoping he wasn't going to miss anything or if something important might clash with it. The Socceroos games weren't until the following weekend, there was nothing on at school, Marianne had no chemo treatment around then, no, he was good to go!

The players were ushered out through the front door and farewelled into waiting cars in twos and threes depending on which direction they were heading, the staff doing a great job of working out who should go in which vehicle. The players were all lost in conversation, the image on their phones had a link which took them to an itinerary, and they were mulling over what was going to be quite a trip.

Jarrod found himself in the front seat with Wes and Ghali. He was the last of the three to be dropped off anyway.

"Have you ever had such a crazy year?" asked Jarrod as Ghali climbed out unsteadily in front of his house. Wes paused for thought.

"I think I must have been building up to this," he replied. "Can it get much better?"

"Oh, it can be much bigger," said Jarrod factually, having played at a higher level but never at the top, "but we're never going to be in this situation again – an owner as mad as a box of frogs, a top class manager, players you would bend over backwards for, fans that travel the length and breadth of the country to follow you. The stars have aligned here."

"We've got to stick together," said Wes, being the first to have said what most of the players had been thinking, "We're the new Crazy Gang."

The Crazy Gang was an obvious reference to the players in the 1980s at Wimbledon FC, a group of footballers who took the word 'team' to a new level and achieved way beyond their means. Jarrod had heard of it, but it had never been used in any sort of comparison.

"You're the man to make that happen," said Jarrod, "I mean, that trophy presentation tonight, could you see that happening at Liverpool?"

"Ha ha, you're right," chuckled Wes, the car coming to a halt.

"See you on the plane!" shouted Jarrod excitedly as Wes put his hand on the door handle to open it. He reached out his hand and put it on Jarrod's shoulder and squeezed.

"It's the start of something beautiful," he said before leaping out and leaving Jarrod in the car with the driver. Wes ran to his front door like an excited schoolboy running home to tell his mum the news. Obviously there was no one awake, all the lights were off, but Wes managed to negotiate the key and made his way into the hallway.

"Been quite a night," stated Jarrod as a conversation starter to the driver. He just nodded and smiled. This wasn't a taxi – there was no meter and only a mounted phone for communications – but the driver was dressed in a uniform, similar to the staff at the party.

"Only a minute or so to the final drop," said Jarrod trying again to initiate some chatter.

"We'll be there in one minute thirty-eight seconds," came the reply in a broad Scottish accent, with a smile but no emotion. Jarrod took that as a conversation ender, and decided that he wasn't going to get anything meaningful in return. It was indeed less than two minutes until they were turning into the driveway, the driver making sure he went slowly to not agitate the gravel too much and wake everyone up.

"Thank you, sir," said the driver and offered his hand, which Jarrod shook with a smile before stepping out and closing the door. Hitting the cooler night air made him spring into a jog to the front door. The car drove off slowly before speeding away as it got onto the road.

Chapter 10

KILLER

The house was in darkness. Jarrod flicked on the light. He sensed that he was still very awake - whether it was the drinks, or the food, or even the air - something had given him an undeniable buzz, and he was nowhere near being ready for sleep. He sat on the sofa, hoping that the comfort and softness would have its usual effect of dampening the senses and getting him ready for sleep. He flicked on his mobile phone, the screen still displaying the itinerary for later in the week. A news feed also popped up :

TOP FOOTBALLER MURDERED

That prompted Jarrod to see his own message feed, and he saw that he had a raft of text messages intermingled with news items of a similar subject, the murder of a famous footballer. He clicked with trepidation and excitement on a link that was to the BBC, surely the most reliable and trustworthy source of such an alarming headline.

ANDRÉ RAMBOUILLET FATALLY SHOT

Jarrod was now sitting bolt upright with his legs curled under himself, halfway to standing up. André Rambouillet was Newcastle United's star midfielder, brought to the club three years ago from unfancied Reims in France. He had secured the captain's role in his second season at St James' Park. He had though been implicated in a betting scandal towards the end of the season, but was more of a bystander than a main actor in the alleged crime. Now he had been shot and killed. Jarrod read on.

...A LONE GUNMAN...

...SINGLE GUNSHOT TO THE HEAD...

...SHOCK AND HORROR IN NEWCASTLE CITY CENTRE...

Jarrod was reading frantically, flicking between links and websites. He could decipher through all the noise and filler in the stories that André Rambouillet had been walking with a friend up Grey Street after leaving a restaurant in the early evening. A man thought to be in fancy dress had come up alongside the pair and asked the player if he was indeed André.

Being the gentleman that he was, and always ready to give an autograph where needed, he had offered his hand to the man who instantly produced a gun and shot him in the side of the head. The man had then fled on foot and was still at large. A number of witnesses had seen or heard the gunshot. Despite the efforts of his friend and a doctor who was passing in his car soon after, the Newcastle playmaker was pronounced dead before the emergency services arrived at the scene.

Jarrod had hardly taken a breath, his heart was racing. This had happened tonight, only six hours ago. He had come across Rambouillet in a pre-season game many moons ago when Gateshead entertained Reims. He was a very good prospect then, and Jarrod remembered having a good tussle with him in the middle of the park, including a moment when they had run into each other by accident and both ended up winded on the ground.

He was a star of Match of the Day, the presenters loved him and he was a revered member of the Newcastle team, one of the players that the fans had instantly warmed to. Now he was dead.

Jarrod switched on the TV and turned to the satellite news channel which was coming to the end of the fifteen minute cycle. After a round up of the headlines and a couple of ads, the programme returned with a solemn-looking presenter announcing the passing of the Newcastle United star.

Police had already released very clear footage from a CCTV camera in an attempt to strike while it was fresh in everyone's mind. Jarrod watched on in disbelief as the man, dressed in black and with what looked like face paint on both cheeks and across his nose, walked up behind and then beside the pair. There was a brief conversation before the man quickly lifted a gun to the footballer's temple. His head jerked violently sideways. The lack of sound in the footage meaning there was no accompanying loud bang.

Rambouillet staggered backwards as his friend went to catch him and the assailant immediately took flight, without waiting to see if his victim was still moving, a suit flashed from under his long coat. The CCTV footage had the action right on the edge of the screen, the footballer lying prone just off the screen, his feet showing. His friend was frantically using his phone to presumably get an ambulance on scene fast.

Jarrod was horrified. He touched his face. It still had the face paint smeared across his cheeks. The paint had survived the whole night and it was only his nose that had succumbed to the slightest smudging after blowing it while it must have still been a little wet. What was this? Was this a set up? He immediately got to his feet and tip-toed guiltily to the bathroom, where he stood in front of the mirror. He had a pick at the face paint.

It took a few goes, but he managed to prize off a little flap at the corner. His skin slowly released itself from the glue-like grip of the face paint. This was not going to be an easy task, and he would be lucky not to leave a red mark or even rip his skin if he wasn't careful.

His mind was racing. He felt like he was the killer, and he had to stop himself from going too fast. The left side of his face was looking clear. He was glad that he had shaved before going to the party, as this could have been a whole different ball-game. He pictured Raynor Gunn with his ten-day growth trying to get this stuff off. It was like taking a stubborn sticker off a new frying pan, one slip and there'll be a huge patch of glue and a thin layer of paper where the label used to be.

Luckily the patch over his nose had joined up with the left side, so he kept teasing at the face paint and it continued to release the skin across his nose. Jarrod didn't look at himself in the mirror that often, not for an extended period of time like this, and he could see some heavy bags under his eyes. His eyes were bloodshot. It could have been the pain of the process or the sudden realisation of how tired he was, but it made him look as if he had been crying.

He started on the other side, unable to lift the section that was right on his eye bag, the skin being too stretchy. He picked repeatedly at a different part and managed to get some traction. He pulled way too quick this time and the pain stopped him. The skin under the paint was looking quite red now and he needed his other hand to pull away the skin as he peeled back the face paint. It was like a beauty treatment at this point. Jarrod had seen Marianne go through something not too dissimilar at her day spa. With one final tug, there was separation.

He made sure he screwed up the pieces of face paint and walked to the kitchen and put them in the bin – as if he was getting rid of the evidence. He returned immediately to the mirror in the bathroom, surveying his skin for damage. He looked a whole lot fresher at this point, and swooshed some water across his face to wipe away any last traces. There was definitely a red patch on the right side of his face where he had been too impatient, but he was happy that the face paint was off. That was one hell of a batch of face paint, Jarrod thought. He'd hope that was never used on the kids at school fetes.

Jarrod was still snappily dressed in his dinner suit, and if his memory served him right, the assailant in the CCTV footage was wearing something very similar. His eyes by now had begun to grow very heavy. The adrenaline had worn off; he conceded that it was almost three in the morning and he was absolutely ready for bed. A quicker than usual brush of the teeth and the removal of all but his undies, he then swapped the stair light for the living room light and made his way up to the bedroom. Marianne was breathing heavily and looked very contented once Jarrod's eyes adapted to the dark again. Jarrod slipped in under the covers and gave his wife a pat of the bottom before finding his pillow and sinking his head into the fluffy down.

Chapter 11

AFTERMATH

There was not a sound in the house, but Jarrod's sleep was already over. It was only three hours since he'd gone to bed. His mind though had kept working and had given him a jolt from which he would never get back to sleep. He was very tired, his eyes grainy and heavy, but there was so much whirring through his head that he had to concede and ease himself out of bed. He checked his face in the mirror on the chest of drawers by the window. In the meagre light he could see that he had a red patch on the right side of his face. It was about the size of a ten pence piece and it didn't look as if the skin was broken. That would be gone in a day or two.

His thoughts turned to the party at Gerry's last night. What a crazy night. They had it all, skydiving, ice sculptures, fancy food and drinks, artistes, suits, some outlandish carnival attractions. All this must have come in at quite a cost. Being a self-professed mathematician, Jarrod started to add things up. There must have been at least thirty staff there all up, so let's say six hours at double time, then hiring a skydiving dome with instructors, that would be at least a two grand expense. If the fancy spirits were as expensive as he'd been told, then that would have added a pretty penny, although Gerry wouldn't have minded digging in to his personal collection one bit to pull off the most extravagant party on record.

All up, with a premium for the organising company, and a hefty taxi bill, as well as the restaurant beforehand, he would be surprised if the total spend came in at anything less than 50K. How the hell did Darlington FC, a small club in the North East of England, end up with a party that cost fifty thousand pounds?

He remembered Caroline buzzing around the room taking heaps of photos – that was a little strange, especially given the questionable content and some potentially damaging photos ending up in between the more formal team and player shots. There were even paparazzi photographers there, although they didn't have any cameras. In fact, no one there had any form of communication. Well, the players definitely didn't – they had surrendered their valuables at the door.

Jarrod couldn't recall any mobile phones being on show, or anyone other than Caroline taking photos. The party-goers would have been totally cut off from the outside world. He hadn't even noticed at the time, but he did remember that there was an appetite for mobile phones when they were leaving the venue, and it was the mobile phone that delivered the startling news of a friendly game in Dubai.

Thinking back, he remembered that the guest list was very Newcastle-centric – all of the TV and sports stars at the event were Newcastle based. How did this happen? What was the significance? Jarrod was starting to get a feeling of paranoia. Was there a higher force at work here, was this party a front for something else. A cover-up maybe?

And what was with the face paint, or warpaint as it had been suggested in the news when describing the assailant in the early morning news bulletins? Was that to implicate all the players in the crime? Was it to flood the crime investigation with suspects? He did recall the make-up artist being very insistent that everyone had to have the same markings, two big marks, one on each cheek, and an Adam Ant-style brush across the bridge of the nose. And it wasn't your typical face paint either – it dried hard, and there was little chance of it coming off. In fact it had taken him a lot of careful teasing to get it off his face only a few hours ago.

Who were those Russian dudes too? Jarrod remembered that they were very insistent that Jarrod was on Newcastle's radar. Who on earth were they? They obviously had a good grasp of the English language – he couldn't ever remember anyone who was not of English native tongue wishing someone 'luck in their endeavours'. Jarrod would love to know who they were and why they were at the party in this first place.

The event staff was another thing that Jarrod had noted – being in Darlington, it was difficult to go to any event without running in to familiar event staff. In fact these people didn't have any branding whatsoever on their uniforms apart from a barely-noticeable 'Viktor A', and none of them seemed to be from the area.

The taxi drivers too weren't real taxi drivers – they had similar uniforms to the rest of the staff and their vehicles seemed to be hire cars as opposed to dedicated taxis. That suggested an event management company was in charge of the whole thing. Nothing like that existed in Darlington, at least not to that extent.

Jarrod hadn't yet made it out of the bedroom and had been staring at himself in the mirror. He eventually moved and made his way downstairs to make a coffee, flick on the TV and get reacquainted with the big news of the day. Adverts were screening on both news channels, it was obviously just coming up to the half hour.

The family hadn't yet started to stir – they wouldn't for a half hour or so. It was school today, so Jarrod set about getting packed lunches together, opening the fridge. He was thankful to see that Marianne, or his daughter Aneka, had prepared everything the night before; the lunch boxes were the first thing he saw when he opened the door. He would just need to put together a sandwich each to complete the box, and that would involve a bit of luck getting the filling right as both kids liked to choose in the morning. There was just enough bread to make them too, and luckily it was still soft after a few days in the house. Jarrod was happy for a moment of reality after an evening completely devoid of it.

When the BBC news came on, the lead headline was of a hurricane in the United States, so Jarrod quickly flicked on to the local news, where the bulletin had started with the chilling CCTV footage that he had seen previously during the night. The footage stopped on the face of the gunman. Perhaps that wasn't paint on his face at all. It was very pixelated and with the dark skin of the man, whether or not it was simply in shadow or not, he couldn't be sure that there was face paint at all.

To be fair, Jarrod's eyes were still very heavy, so there was an extra layer of blurriness to contend with. That element of doubt seemed to strangely calm Jarrod. Maybe his over-stimulated mind had been playing tricks on him earlier. The footage then cut to a second CCTV feed that showed the man sprinting up Grey Street at a fair lick. It was only a brief second of footage. He could definitely run. Jarrod couldn't place the running style on anyone in particular. No pointed fingers like Dec Hines, no flailing arms like Ghali Barbera. Again, Jarrod seemed to relax ever so slightly.

The news reporter on the scene went on to describe the last few days for the victim. Newcastle United had been on a post-season mini-tour in Japan after the end of a dismal season. Jarrod recalled what a dismal season it was. They had to sweat through the final day hoping that their relegation rivals wouldn't get a better result and send them down. In the end, a toothless goalless draw at home to already relegated Derby County was enough to see them stay up. Brighton had roared back to draw 2-2 at title also-rans Liverpool, thus matching the result. It was Brighton and West Ham, losing 5-4 at home to Chelsea in an outrageous see-sawing game, who went down in a blaze of glory on goal difference.

Newcastle also had ownership turmoil to deal with, the current owner unable to offload the club at any price, finally selling the club to the Supporters Trust. The reporter continued. The squad had flown back in on the Friday. Rambouillet had been interviewed by police on the weekend in regards to the betting scandal that was enveloping British football, but there had been no charges. There was nothing formal from the Premier League either. The night out on Monday night was with a close friend, and he was making his way home relatively early when he was gunned down in cold blood in the street. Investigations were continuing.

This was some serious news. Jarrod couldn't help thinking that Newcastle's coincidental interest in signing him was in some way linked. This could have been some Andrés Escobar style shooting by a betting syndicate that had lost money due to a failed transaction. It could even be a way of clearing the Newcastle midfield of a similar style player, paving the way for a replacement to be brought in. This was potentially something that transcended Jarrod's simple black-and-white understanding of football, and he was keen to shut down these thoughts.

Purely coincidental, he thought to himself, but he got the urge to text an old teammate from his early Gateshead days, goalkeeper Freddie Hughton, who was enjoying a similar renaissance in his career at Sunderland.

HEY FREDDIE, HAVE YOU SEEN THE NEWS?

Barely five seconds after sending the text, Jarrod's phone buzzed. It was still on silent. Night-time mode wouldn't finish until seven. Jarrod quickly dashed into the bathroom and closed the big wooden door so he could talk without waking anyone up.

"Oh my god, Jarrod, have I seen the news?" came the voice down the line, "This is massive. I started getting texts during the night."

"Yeah, I was offline at our end of season party last night," said Jarrod, "I didn't know about it until I got home and checked my phone. It's some serious shit!"

Jarrod wasn't one for swearing, but it felt appropriate under these circumstances.

"Hey, we had our club party last night too," said Freddie, "It was huge. I don't think I've ever been to a party quite like it."

Jarrod felt a cold shiver running over him.

"It was like a circus," Freddie continued, "we had performers and fancy champagne and it was a pure riot. We had to swim to the party across a river, and when we got there, they gave us brand new suits and painted our faces. It was incredible."

"Jesus," said Jarrod, "sounds outrageous!"

He felt the urge not to compare stories, but to hear more about Freddie's night before making any conclusions.

"It was," said Freddie, getting into a groove, remembering what a crazy night he'd just had. "It was, there were loads of famous people there too, and we partied until the wee hours."

"You'll be pretty tired today then, sorry for getting you up so early," said Jarrod.

"No, no," said Freddie, "When I heard all of this Rambouillet news, I couldn't sleep. I haven't been to bed yet, I've been watching the news all night."

There was a pause. Jarrod wasn't sure what was happening.

"Hey," said Freddie, "That's Haz on the other line. I'll ring you back."

By 'Haz', Jarrod was probably referring to their old Gateshead team mate Harry Lowndes. He had been reserve goalkeeper there, way back when they were all going through the youth set up and breaking into the reserves. After a long career in Scotland with Dundee, Harry had returned this season to finish his career in his home town.

"Hey, Freddie," said Jarrod quickly, "let's do a three-way call. Patch him in …"

Jarrod was sure he'd never used that terminology ever, but it seemed to suggest the right thing.

"Ok," said Freddie and there was a momentary silence before Jarrod could hear background noise.

"Haz, you there?" asked Freddie.

"Sure thing. Jarrod, you there too?" asked Harry.

"All present and correct." said Jarrod. "Now, let me guess, you had an end of season party last night too, right?"

"Last night and this morning, more like," said Harry. "It was something else. We went on a team building trip to an Outwards Bound place out in the wilds. We thought it was going to be tramping through streams and carrying logs and all that shit, but after we'd got settled in to our accommodation and got changed, they drove us in a couple of army trucks to this big hall on a hill in the middle of nowhere."

Jarrod hadn't spoken to Harry for many years, but he remembered now that once he started speaking there was no chance of breaking his flow. And he spoke so well too.

"The trucks pull in and we pile into this room," he continued, switching tenses, "and lo and behold there's suits waiting for us, brand new suits. We get changed into them and get ushered into the next room where there's a bar and ladies and all sorts of games for us to play. We thought we'd died and gone to heaven. They had this bar thing where you would put your glass in and it would shoot around these tubes to all the ingredients of your cocktail and it would make itself. Unbelievable."

"Hey," said Freddie, "We had something like that too!"

"Sounds like we've all had pretty good nights eh?" said Jarrod, who had now affirmed that something was afoot and that they were all part of something bigger than a simple party.

"What about Rambouillet?" said Freddie, with emphasis on the 'oui' to make it sound as if he knew how to pronounce it, even though he was totally off the mark.

"Yeah, that's mad!" said Harry. "Shot right in the head in the middle of the street. He must have done something pretty bad to annoy someone."

"Hey, Harry," said Jarrod, changing the subject as Sebastian had just opened the door to go to the bathroom and got startled by his dad's presence, teetering on the edge of the bath. Jarrod moved out into the kitchen and let Sebastian close the door behind him, while still talking.

"How was Gateshead this year? You were close to a spot in the six."

"Ah, Jarrod," he said, "it was a great season, we played some fantastic football. It was December that stuffed us up, losing Ferrazzo and a few others to injury and going on a run of defeats that left us in the bottom half. By the time we'd turned it around and everyone was back, we were chasing the top six, and we just couldn't catch up."

"Great place though, eh?" said Jarrod.

"Certainly is, my friend," said Harry, "I've just signed a new deal to keep me here for two more years. I thoroughly enjoyed the season, but I think they missed you in the middle of the park."

"Yeah, it was a tricky situation last year," said Jarrod, "I would have loved to see Gateshead power up to the Premier League. I thought they might after I'd gone."

"Well if you're looking for another move," said Harry, "we'll have you back in a heartbeat."

"Yep!" said Freddie, "And don't think Sunderland haven't noticed your performances this season."

"Ha ha," said Jarrod, "you two clowns … Listen, I'd better go, but if you hear anything on the grapevine about Rambouillet, shoot me a text. I'm intrigued."

"Righto, Jarrod, see ya mate" said Freddie, "Hey Haz, stay on the line, I'll fill you in on our party last night."

Jarrod put the phone down as Sebastian walked back out flicking his hands dry and smiling at him.

"Look at your eyes, Dad," he said, "you look out of it!"

"Good morning to you too," said Jarrod. "You'd look like this too after three hours sleep."

The morning rush was on, Aneka appeared next, then Marianne in quick succession and they were both way more switched on than Jarrod.

"Darling," said Marianne reaching in for a kiss and stroking the red mark on his cheek, "I can tell how tired you are. Now, how about I run the kids to school and you get some rest?"

Jarrod was caught in two minds. Did he talk about the night last night, did he mention Rambouillet, or did he just cave in and head back to bed where he probably should have been for the last half an hour. Marianne had just had a big weekend with Jarrod and the family in London, was still recovering from major surgery and was in the midst of chemotherapy treatment, so she was in no way qualified to be the less tired of the two.

"No, no," said Jarrod, enjoying the closeness with his wife, "I'll do the school run. You take it easy. You'll need all your energy later in the week when I head off on our post-season tour."

Jarrod looked at Marianne with that face, tongue in cheek and eyes darting around aimlessly with the hint of a smile.

"Post-season tour, eh?" she said with a smile. "Partners?"

"No partners this time," he said, to which Marianne feigned disgust and slapped her hand on the table. "We're off to Dubai on Thursday."

"Oh wow!" said Marianne. "That's amazing. Then you've got your international weekend after that. Where are you going for that?"

Jarrod was impressed that Marianne was up to date with his movements, if not the details.

"We're meeting next Wednesday night in Prague," said Jarrod. "We've got a game against the Czech Republic before we move to Switzerland for a game against Peru. It's going to be a big couple of weeks."

"Last chemo session is next Tuesday, remember," said Marianne. "You might need to write your tour on the diary." She turned to the diary on the wall that Jarrod had insisted they start to use, her finger pointing at a busy weekend coming up that was now shot to pieces. Jarrod knew that Marianne had to be flexible and bow to pressure from Jarrod's footballing commitments, but this one was after the season when they would traditionally be preparing to go on holiday.

"Wouldn't miss that for the world," said Jarrod, relieved that the tour only clashed with some catch ups and kids sporting events. He kissed Marianne.

"Wouldn't miss that for the world."

Chapter 12

RUMOURS

Jarrod found himself home alone now. He had been bright and cheery when he was doing the school run, but now he had come home to an empty house. Marianne had passed Jarrod going the other way up to the Golf Club with her parents. He could feel the tiredness taking over. The logical thing to do was to sit on the couch, flick on the TV and take in more of the news until he succumbed to sleep.

That was the intention, but he caught the start of the news headlines again and found himself absorbed in it, much like his mum had described the moments the Twin Towers were under attack all those years ago. Taking in the repetitive news cycle, he couldn't peel himself away from what was a truly amazing piece of news. The newsreader shared some banter with one of the hosts of the morning show, giving his version of what could have been the reason – Rambouillet had been interviewed just on the weekend by the police and perhaps he had been a little too forthcoming with accusations. Jarrod couldn't believe what he was hearing – tittle tattle on prime time TV – where did this come from?

There was yet another piece of CCTV footage, this time from a different angle, which the news had to blank out at the moment the shot was fired. It must have been too graphic as the presenter winced as the camera came back on him. The CCTV of the aftermath was run, showing the attacker sprinting towards the camera before ducking down an alleyway. Jarrod could definitely make out something on his face, perhaps it was scarring even, but this brought back some nervousness. He flicked the TV back a few seconds and played it again, trying to stop it at the best moment to see the gunman's face. Two or three attempts later, he couldn't get anything but a blurry frame so just let it continue, watching the well dressed and athletic man dash at full pace out of shot.

Social media was rife with accusations, rumours, but mainly reaction. The usual go-to source of instant reaction, Twitter, had many posts from Jarrod's 'follow family'. He read through them, starting logically at the earliest, not long after the news had broken and the death of the star footballer had been confirmed. There was one just prior to that from a news channel, headlined 'Breaking News', then a long run of reactions, first shock and anger, then condolences.

There was one in there from Darlington FC. Jarrod could hear the words of Pauline Huck, the Head of Media at the club, clearly in his head – 'Don't ever post on twitter without running it past me first', and knew that she would have been the author of the post. Jarrod thought for a moment, flicking over to Facebook to be bombarded with adverts. He navigated to Pauline's number, hesitated for a second then dialled. She was, after all, the closest thing he had to a confidante at the club.

"Good morning Jarrod," said Pauline in a very cheery manner, "up and about early for a day off."

"Hello Pauline," said Jarrod, "how did you go after last night?"

"Ha ha," said Pauline, avoiding the question, "it was a great night, don't you think?"

"It was an absolute blast, alright," said Jarrod truthfully, conversations and events that took place during the evening dashing through his memory, "but what about André Rambouillet?"

"Oh my goodness," said Pauline, slightly theatrically, "that has shaken us all up."

"I saw your Tweet," said Jarrod.

"Yes," said Pauline, "Gary was in touch and wanted us to put something out. I think there was some sort of connection between Gary and his agent."

"Look, Pauline," said Jarrod sharply, seizing the moment, "I've talked with old teammates from Sunderland and Gateshead this morning, and I reckon something's up."

"What…" There was a rustle and a pause. "What do you mean?"

"I mean," continued Jarrod, "how come they had their end of season party at the same time? How come they did almost the same thing? How come no one had mobile phones? How…"

"Jarrod," interrupted Pauline, "I'm in the office. Come in."

"Now?" asked Jarrod to confirm.

"Now," replied Pauline and she put the phone down, as if they were going to continue this conversation very soon. Jarrod's senses were all of a sudden peaking. He raced out of the house and jumped in his car, roaring out of the driveway in spectacular fashion. He would be there in ten minutes if the traffic lights let him. As he passed the bunch of dried out flowers on the side of the road on the way into town, signalling the spot where a young boy had been mowed down a few years earlier, he started to ease off the accelerator and gather his composure.

There were four cars in the car park, Jarrod recognised

Pauline's. He'd given an interview in that car recently over the phone with the BBC and he remembered getting quite sweaty on the beaded seat covers during the call. All the players and staff had the day off, but there were things to be done, so a few hardy souls had made their way in to get ahead.

Jarrod knocked at Pauline's door, even though she would have been expecting him. He waited for her to answer the knock. As usual, her ear was pressed to her phone and she had a small tablet computer in the other hand looking at some documents. Jarrod remembered he had left something in the car and excused himself before he sat down, and jogged back to the car. Pauline's door was open when he returned, and she was wrapping up the call.

"A present for you," said Jarrod, handing over a small gift-wrapped box.

"A present?" asked Pauline in surprise, "Intriguing! Do I open it now?"

"Please do," said Jarrod. "You'll get hours of joy out of it!"

Pauline flicked off the ribbon and found a gap to prise open the delicate wrapping paper. Jarrod remembered how his sister Anna would open presents very methodically too. He smiled. She opened the paper to see the contents.

"Oh, my, how thoughtful!" she said, breaking into a relaxed smile, "Thank you so much!"

Jarrod had been given a set of wireless earphones as a promotional gift, and had instantly thought of Pauline. She was constantly in that awkward position, left shoulder crunched up to hold her mobile phone to her ear while she multi-tasked with her hands. Jarrod had gone out and bought a set last week and he had it wrapped and in the car for such a moment.

"You'll never be able to tell now whether I'm talking on the phone or not!" she continued, "Ah that's so sweet, thank you."

"Think nothing of it Pauline," said Jarrod. "Let me know if you need help setting them up."

Pauline smiled and walked around the table to give him a hug before retreating to the other side to take her seat.

"Good mood changer too," said Pauline, still smiling.

"Yes, right," said Jarrod, sensing he was being prompted to get on with the reason he was there. Before he could continue, Pauline broke out, as if she was admitting to all her sins.

"We were given a tip off that something was going to happen, but we had no idea what it was. Gerry had received an offer earlier last week to host a party and that it was in the club's best interests to take up the offer. I don't know who made the offer, but Gerry was straight on it, and got us all together to announce it. We were going to make it our end of season celebration. Problem was, we'd already paid a big deposit on Rosco Pronto and Gerry wasn't going to let that go …"

"So that's why we started there … and finished off at Gerry's place," said Jarrod thoughtfully.

"Yes, right," said Pauline looking at Jarrod as if he was being Captain Obvious. "Now, Gerry had to give the keys to his house to this event company and move out into a hotel for the week. Didn't really matter, as we were in London anyway on the weekend."

"So that's why we got the hotel for the weekend in London after the play off final?" asked Jarrod.

"Oh, don't be fooled into thinking Gerry wasn't planning that anyway," said Pauline. "He's an unbelievably generous man."

"No, no," said Jarrod putting his hands up in front of him, "I'm not questioning that at all. I've had nothing but a good rapport with Gerry. Loves life, lives large, I get it."

"Anyway," continued Pauline, "we got wind that the same offer had been made to all clubs in the area, from Berwick Rangers down to Middlesbrough. Even Blyth Spartans had one."

"Let me guess," said Jarrod, "It was only Newcastle who didn't have one."

"Yes!" she said, loving the opportunity of talking about this openly, "You're seeing the connection, aren't you?"

"Wow!" he said, "Absolutely!"

"Now, we're trying not to be alarmed," Pauline continued, "We're hoping that this was simply a way of keeping all players with their own clubs for the night and out of Newcastle."

"Seems a little tenuous though," said Jarrod after a moment's thought. "Why would someone go to so much trouble and expense?"

"Yeah, we don't understand," said Pauline, "but that sounds like the best version of the truth to believe at the moment."

"So, what about the painted faces and the suits?" Jarrod asked, "The killer had a similar suit and a painted face."

"It would appear so," said Pauline, "but all players were at parties across the region, so it couldn't be one of the players from any of those clubs. Gerry made sure that Caroline was capturing as many players as she could over the course of the night, just to be sure."

"Christ," said Jarrod, starting to think a bit more about this mad situation, "maybe it *was* one of the players?"

"Well," said Pauline, "whoever it was, and there's plenty of people it could have been, they would have a watertight alibi. I'm thinking it's a total decoy, and the killer has used the decoy perfectly."

Jarrod looked at Pauline and smiled. He was a little bit lost. The killer was dressed like one of 150 or so men who were at one of seven or eight parties around the region, all of whom would have been photographed throughout the night and who would have had no way of getting to Newcastle to carry out a murder.

"Well, thanks anyway for a great party," said Jarrod, changing the subject slightly. "Can you keep me informed? Marianne will have heard the news by now and she actually knows Rambouillet's wife. If there's anything you can share with me, I'd love to know."

"I'll keep you up to date," said Pauline. "Hopefully the rest of the guys don't put the pieces together and start asking questions like you."

"We'll find out tomorrow, I guess," said Jarrod, remembering that the whole squad was due at the Arena for the sponsorship day.

"Ah yes," said Pauline suddenly, "before then I have a job for you."

"Is it going to implicate me in a crime?" asked Jarrod jokingly.

"Hardly," said Pauline, "but it's definitely going to be a great service to the club as captain. I need you to ring four of our players and get them to bring in or scan through their passports in time for our departure on Thursday. We can do a mercy dash on Wednesday to get last minute passports, but I'd rather we have 100 per cent attendance at our sponsorship day. I just can't get these players to get it done. Has the fine system ended?"

"We can definitely enforce it for this one," said Jarrod. "Who are the four?"

"I'll give you the list, I've printed it out here," said Pauline handing over a hastily printed list of things they needed. One of the players, young forward Jason Glenn, even needed a permission slip from a parent as he was under eighteen.

"I'll get right on to it now," said Jarrod, pointing. "Can I use the office next door?"

Pauline stood and held her arm out to indicate that he could.

"Thanks for coming in," she said, "and thanks for the present."

"There's something weird going on, Pauline," said Jarrod, "I don't think we've heard the last of this."

Jarrod left the room and walked into the vacant contracts office next door and started the task of rounding up the required bits and pieces from his team.

Chapter 13

SELL

Marianne's mum Mireille was up and about very early, clearly anxious that this was the last opportunity she would have to be spend time with her daughter before heading back to France. Marianne hadn't got the memo though and wasn't stirring. Jarrod had woken early too and the two of them found themselves having a rare conversation in the kitchen over their oversized mugs of coffee. There had always been a mutual respect between the two of them, but the opportunity to talk one-on-one, Jarrod with his limited French and Mireille in her almost non-existent English, almost always eluded them. It was heart-warming and frustrating in equal measure.

"Thank you for take care of my Marianne," said Mireille slowly and in surprisingly good English. She was referring to her daughter's battle with cancer and the big challenges that were being thrown her way.

"No, thank you Mireille," said Jarrod in response, "this has definitely been a team effort. This would have been much tougher without you here."

Jarrod knew that his sentence was probably a little complex, but they sat in silence for a moment before Mireille again spoke.

"You have a beautiful family, Jarrod," she said, rolling the 'r's and emphasising the 'rod' in his name. "We look forward to see you more often."

There was sadness in her eyes. Jarrod stood up and offered his arms to Mireille. She stood up and they hugged their longest hug ever. Jarrod could feel the helplessness of his mother-in-law, who had seen her daughter at her lowest ebb, and was now leaving her in what she still considered her time of need.

They were both welling up when Jean-Jacques walked to the top of the stairs and slipped on the first step, thumping on to the second and only just catching the bannister to stop himself making the grandest of entrances. They could always rely on Marianne's dad to detract from the seriousness of any situation, and as he gathered his composure, muttering to himself with no doubt a number of *gros mots*, Jarrod and Mireille uncoupled from their embrace and smiled warmly at each other.

The thump at the top of the stairs stirred the rest of the family, Aneka the first to appear with a quizzical frown on her face, followed by a weary Sebastian and finally Marianne who was chuckling as she asked "What was that?" This would signal the beginning of a final breakfast together. Mireille and Jarrod made a point of setting the table for a feast, and making this a celebration rather than a day of sadness and mourning.

Jarrod was first to leave, Marianne and the kids would do the run to Teesside Airport a little later. Jarrod had an eleven o'clock start for the sponsorship day, and he was keen to get there a little earlier and was also keen to miss the floods of tears. This was an event that he had never experienced, but he was aware that it was becoming a thing in football circles.

A club would invite all its current and prospective sponsors to an open day, give them their undivided attention and try and portray as positive an image in the hope of attracting more cash injections to the club's finances. This would surely be a big one – Darlington had after all won promotion in successive seasons, a recent Wembley appearance with all the nationwide exposure, and boasted a team that was full of raw, untapped sponsorable talent. Coupled with a notoriously generous owner, a household name for a manager and a high profile international in Jarrod, this could be the moment that Darlington needed to move to the next level.

All the players arrived around the 10.30am mark, Pauline having told the squad to be there in time for an 11am start. Jarrod took this as an opportunity to check on the four players that were on his hit-list from the previous day. Dan Collier had his passport with him and Jarrod asked him to give it to Pauline when he saw her, Ghali and Mitch assured Jarrod that they had handed over their documents the day before and that left Connor Naughton.

When Connor walked in through the automatic door and clocked Jarrod, he stopped in his tracks, knowing that he had forgotten something. He was straight on the phone before Jarrod had a chance to ask him, and the process of finding his passport and getting it to Darlington was underway. He stood as his Mum remonstrated with him on the other end of the phone when she had to go through the Twilight Zone of her teenage son's room.

The players were invited out onto the Arena pitch. Pauline welcomed them and gave a quick briefing.

"Gentlemen," she started in a professional voice, "welcome to the first Darlington FC sponsor day. Each player has a booth. That booth also has an attraction next to it for the kids. You are expected to be at that booth for the duration of the event, which will begin at eleven and close at two. If you need to go to the toilet, now is the time."

The players were looking around at each other, a little bemused at being considered on par with kindergarten students.

"Today, you are all salesmen," she continued. "Today, you have the opportunity to sell your own personal brand to hundreds of current and prospective sponsors. They are looking to give money to the club and enjoy the ride as we continue our incredible success."

The squad seemed to be warming to the idea.

"At the end of today, we would like all of you to have a sponsorship deal for the season. We expect to attract shirt sponsors, sleeve sponsors, programme sponsors, you name it. Your undivided attention is required. Your professionalism and willingness to help our club move forward is absolutely essential today."

Jarrod was impressed that the players were being given the responsibility of selling themselves.

"Do you have any questions?" asked Pauline. A couple of hands went up.

"Are we competing against each other?" asked Wes after being prompted by Pauline. That was an interesting question, thought Jarrod.

Pauline responded after a moment of reflection.

"We are definitely not competing with each other, but some of you will attract bigger deals than others. We will keep you up to date during the day with who is needing some help in attracting a sponsor, and those of you who have already attracted a sponsor can direct prospective sponsors to your fellow players."

There were some nods of heads. Jarrod still couldn't quite believe how much trust was being put into the players to essentially 'not f- it up'.

"Grab a quick bite to eat," said Pauline by way of wrapping up the intro. "Our main sponsors are watching a video in the function room as we speak, and that's due to finish right on eleven. There will be many others joining us then. Thanks for your attention."

A delicious breakfast snack of crusty rolls filled with bacon and eggs and bottled water was very welcome before the players all took their positions. The first of the invitees for the day came walking down the main stand from the function room and made their way over to the makeshift starting line that would take them through this magical maze of booths and fairground attractions.

The route would take them to the refreshments area at half way, and the young players were all positioned close to the snack bar so they would get maximum exposure and through traffic. Jarrod was relieved not to be first in line, but he was a little disappointed to be almost the furthest away from the main hub.

Jarrod's first 'customer' was a sharp-looking man with two pre-school age kids, and he sent the kids off to the attraction next door before collaring Jarrod for a chat.

"Jens Lermann," he said, offering his hand before producing a business card. Jarrod almost did a double-take before realising that it couldn't be the former Arsenal goalkeeper with almost the same name.

"Hi, Jarrod Black, club captain" replied Jarrod confidently, taking the card, reading the title 'Managing Director' and placing it in a shallow dish that was meant just for that purpose. "Are you a current sponsor?"

Jarrod wasn't sure of how forthright he was meant to be, or whether this should simply be a chance for idle chit-chat.

"Not yet," replied the slender Mr Lermann, his Scandinavian accent becoming a little more obvious. "We are one of the biggest employers in the region and we are looking to partner in the success of your club. I have lived in Darlington for two years and we have heard nothing but good things about the football club and the people they have running it. I understand you are even going overseas to play this weekend?"

"It certainly is a whirlwind," said Jarrod with a smile. "The club snatched an unlikely promotion to the Football League the previous season and now we find ourselves already in League One. Remember Sunderland have been here before and look where they are now."

Jarrod was feeling pleased with his answers. The chat was positive and he felt as though he was initiating Mr Lermann into how good a club this was. When his two kids shouted for him to come join them, he finished the conversation.

"Thank you Jarrod. We will be in touch."

It felt like an unclosed deal, letting him walk away just like that but Jarrod felt he had done enough to leave at least a good impression. Who knows, this guy could be the head of a large organisation, and he could have been responsible for winning a game-changing sponsorship deal.

Jarrod checked in with Raynor Gunn in the next booth who had just finished a chat with a potential suitor.

"Hey Jarrod," said Raynor, "I'm thinking I should be a salesman when I finish my playing career. How are you doing?"

Jarrod smiled. Not only was this giving responsibility and ownership to the players, but it was actually making them feel good about themselves.

The contracts lady June started doing her rounds midway through the day. Word had got around that they had signed up several major player sponsorship deals already, and that now there would need to be a concerted effort to get some of the up and coming players involved. The senior players were instructed to go on the charm offensive. It wasn't long before Jarrod was spinning Jason Glenn to a potential sponsor who had made it clear that Jarrod was out of his league.

"Let me point you to our young centre-forward Jason," he said, leading the way through a shortcut to the booths near the snack bar. En route, he filled the sponsor in about how Jason was looking to break into the first team in the coming season and how he was being touted for possible England youth honours. He left the sponsor with Jason beckoning June over to help answer any questions.

The sun was shining through the clouds and the party was starting to get going at the snack bar. The official end of the day was signalled at 2pm, all players joining the party to mingle with the remaining guests. Jarrod ended up staying until well after 5pm. He knew he should get back to his family, as he was going to be away for the next few days. He excused himself as the final guests were making their way out, guiltily leaving behind all the clearing up to the rest of his Darlington family.

What a great day, he thought, as he drove home. The players had been more than willing to spruik their club. It was clear that they were as proud of their club and their town as Jarrod. There had been companies from around the world at the event. There were multi-national companies as well as local family-owned businesses, and Jarrod was sure that everyone had come out of the day with an appropriate deal.

The club events were coming thick and fast. They were due at Newcastle Airport at 10:30am the next day for the end of season trip to Dubai. This fit in so beautifully with Marianne's scheduled visit to the oncologist at 8am – Jarrod couldn't believe his luck at the timing - and Marianne was able to drop him to the airport after the appointment. They shared a passionate smooch as Jarrod went to get out of the car, so much so that there was eventually a beep from behind. Jarrod quickly scrambled out, grabbing his bags from the back seat only to notice that it was Freddie Asquith being dropped off.

Freddie was laughing and turned his back and gave Jarrod the self-smooch, running his arms up the sides of his own body as if he was himself in a passionate embrace. They clasped hands and shared a laugh. This was going to be a great trip.

Chapter 14

TRAVEL

The players met at a check-in desk that had been reserved especially for them and there were a few interested onlookers. Jarrod recognised the one photographer there, a source of much ire of North East players over the years, but someone with whom Jarrod had enjoyed a good working relationship over his years at Gateshead.

"Jarrod Black," stated the photographer, not sure as to whether to hold out his hand.

"Hello there," said Jarrod offering his hand which was accepted. "I've never known your first name, Shorty. I feel as though we've never been formally introduced."

"It's John," said the photographer, "John Short. Good to see you, Jarrod. I was waiting for a couple of Newcastle players who are due to fly out of here today."

"Don't say that," said Jarrod. "You were waiting for the mighty Darlington, embarking on their first overseas tour …"

"Of course," said Shorty. "Of course."

"Would you like to take some photos?" asked Jarrod. He was revelling in the fact that John would have had little or no interest in taking a photo of Darlington FC, so was mischievously keen to make this as awkward as possible. "Come on, I'll get the lads in together and you can get a few snaps."

"Okay, okay," said Shorty, fumbling with his equipment.

Jarrod corralled the troops and got them into some sort of order and Shorty started firing off a few shots. Jarrod had spotted Newcastle players Milos Sarovic and Hector Felipe arriving and checking in behind Shorty.

"Oh, I think I had my eyes closed on those," said Jarrod. "Let's have a few more."

Shorty's shoulders slumped. He went to take another round of photos he knew he wouldn't be using. The two Newcastle stars were still at the check-in desk.

"Can you get some of the youth players all together too?" asked Jarrod.

"Sure, sure …" said Shorty with a resigned look on his face.

Ghali and Sam Basaan had cottoned on to what was at play, and started fussing over the youth players, asking Shorty if they looked good. When they saw the Newcastle players ready to walk off, Shorty started impatiently snapping away again. The two players were just about to head up the escalator to departures.

"Oh, look Shorty," he said, pointing, "there's Sarovic and Felipe, just about to go through customs."

Shorty turned to see the two players, who were jetting off to their respective countries to join up early with their international squads. He looked back.

"Bastards," was all he could muster before racing off after the two players. He caught up with them just in time and managed to get the photo he was looking for. The Darlington players looked on. When the two players eventually got on the escalator up to the next level to customs, Jarrod and the Darlington players let out a cheer and a huge round of applause. Shorty's one finger salute had them in stitches as he marched off huffily in the opposite direction.

Jarrod felt a tinge of guilt for jeopardising a good photo but felt vindicated by all the times Shorty had bugged him over the years. It set the scene for a light-hearted journey to Dubai. After spending the usual unproductive time in the airport, they eventually boarded in the early afternoon.

It was early morning by the time they filed off their coach and into the hotel, and this was some place. The foyer was full-on marble, as ostentatious a place that Jarrod could ever remember visiting. The expectation of crappy rooms hidden behind this outrageous façade was dispelled. The rooms were all magnificent. The club had an entire floor, and the players shared in twos and threes. Jarrod ended up with the Dads club of Martin Howard and Dario Reilly.

It was at this point that the absence of defender Mitch struck him. He hadn't even noticed that Mitch wasn't there, as he was always there so it was never a question. Jarrod went to find Gary, and found him already downstairs in the lounge.

"Hello Jarrod," he said with a smile, a waiter coming across to bring a pot of tea. "How was the flight? I always have a cup of tea before bed."

"Hey Gary, where's Mitch?" asked Jarrod, still a little annoyed that he hadn't noticed earlier.

"Ah yes, Mitch," said Gary, pouring from the ornate teapot, "Mitch decided that he wasn't coming. I don't know what his agenda is, perhaps he doesn't like flying, perhaps he's got something going on at home, maybe he doesn't have a passport."

"He assured me he'd given his passport to Pauline," said Jarrod incredulously.

"Nope," said Gary, "and he let us know only this morning too, so Gerry is pretty angry. Seats on a plane to Dubai can't be cheap."

"Ah, I'm annoyed," said Jarrod, "why would he do that?"

"Don't get yourself involved Jarrod," said Gary. "Just let the club deal with it. I do know that some of the players have been subject to enquiries from other clubs. Maybe that could be it."

Jarrod left it at that and bid Gary goodnight. Having been sitting down for most of the day, Jarrod was a little reluctant to be going to bed. The sight of two fellow dads fast asleep was enough to send him off to his own sleep as soon as his head hit the pillow. A big day was ahead, so this was probably for the best.

Chapter 15

FIGHTBACK

It was Friday evening. After a low-key training session at the Zabeel Stadium earlier in the day and a relaxing afternoon at the hotel, they returned to the same stadium to play the first of their two games against highly rated Al-Wasl. The build-up was very surreal.

The players all congregated in the immaculate centre circle and Gary gave them an early team talk. He emphasised that they were the complete underdog. Their opponents had only just finished their season too and had underachieved, only snatching fourth spot on the final day of the season. Most commentators and fans had been expecting them to be challenging for the title.

"Diego Maradona was manager here," said Gary, "that's a club that has some pull in the football world. And this place is pumping on a match day. Hopefully we'll experience some of that."

The fact that Maradona had graced this stadium gave it a sense of occasion, and the players knew that they would be up for a big game. Nolan Parkes had brought a mate Davy along who said he lived in Dubai. He was tagging along, and looked the part in his tracksuit, cutting quite a sharp figure. They started to kick the ball around in the centre circle, Davy keen to get some touches and continue the impression of being a professional footballer.

The players were starting to get a tempo up in the traditional circle game, the two in the middle trying to get the ball off the guys on the outside who were limited to one touch. Dario played a ball a little short and Davy raced after it. Gav Selley reacted late and just managed to toe the ball to a teammate. Davy fell to his knees and then collapsed on his face, holding his left knee. The players were all having a chuckle, the non-professional being found out. No one realised, not even Nolan, that he was actually in a lot of pain.

A few passes later, Davy was still on the ground and was starting to groan. Nolan raced across to his mate, and crouched down to ask what the problem was.

"Ah man," he said through gritted teeth, "I reckon it's busted!"

"Just stay there," said Nolan, quite sure that he wasn't going anywhere. "I'll get Sash."

Nolan raced over to the bench, where Sash was rummaging through some bags to make sure he had everything for the game. After consulting with the patient and visually checking to see that the knee had started to thicken up with swelling, Sash decided it might be a good idea to get an ambulance.

"Are you kidding?" Davy pleaded. "An ambulance would cost me a year's wages. Just wait a sec and I'll hobble over to the side with you."

Gary instructed his players to return to the change rooms, the first of the fans having started to filter in, a little bemused at the sight of a player being carried across to the sideline to a waiting car that would take him off to hospital. Time was starting to tick on, and none of the players were even in their kit.

That incident seemed to knock the wind out of the players' sails, and there seemed little enthusiasm, even when they stepped out just before kick-off to a raucous welcome. That changed when Wes went to his goal and caught sight of superfan Alex Horsley behind the goal and ran across to give him a welcome hug. The rest of the players saw this and there were waves and thumbs up from the rest of the team as the referee completed the coin toss. This brought them back into focus and there was a sudden invigoration of the team. Even Jarrod could feel a twinge of nerves and a big game feeling.

The scene of utter devastation at half time though was testament to the weariness that they were feeling. Al-Wasl had struck in the eighth minute, and again on ten minutes, before adding a third just before half-time to assert their complete domination over Darlington.

Two of the goals were simple square balls into the penalty area where the attacker had reacted first, the other was a cracking shot from a full 30 yards that sailed over Wes into the corner of the net. Gary was irked. He was pacing the change room, not saying a word. Gerry had been in and out of the change room in a flash, and was clearly annoyed. This feeling permeated to the rest of the room, and Jarrod felt he had to say something to try and turn it around.

"Right, lads," he said. "We're three-nil down at Old Trafford in the FA Cup third round. They're going to take it easy in the second half, make some changes and not treat us with any respect."

Players were looking at each other and not following.

"Come on lads," said Jarrod. "Let's make a go of this. If we're going to go down, let's go down fighting. Let's shut this Old Trafford crowd up, and give them the shocks of their lives."

Gary had his eyebrows raised. He decided to go along with it.

"They've got 73,000 fans and we've got our allocation of 3,000 die hards, who are waiting for us to pull something out of the bag."

"Who's coming with us?" said Jarrod, looking at Gary. "Who's going to be the heroes of the back page of the paper tomorrow when Darlington's name is in the hat for the fourth round?"

None of the players in the room had played at Old Trafford before, Jarrod had been there a couple of times when he was taking friends from Australia to games at the shrines of English football, so he knew what it was like. He'd even seen Swansea take a point there, and knew what that feeling was.

The players bought into the ruse, and Jarrod led the team confidently out for the second half. The crowd had passed the fervour stage, the one-sided scoreline making it less buoyant than it could have been, and the game kicked off in relative quiet.

It wasn't long before the crowd was totally stunned. Jarrod picked the ball up in the middle of the park from a stray pass, shaped to shoot from way out before dinking a delicious ball through for Ghali. He himself was surprised by the amount of time he had, and coolly slotted the ball just past the goalkeeper's right hand to notch what was either a consolation or the start of a comeback. A quick glance to the assistant referee to see if he was indeed onside and Ghali raced over to the single Darlington fan that stood in the away enclosure, Alex having leapt up to celebrate the start of an unlikely fight back.

The Al-Wasl bench looked like it was going to erupt at any time, bickering and gesticulation in bucket loads, and Darlington could sense that their heightened concentration and desire had given them a chance of getting right back into this one.

Just as Gary was urging the team to slow the play down and get some touches on the ball, a huge throw from Wes sent Connor down the right and into quite a bit of space. At the point of meeting the defender where he'd normally check back and play the simple ball, he surprised everyone with a shimmy that took him wide. He then slotted the ball through the defender's outstretched legs and made for the byline.

Will Telfer was racing to keep up with this surprise attack, and when Connor looked up for options, he drilled the ball square across the goal into Will's path. The Darlo striker swept his foot at the stinging ball and got the slightest touch on it, diverting the ball onto the shin of the covering defender. The ball seared into the top corner of the net for an outrageous own goal, the goalkeeper given no chance. Connor and Will continued their run to the away enclosure, where Alex had already got his phone out, and waited for the rest of the players to arrive before getting the best selfie ever with half of the team.

Darlington were playing some of the best football they had done all season. They had now remembered just how well they could carve open a defence with their intricate passing and powerful running. Gary made a couple of subs, Julien Favot coming on for Ghali and Will Jevons replacing Sam Basaan. This took them from a trusty 4-4-2 into an all-out 3-4-3 attack formation.

Gary sent the rest of the bench to the away enclosure to make a bit of atmosphere. Only himself, Des and midfielder Jackie Thomas remained in the dugout. The intention was clear, they were going for it. A slick attack by the home side saw Darlington's comeback derailed almost immediately, Wes somehow managing to get a foot to the ball after a deflected shot looked goal bound. The ball spun precariously over the bar and onto the roof of the net where it nestled much to the relief of the visiting players. Wes afforded himself a moment to blow out his cheeks and ponder.

There were six minutes left and the game was on a knife-edge.

This game was meant to be a post-season knock-about friendly encounter, where the quality home side would be able to sign off on their season and thank the fans with a few goals. As it stood though, their fans were increasing in agitation as the minutes wore on and the volume was rising.

Freddie Asquith intercepted a promising attack from the home side and found himself at the start of a potential counter. He flicked the ball nonchalantly to Jarrod. He looked up and sent a raking ball over to the far side where Connor delicately brought the ball under control and raced for the byline. His cross was straight from the textbook, into an area between goalkeeper and attackers. Julien stretched and tried to get anything on the ball, but it was Will behind him who stooped low with a diving header and caught the ball perfectly.

The header skidded off the damp turf and into the net at the near post for an amazing equaliser. Wes ran all the way from his own half to join the celebrations in the away end. The players, coaching staff from the bench and even the physios were all making a real racket. As the players peeled themselves away, the chant went up "Nah nah nah nananah-nah, nananah-nah, Darlo!"

There was still time for a winner for either side, and the home team's fervent support was baying for blood. The white kandura robes of the mainly male crowd gave a conservative appearance that was counteracted by jumping and shouting like banshees. They were even throwing things on the field, and these were season tickets.

Even though the season was over and there were no more tickets in the season tickets, it was a gesture that expressed perfectly their disgust. In the end, a five-minute period of keep-ball by the away team was enough to see the game through.

Darlington had turned around the half time deficit to score three unanswered goals against Diego Maradona's former team.

The post-match mood was one of utter exhilaration, and even a dry bar afterwards didn't deter the players from having a great time re-living the second half. Superfan Alex had been invited into the players' lounge and was having a ball, chatting with all the players as he had done earlier that week and getting selfies with everyone.

Jarrod couldn't remember feeling this way after a friendly game, and he was still buzzing as the team coach took the team through the now deserted car park and the few kilometres to the hotel. His phone had a bank of messages when he finally checked it. There was even one on there from Socceroos coach Mike Jerszek, a proponent of the UAE football scene, congratulating him on his team's result.

Chapter 16

MEGS

This mini-tour was already clearly a success, the low expectations he felt for Dubai on the Saturday morning were begging to be exceeded. The team met at 8am in the hotel lobby after an early breakfast and were ushered onto a trio of slightly unnerving mini-vans for a short journey out into the desert.

It was only five minutes before they left the sleek modern streets and found themselves surrounded by barren sandy building lots which then in turn gave way to flowing sand dunes. The players stared wide-eyed through the windows and hung on tight to the seat in front as the vans veered a corner at high speed and shot along a dead straight road to their final destination. They arrived at a camp where there was a fleet of large white four-wheel drives, each with a driver standing at the door in a perfect line.

The squad got out of their mini-vans and were guided to their vehicles, parties of four per car and they were all set for an adventure. Jarrod was in the front seat, buckled in using a proper racing harness that crossed his chest, his fellow passengers buckled in using standard seat belts in the back for what promised to be the ultimate wild ride.

The driver propped an iPad on the dashboard and played a safety briefing, much like the one they had half-listened to on the plane on Thursday, but this one was a little more graphic. Jarrod was sure the message had sunk in that all body parts must remain in the vehicle and that seat belts must remain fastened at all times. As soon as the message finished, the cars all raced off in unison, and Jarrod and his teammates were off on a half-hour scramble through the dunes.

The squad reassembled under a shade and swapped stories. Will had dented the roof with his head after their car got airborne. The car that Wes and Freddie were in had fallen on its side and had to be winched up, a process that took about half a minute. Sam Basaan's car came in full of sand after one of the passenger windows shattered. There was a lot of adrenaline pumping, and that made the next part of the challenge even more tempting – camel riding!

Jarrod had never been anywhere near a camel, he'd only ever seen them on TV, and he could not remember any good stories that went along with them. The players' heightened senses after the thrill of the crazy sand dune safari gave them all the required bravado to get up onto the camels. Gary, Des and the rest of the staff were looking on, so was midfielder Roni Verelo, who had put his hands up straight away and refused to do it. Jarrod got up first time and took his place on the precarious saddle, and it wasn't long before they set off.

If someone had told him this time last year that he would be in the desert riding a camel with Darlington FC, he would have laughed. But here he was, being filmed from every angle as he lolloped around untidily on the back of the huge beast. The players were still hyped when they negotiated the dismount. Only Ghali had trouble getting off. He missed the big wooden step and went tumbling into the sand which attracted a big roar of laughter from the onlookers.

There was time for some extra strong coffee and Middle Eastern sweet treats that were not exactly devoured. Baklava was the only one Jarrod recognised, a treat seen at many teammates' houses when he was growing up back in Sydney, but he wasn't game to try it. It was now almost midday, and Darlington had their second and final game late in the afternoon. Pauline was keen to get everyone packed up in their mini-vans and back to base camp to head off to the stadium, and made quick work of rounding up the players.

After lunch at the hotel, it wasn't long before they were assembled and ready to head off to the Police Officers Stadium for the low-key fixture against unknowns Hatta Club, who themselves were travelling from out of town for this game.

Gerry was first off the coach and straight into an embrace with a tall Indian-looking lady, either a staff member of the opposition or someone from the Police Officers Club. Jarrod couldn't help thinking that Gerry was the quintessential guy who 'knows everyone'. He walked down the steps from the air-conditioned bus and the heat hit him. It would definitely be tough if the temperature stayed like this during the game. It was not something totally foreign to Jarrod, but it had been about twenty years since he'd played football in these conditions.

By kick-off, after a leisurely warm up and a swim in the adjacent pool, the heat had subsided somewhat, but it was still in the low 30s. It was decided to play the game in four quarters, allowing the players to take on fluids in a two-minute break on 22 minutes. As a result, the game was a little disjointed, and the players, especially the Darlington team who had played a high tempo game the night before, were struggling to put any meaningful passes together.

Gary had totally changed the team, Roni in midfield with

Jarrod, a totally fresh front three of Jason Glenn, Julien Favot and Will Jevons. The idea was to get the young guys to do the running, and it worked to some extent, but the quality of the play once they got the ball up there was sadly lacking.

At half-time the score was unsurprisingly locked at 0-0 and Wes had been working as a central defender with little to do other than distribute the ball and get it back again. They needed something to pep up the game. They had tried the analogy of the FA Cup third round tie last time, what would they come up with this time?

Gary had the answer, and he gave the players a challenge, totally canning his usual tactical half-time speech. He wanted every player on the field to do a nutmeg in the second half. The players looked at each other excitedly. There was an immediate shift in the mood.

"So, we're looking for goals too, right?" asked Ghali, who was happy warming the bench but all of a sudden interested in making an appearance.

"I'd like to win this game," said Gary, "but I think we need to do it with a little bit of fun. We'll take you out to a bar that serves alcohol tonight if we can get all eleven players who start the second half to do at least one nutmeg each."

"You'll substitute us if we're close," said Wes.

"No, no," assured Gary, "there's your challenge. Don't know about anyone else, but this dry heat is making me thirsty!"

The players were up for this, it was obvious. It was as though this was the last day of the regular season and half-time scores were going their way to give them a chance of winning the league.

"No goals, Wes," said Gary. "Don't let us down!"

The players strode out onto the field from the impressive

arched main stand, looking like a different team. There were no changes at half-time, but this didn't mean there wouldn't be many in the second half. Jarrod was a little concerned that this could be the most farcical second half on record, but he was excited by the challenge.

Hatta kicked off and kept possession for a good two minutes, looking to continue the theme of the first half. The front three though started to press and it was Julien who stole the ball and laid it right back to Wes from well inside the Hatta half to allow Darlington some quality possession of their own. The challenge was at the forefront of everyone's mind, but to do nutmegs, 'megs' or 'nutties' as Jarrod grew up with, they had to tempt the opponents on to them and stretch the game.

Wes toyed with the ball and rolled it to Freddie who dallied intentionally on the ball and sucked in the challenge from the attacker. He managed to roll it back to Wes, who was faced with an on-rushing forward and feigned to thump the ball long before delicately touching the ball through his legs as he braced for a hit. The cheer from the players was huge, the attacker had no idea where the ball was and Wes saluted with one finger in the air. He was off on a FIFA-esque goalie run up the field before remembering where he was and laying a simple ball to Raynor to continue the move.

By the time three-quarter time had been called, the count was up to seven, and they had still kept their challenge a secret from their opponents. Julien had done the best one, jinking to his right, shaping to shoot, and then scooping the ball through the outstretched legs of the defender who was trying to block the shot. That gave him a great chance on his weaker left but he fluffed his lines. The score remained goalless as the ball bobbled harmlessly wide of the goal.

The players were geeing each other up, there were a few substitutions at this point, four players who had achieved their goal were sacrificed, and some of the more senior players were coming on for the last quarter. Four more players and their evening would be very different.

When Hatta scored from their first real attack with 15 minutes left on the clock, Gary was up out of his dugout and was furious. He was barking at his players to concentrate. He needn't have worried though, as directly from the kick-off, Dean and Ghali combined down the right and a beautifully weighted cross was swung straight onto the head of Will Telfer, the tall striker making no mistake from eight yards out.

A few more nutmegs and Darlington had one more player to make the full eleven. The game was poised at one goal a-piece and there were five minutes left. The choice was there to go for the win or go for the full house. It was clear that the missing nutmeg would be the goal. The players started to concentrate on manufacturing situations around Freddie. The central defender was the least likely by his own admission to dummy a player, and he seemed unable to work out a situation by himself.

It took a piece of trickery from Roni, who dummied a pass from Jarrod, causing Freddie to panic and stick out his leg instinctively to divert it, and it slipped perfectly through the legs of the Hatta attacker. Freddie leapt into the air in shock. The Darlington players, free of the shackles of the challenge, scrambled into position to transition onto the counter attack. They streamed upfield with a flowing move that saw Connor skip past his marker and romp down the right.

He glanced up to see Roni scuttling to the far post and arrowed in a swerving ball with the outside of his left foot, Roni meeting it with a slide. The ball looped up and over the keeper before nestling in the back of the net for what would surely be the winner. Roni was straight up and looking for players to celebrate with and the whole team raced to him and joined in a joyful pack of bouncing players.

The Hatta players were looking around perplexed by the magnitude of the celebrations, and it took a good two minutes for play to restart. Darlington went on the ultra-defensive again, Wes and Sam playing keep-ball as the Hatta players barely broke into a stride to try and win the ball.

A long aimless ball upfield was enough to see the 90 minutes up, and the referee blew for time with no injury time. Darlington had again come up with a win. The players were full of endorphins at the end of this one, sharing stories in the changing room about whose nutmeg was the best, and making plans for the evening ahead. Gary had created a fighting spirit in the players that would never have come about organically. Jarrod was reminded of a YouTube video he'd seen of the England team trying to slip in as many song titles into TV interviews during a World Cup, and felt that this one was a close rival.

The players were transferred back to the hotel almost straight after the game – the fact that they were not in fact being hosted by Hatta meant that there was not an official post-match function, so the players were back at the hotel by 8pm. Gary was first up to get off the coach, and instead grabbed the microphone and announced that the hotel lobby would be their venue for the evening after receiving advice from the hotel staff and UK consulate advisors.

There were groans from the back seats. Jarrod had read up

about alcohol in Dubai, and was instantly relieved that the players would be confined to the hotel, where any sort of booze-fuelled nonsense would take place within the walls of their accommodation. A squad of players venturing out into Dubai after a few drinks was possibly one of the toughest assignments imaginable for a club captain. The first person they saw was Davy, sitting at the bar with his crutches, waiting for the party to begin.

The hotel had organised finger food and there was a free bar. Someone had obviously made a few calls and there were gradually more and more people turning up to join the party, the ex-pat network being quite a reliable source of partygoers if there was a sniff of a soirée. The evening was excellent, the players continued their jovial spirit which got them the victory today and the Darlington staff were more than happy to enjoy a few beers for the final night of the tour.

Gerry was his usual self, his tie getting looser by the hour until it came off and the impromptu dancefloor erupted when the latest David Guetta hit was pumped through the speakers at full volume. Jarrod was getting used to this party vibe. After all it was only last weekend that they had partied after the play off victory and only five days since the Monday night madness that Gerry had put on.

Some sore heads were in the lobby at 4am as the check-out process started, and there were some bleary-eyed players making their way onto the coach to the airport. Jarrod felt a little strange not to be continuing on to Sydney, as he had done every other time he'd flown in to Dubai from Newcastle. The fact that this was the end of the season made him a little annoyed that he hadn't thought of doing so.

This had been an epic tour, one that would go down in history with the players. They could do no wrong, they had shown they had the magical recipe for pulling results out of a hat, and they were as tight a bunch of players as Jarrod had ever been amongst. There were question marks over Mitch's absence but he was sure that everyone else felt the same as himself.

The bus back from Newcastle airport arrived around 2.30pm into the Arena. This was the definitive end of the season now, and the players knew it. There were hugs and pats on the back between players. The staff were enjoying a final laugh, and Gary was being liberal with his praise and wished everyone a happy holiday. They had effectively four weeks off before the official start of pre-season, and most players had booked to go away. Marianne had booked that trip to Geneva, albeit only just over a week, but they had to change the dates to work around Jarrod's surprise call-up to the Australia squad.

There were a few Mums and Dads doing the pick-up, but most of the players had their cars in the car park ready to go. Jarrod remembered that he was not on the coach to the airport last Thursday and hollered at Wes to give him a lift home. His tired-looking teammate simply stuck up his thumb and let Jarrod run after him to join him in his car for the short ride home.

Chapter 17

INSPECTOR

Jarrod was effectively now on holiday. He did have two days before he would join up with the Socceroos squad for their games in the Czech Republic and Switzerland. The gym at the Arena remained open, staffed with physios still working on players from both the football club and the rugby club.

The Sunday afternoon had been fun, catching up with the family after the few days away. Jarrod had offered to do the Monday morning routine and the school run despite being very tired. He continued on to the Arena and, about half a mile from his destination, received a call from Pauline. She was at the Arena on speaker with June, which she announced before they even said hello. Jarrod was intrigued.

"Jarrod," said June, cheerily, "what are your plans for today?"

"Hi June," said Jarrod, trying to match her enthusiasm. "Just on my way in, as it happens. Should I be turning around and going home?"

"No, no," said both Pauline and June together, "we just need to see you for maybe half an hour before your gym session."

She obviously knew already that he was coming in.

"No problem," said Jarrod. "No problem at all. See you in five minutes."

He hung up and the radio came back on, just after the start of the sports report. It wasn't long before talk turned to transfer dealings, and there was talk of Mitch being courted by Rangers in Scotland. That would be a big move for him. If there was any substance in the rumour, it would not be a surprise that Mitch hadn't made the trip to Dubai. The sports reporter also alluded to an earlier item in the news about André Rambouillet, mentioning that Newcastle would be looking for a midfield kingpin to fill the space left by the late French superstar.

Jarrod arrived in the mostly empty car park. He found a car spot near the front door and made his way in. There was no one in reception, so Jarrod made his way up the steps to the contracts office, where there was some chatter. There were some male voices, which gave Jarrod a bit of a surprise.

He walked around the corner into the doorway and saw June and Pauline on one side of the desk, and two professional looking gentlemen sitting on the other, with a chair beside them. Jarrod smiled at the two men, before June took control of proceedings.

"Jarrod Black," she said, half as a greeting, half as an introduction. "Detective Inspector Allison from Northumbria Police."

She glanced at the business cards in front of her, "and Chief Superintendent Suwaris from Scotland Yard. Gentlemen, if I got any of that wrong, I do apologise."

The more exotic-looking of the men, the one closest to Jarrod, stood up and offered his hand, by which time his colleague had also got to his feet to greet Jarrod.

"Dinesh Suwaris," offered the tall Indian-looking man, "but you can call me Dennis."

They shook hands.

"And this is D.I. Allison," he continued. "You can call him D.I. Allison."

The shorter of the two men, the D.I. had the look of a local, or at least from somewhere nearby.

With introductions over and done with, Jarrod didn't need prompting and took the third seat next to the two policemen. He was puzzled as to what this could be about. His first thought was one of his teammates, but this was someone from Scotland Yard, so it must be something London related.

"Right," said Jarrod, breaking the silence, "what can I do for you ladies?"

He hoped it didn't sound too flippant. That wasn't his intention.

"Okay, right," said June, "let me start this off by saying that Newcastle United have made an enquiry to sign you."

Boom! Strike to the heart!

"Wow!" said Jarrod, sitting upright immediately but trying to maintain a level head.

"That's just the start," said June in a tone that suggested she was giving him a warning rather than getting ready to reel off more interested parties. "We had responded that our star player Jarrod Black was not going anywhere at any price, and we thought that was the end of it. That is, until Dennis and D.I. Allison became involved."

"Keep in mind," interjected Pauline, "that this just happened yesterday after we got back from Newcastle airport."

Jarrod turned quizzically to the two men next to him. Dennis started.

"Please treat everything you hear today as strictly confidential," said Dennis.

"Of course," said Jarrod.

"We are investigating a criminal gambling organisation, one that has been implicated in the death of a fellow footballer, André

Rambouillet, last week in Newcastle."

"Okay …" stumbled Jarrod, unsure as to the direction of the conversation.

"The link between the death of Mr Rambouillet and this organisation is not public and we would like to keep it that way."

"Right …" agreed Jarrod, not quite able to comprehend the unfolding scenario.

"We would like you to join Newcastle," said D.I. Allison, "and become our man on the inside as we investigate further into this link. We feel that we are very, very close to bringing down this organisation, and with Rambouillet now out of the picture, we see you as the perfect person to bring this investigation to its conclusion."

Jarrod's jaw had dropped a little and he felt that he was breathing in through his mouth. He was absolutely stunned. Signing for Newcastle? Helping the police catch criminals? Step in to a role where the last person had been shot and killed? Are these guys for real? Jarrod held his tongue and looked pleadingly at June and Pauline for support or guidance. They were clearly as perplexed as him.

"Rambouillet was shot in the head in broad daylight," said Jarrod. "Does that sound a little worrying for a father with two kids and a sick wife?"

"Let's go through the basics first," said D.I. Allison, shifting in his seat and launching into an instantly likeable broad Geordie accent. "We believe Rambouillet was responsible for manufacturing on-field situations. We've been through all his games this season, and there are three incidents that stand out when correlated with spikes in betting activity."

"I think I know one of them," said Jarrod, "Everton away."

The two men nodded either in anticipation or agreement.

"He smashed the ball into his own player and conceded an own goal," continued Jarrod. "It was comical."

"You might be surprised to hear that it was that game, but not that incident," said D.I. Allison. "Newcastle battled well to come back in that game, and won a penalty late on to win it. I know, I was at the game. The Newcastle end was going off at that point."

"And Rambouillet who normally takes the penalties, gave it to Szczepanski instead, who scored the winner in the last minute," continued Jarrod. He was feeling rather pleased with himself and was warming to D.I. Allison who was obviously a football man.

Jarrod sat in contemplation for a moment.

"So why was Rambouillet shot?" he asked.

"Rambouillet had refused to go to the next level," said Dennis. "He wasn't prepared to make obvious mistakes and we think he had openly refused to manufacture a situation in a big game where there was a lot of money riding on his actions. We don't know exactly when and what he was meant to do, but we do know that he was a marked man for about three weeks before being murdered."

"Is any of this linked to the party we had last Monday?" asked Jarrod.

The two men looked at each other.

"There could be a link," said Dennis but he wasn't prepared to go any further.

Jarrod looked at Pauline, whose nostrils flared as her chair creaked.

"Of course there's a bloody link," exclaimed Jarrod. "Why the hell would we be at a party with paint all over our faces, doing the same thing as Middlesbrough and Sunderland, Gateshead and even Blyth bloody Spartans."

The two men continued to remain calm as Jarrod took his opportunity to spill everything that he'd been holding on to.

"And it just so happens that at the same time," Jarrod said, taking a quick breath, "at the same time, a man with the same paint on his face is filmed in broad daylight gunning down a Premier League superstar."

He was standing up now, unsure as to what to do with himself.

"Can you see why I'm a little edgy?" asked Jarrod to his captive audience. There was no reply. Jarrod took a deep breath and sat down, his body language as closed as it could be, arms crossed, legs crossed, sitting back in his seat and not looking at anyone in particular.

"Jarrod," said D.I. Allison, careful not to be irksome, "your career is coming to an end in the next couple of years?"

Jarrod looked him in the eye. No time for sentiment.

"Two years if I stay injury free."

"And so, with interest from Newcastle United …" continued D.I. Allison.

"And a lot of love for Newcastle United in your family…" added Dennis, which caused Jarrod's eyebrows to lift.

"… you would be crazy not to take this opportunity to finish off your career at St James' Park," said D.I. Allison. "I mean, what an honour. What a news story. Thirty-five years of age and signing for the only club in the country where twenty-eight is the usual use-by date."

Jarrod sat staring ahead, clearly agitated, but his arms had dropped and his legs were straight out in front of him. After a long pause, he spoke.

"So what's in it for me? I go to Newcastle, we get the guys, you make arrests. What happens to me then?"

"We'll take you back," said June, very matter-of-fact. "If you want to come back that is. This will be a loan move, if it makes it easier."

Jarrod looked at June.

"And when it's all over, I just come back?" he asked.

"Well, it's not unusual," said June, "to go out on loan and then the loan agreement ends. End of story. No one loses, you get a handsome pay cheque for a few months then you come back."

"On the other hand," interrupted Pauline, "you could have a blinder at Newcastle and they keep you for the season. Remember that they do legitimately want you."

Jarrod couldn't help feeling a sense of duty, but most of all he had a feeling that he really wanted to play for Newcastle, the club he had supported all his life, the reason for his late nights and early mornings growing up back in Sydney.

"Okay, so it's a loan deal," he said. "Are we talking right now? Today?"

"No," said D.I. Allison. "You have international duty and also a holiday to take. Let's keep it under wraps until that's all out of the way."

"Things will happen very quickly though when you return," said Dennis. "You will be transferred to Newcastle on a loan deal, as discussed, and you will join up with your new club for the start of pre-season, which is scheduled for the first weekend in July."

"Then what?" asked Jarrod curtly.

"Then we get you talking to the people we need to get you talking to," said D.I. Allison, "and you build up a similar relationship to the one Rambouillet had."

"Rambouillet's dead though," Jarrod reminded them.

"Yes, but we're going to be involved every step of the way," said Dennis. "and as soon as we have the information we need, we will make the necessary arrests, implicate the necessary people in the crime, and you will be free to follow whichever path you choose."

"Won't these people be laying low right now?" asked Jarrod. "I mean, someone killed someone, and there'll be quite a few of your guys looking for him, I imagine."

"These people will try to lay low," said Dennis, "but the sniff of a payday and the thought of having got away with it will be enough to coax them into resuming their criminal activities."

"You do know I'm a really bad liar," said Jarrod, changing the subject completely.

"That's not a bad trait to have," said D.I. Allison, "but you'll surprise yourself if you get put in any tricky situations."

"Do I get a choice in all this?" asked Jarrod.

"Of course," said D.I. Allison. "You can choose to say no and we take a few steps backwards and try a different approach. The timing though is so good, and this is your chance to remove an element from football that no one in this country wants."

"And what would your dad say?" asked June.

Another shot to the heart.

Jarrod left the room with a hug for Pauline, a firm handshake for June and the two policemen. Pauline was clearly torn by this – her go-to man for a quality interview, the club captain, a player who had brought his team together to perform in his mould, was set to leave the club. And yet she was so pleased for him. Jarrod realised he'd been in there for over an hour, and started jogging to get to the gym.

There was a lot of activity in the gym, a couple of first teamers in there, and just as Jarrod walked in with a determination to get stuck in to some weights, Mitch Short appeared behind him.

"Mitchy!" exclaimed Jarrod, delighted to have someone to take his mind off the bombshell that had just landed at his feet. "Tell me everything!"

They clasped hands and hugged.

"What a whirlwind," said Mitch, looking excited and agitated, not sure where to be looking or how to be standing. "I got a call from Gary to say that Rangers were keen to talk to me. I was all packed and ready for Dubai."

"We were wondering where you'd gone," offered Jarrod.

"I didn't have any idea anyone was interested," said Mitch with brutal honesty. Jarrod definitely knew how Mitch was feeling. After all, he was in the same situation himself, only he couldn't say anything.

"So, does it sound attractive?" asked Jarrod, knowing very well that Mitch would be very interested indeed.

"Oh my god, Jarrod," he said, "attractive? It's like being offered an upgrade from a Nissan Micra to a Bentley. Have you seen Rangers training facilities?" He kept that last sentence a little quiet, given where they were standing, not wanting to sound ungrateful.

"This is your big chance, mate," said Jarrod, giving him a rub of the arm, "we'll miss you."

Mitch was distracted by one of the physios who was pointing at his watch and beckoning him over. He smiled at Jarrod and blundered over apologetically to the physio. Jarrod made his way to one of the weights machines and got in to position ready to expend a great deal of energy and to get his mind elsewhere.

Chapter 18

DUDDY

"Jarrod," said Dad, answering the phone in a jolly mood, "great to hear your voice. Lots of rumours going round. What's happening?"

"Hello Dad," said Jarrod, "I'm fine, thanks for asking … "

"Ha ha, don't give me that," said Dad. "Stop being so Australian. Now, where are you calling me from?"

"Deepest Darlington," said Jarrod, still sitting in the car, not having left the Arena car park yet after the gym session. The windows had started to fog up from his sweat. He wound the window down a touch to let some fresh air circulate through the car.

"Thought you might be in Czechoslovakia," said Dad, trying to sound all retro cool but coming across all old and uncool.

"Not yet," said Jarrod. "Still a couple of days before I head out. Say, have you spoken with Mr Leonard recently?"

"Mr Leonard?" asked Dad suspiciously, sensing some news. "Now why would I speak with Mr Leonard?"

"I'm just after a little advice," said Jarrod, "and I would like to run something past him. You do stay in touch with him, don't you?"

"Of course I do, son," said Dad emphatically, "he's a hero in my eyes. Got you your big break. Now, what's this all about, and why are you asking me and not him?"

"Well," said Jarrod, pausing for dramatic effect, "there is a possibility that St James' Park might be my next stop."

Jarrod left it at that and there was silence. He could picture Dad punching the air and racing across the room in Alan Shearer fashion.

"Ah that's great news," said Dad, trying to keep quiet and not to wake up the whole house. "I'll give him a ring now. It's not too late. He'll be intrigued."

Jarrod looked at his watch in horror.

"Ah shit, sorry Dad. Did I get it all wrong? Nine hours ahead aren't you?"

"No, you got it spot on. Your mum's out tonight with the girls. She wanted me to go and pick her up, so I'm up for a while yet. You know how she says she'll not have a late night when she goes out. I'll be good for another few hours yet. I'll ring him now …"

Dad hung up and Jarrod was left listening to a dial tone for a few seconds. He hung up and checked the news on his phone, navigating through to the Chronicle website and the Newcastle United news. Rambouillet still led the headlines but there was plenty of other news, and lots of transfer activity and rumours. Nothing about Jarrod though and that's the way he expected it to stay for at least another two weeks. The phone buzzed in his hand, incoming call.

"Jarrod," said the voice on the other end of the line, "my best agent work!"

"Hello Mr Leonard," said Jarrod, recognising his voice immediately, "I hope it's not too late for you?"

"As always," said Mr Leonard, "any time is a good time. How can I be of service?"

Jarrod took a breath.

"Darlington have been approached by Newcastle with an enquiry as to my availability," said Jarrod.

"Wow!" said Mr Leonard enthusiastically. "You're 35 years old!"

"I know," said Jarrod, "but I'm looking good for a 35-year-old, surely? Don't you think?"

"Well, yes," said Mr Leonard, "and a full international. So, they're asking about your availability. That's your call, Jarrod."

"Right," said Jarrod slowly, "I thought maybe I'd get a bit of advice from you, one way or another. You know, a bit of devil's advocate, some friendly cajoling. Anything."

"Well, first of all," said Mr Leonard, "I'm no longer an agent, so you will need to find yourself an agent. I think a move to the Premier League is going to need a good one to get you the most appropriate deal. Secondly, didn't you just win promotion with the club that you took a punt on only 12 months ago? And finally, what would your Dad say. Oh my goodness, if he wasn't proud enough of his son already, his heart would be beating out of his chest at this."

Jarrod was taking it all in.

"Now," continued Mr Leonard, "rewind one year. What would you have done then if Darlington and Newcastle were vying for your services?"

"I think I'd still have gone to Darlington to be honest," said Jarrod sheepishly.

"You're another year older now," stated Mr Leonard. "This will be your final chance to play Premier League football. If I were you,

I'd be taking this opportunity with two hands. You'll not die wondering."

"Where do I get an agent from?" asked Jarrod, suggesting that he would not be dying wondering any time soon.

"Think of the most professional footballer you know," said Mr Leonard, getting into his stride, "one who has made a move in the last year or two. Now get in touch with him and ask who his agent is. Word of mouth. The only way."

"Okay," said Jarrod, "on to it."

"Good man, Jarrod," said Mr Leonard, sure that the decision had been made. "I don't quite see how you tick the boxes for a Newcastle player. They usually go for the young player on a long contract. There is change at St James' Park, so you could be part of the new regime."

"Let's do this," said Jarrod with resolve, happy that he'd been swayed by one of his fiercest allies. "Thanks Mr Leonard. I really appreciate your honesty and knowledge."

"Keep us updated. And strike while the iron's hot."

Jarrod hung up. After his last transfer had got a little complicated and nervy, he knew that he would be in for a tricky time again, and that things would happen very quickly once he got in touch with the Detective Inspector to give him the thumbs up.

Jarrod toyed with his phone, then put it down on the passenger seat and placed his foot on the brake, about to start the car. A slump of the shoulders was all it took to make him realise that he had to make the call now and that any procrastination wasn't going to get him anywhere.

"Jarrod, great to hear from you," came the voice of D.I. Allison on the other end of the line, "I wasn't expecting to hear from you so soon."

"Hello there D.I. Allison," said Jarrod, "can I call you by your first name? It just makes me a little nervous not knowing."

"Aye, sure," said the Detective Inspector, "my Christian name is Marcus. Dennis was just being a bit of a smart arse this morning. Feel free to call me whatever you like, but it's Detective Inspector, not Inspector …"

"Okay, understood," replied Jarrod, a smile in his voice.

"What can I do for you Jarrod?" asked D.I. Allison.

"Right, well I've made a few calls and I'm ready to go," said Jarrod. "There is the question though of an agent."

"Yes, that's something we've had teed up for a while now," said D.I. Allison. "We've got one of the top agents in the North East involved, and he is willing to be on the inside with this too. You probably know his name, Duddy Freiberg."

"Woah, yes," said a startled Jarrod, more excited at the fact that he wouldn't need to worry about finding an agent, "everyone knows Duddy."

The mercurial Mr Freiberg was a most charismatic man, a cross between Rod Stewart and Liberace, a true gentlemen with a lot of bling. He was like the Don King of North East football, always involved in every event in some capacity and always spruiking players as 'the next Wayne Rooney' or 'a future Jordan Henderson'. He was very well liked, and was one of the only football agents you could actually put a face and a name to.

"Mr Freiberg has extensive experience in dealing with Premier League clubs," said D.I. Allison, "and he has been briefed as to what is required and what the situation is."

"Wow," said Jarrod, "this really is turning into a plot for a movie. So how do I contact Duddy? I usually bump into him all over the place, but I haven't seen him for a couple of months. Say, no, hold on. I saw him on Monday at Gerry's!"

"Yes, he's actually been working with us on another matter," said the D.I., "but I think he's keen to get off that one and on to something where he knows the lay of the land. I'll text you his mobile number. Thanks for agreeing to this."

"You do realise that I am jeopardising my career here," stated Jarrod.

"Ha," said D.I. Allison, "if I had the chance to sign for Newcastle, there'd be no hesitation. Just imagine walking out at St James' in front of 50-odd thousand fans. What a blast!"

Chapter 19

CHEMO

It was Tuesday morning. Jarrod and Marianne had dropped the kids at school and made the dash up the A1, getting to the clinic right on time for the appointment. This was to be the final chemotherapy session, and the old terraced house was becoming dwarfed by the new modern building taking shape next door. Marianne confidently burst through the door and breezed in, Jarrod left in no doubt as to who was in charge today. She had been feeling ill the night before but today she had her brave face on – with a great beaming smile, however forced.

After being greeted and informed by the receptionist that there would only be a three or four minute wait, they were invited through to 'the lounge' before they had even picked up a magazine each. Jarrod stayed well back as his whirlwind of a wife strode through behind the nurse, Anne-Charlotte, and took her seat in the comfy looking armchair.

Jarrod spied a few familiar faces from the last visit, but kept his greetings to nods and winks as he trailed behind. The middle-aged man who did the rounds with the tea and coffee looked up and tentatively made his way over, half expecting to be shooed away. Marianne was super friendly and she accepted a mug of tea from his porcelain teapot and even one of the home-made sandwiches, cut into triangles. This was the Marianne that he admired. He crouched down next to her as she started away in conversation in French with the nurse. A quick squeeze of the arm, and he interrupted quietly.

"See you later," he whispered. Marianne turned and smiled. Jarrod got up and walked back out to the reception and into the street. It was time to get his head in the right place.

His meeting with the agent had been perfectly scheduled to fit in with Marianne's chemo session and Marianne had herself suggested that Jarrod should leave her at the clinic. She knew he was meeting an agent, but that was as far as their conversation had gone. It was a ten-minute walk at least and it was ten minutes to the meeting time. Jarrod had, subconsciously or otherwise, chosen a little French café as the meeting spot, not far from St James' Park. He broke into a jog but decided it would be better to arrive just on time than a minute or two in advance and all hot and bothered. He was the client here too, so he could even be late, he figured.

The feeling of all eyes being on him had been a common one in the past, but he was pretty sure he was incognito today, dressed smartly as if he was a worker in one of the neighbouring businesses. There were a few people in the courtyard in front of the café and no heads looked up as he carefully negotiated the tables and went inside. It was a beautiful day. It seemed a shame to be indoors.

Jarrod had been here before and he knew there were a few alcoves and nooks where you could have a bit of privacy, and he walked just past the counter and turned the corner into a small area with only one table and four chairs. Three of the chairs were taken up by the large frame of a man and his two large satchels, and the large table was mostly taken up with paperwork.

"Well hello there Jarrod," came the friendly greeting as the grey-haired man looked up from his reading and realised who was standing in front of him. Jarrod moved closer, offering his hand. After carefully putting down his papers, adjusting his glasses and creaking to his feet, the man standing before Jarrod was about six inches taller than him and had hands like goalie gloves. He plunged his hand into Jarrod's.

"I'm absolutely thrilled to finally meet you in a professional environment," he boomed in his softened anglicised Edinburgh accent.

"Good to see you, Duddy," said Jarrod, who felt as though he was meeting Sean Connery, "I don't think I've ever met you in the daytime."

That was probably true. If there was ever a night time event, an awards ceremony or an organised night out with Gateshead, Duddy would invariably show up towards the end of the night. They had shared a brief conversation at the casino one night, when Jarrod had been touted with a move to the top level about five years ago. Duddy was aware that Jarrod didn't have an agent and, although very keen to offer his services, stopped short of being pushy. He had though made quite an impression on Jarrod. Jarrod felt at the time that Duddy was out of his league, and they had never talked about it again.

"Ha, ha, my friend," said Duddy, "I do my best work at night. Although the man you see today is getting a lot less tolerant of loud bars and nightclubs."

Jarrod took the empty seat opposite Duddy. Duddy popped his head around the corner and caught the eye of the lady at the counter.

"A big bottle of sparkling water …" he requested. He turned to

Jarrod before turning again, "… two glasses, and two Croque Monsieurs, please."

Jarrod couldn't hear the reply, but Duddy nodded his head and returned to the table and sat back in his seat, which creaked loudly under the weight. He had chosen well, the Croque Monsieur conjuring up memories of the multiple trips to France he had enjoyed over the years with Marianne. The bottle of water arrived immediately.

"Let's get down to business," said Duddy, his huge fingers struggling to separate two pages of a document he was trying to fold back to the front cover. He didn't seem the slightest bit concerned that his booming voice could probably be heard out on the street. "I've spoken with our illustrious friends Dennis and Marcus, and they have filled me in on everything. So much so that I feel as if I know you more than your wife does."

Jarrod sat glued to Duddy, waiting for the punchline.

"I've also spoken with June," he continued, "I've actually dealt with June on a number of deals in the past. I like the way she works."

Jarrod was conscious that he was talking without giving away anything about the subject matter, and was assuming a level of knowledge from Jarrod.

"And the last person I spoke to last night was from the cathedral just around the corner from here. He was a little dismissive at first, but when I explained who I was representing, he was more than happy to have a very long conversation indeed."

Jarrod was taking this in.

"In fact," he continued, "I think I might have rebuilt a bridge that had been burned many years ago."

"So," said Jarrod slowly, "what was the outcome of your

conversations yesterday?"

"Well," said Duddy, lowering his voice a little, "that was yesterday. This morning, the nice man at the cathedral rang me back and he was quite excited. He wanted things to happen very quickly. I said 'We can work quickly, no problem, but let's do this properly and I'll get back to you tomorrow' but he was very insistent."

"So, you reckon there's going to be some sort of agreement happening today?" deduced Jarrod. Duddy studied Jarrod for a moment.

"How does three times your salary for a year sound?" he finally asked.

Jarrod's eyes widened, and in his head he cursed himself for letting it happen. All he could think of was why he hadn't trusted Duddy earlier in his career.

"Anything else?" asked Jarrod almost tongue-in-cheek. "You do realise what is at stake here for me."

"Signing on fee, yes," said Duddy picking up the document that he had been wrestling with earlier, "win bonus, yes, appearance fee, yes, goal bonus, no, recall clause, yes. It's all here on page two."

He handed the document to Jarrod, who deftly turned the page that Duddy had struggled with just a moment before. Jarrod made out that he was reading it, but in fact he was just scanning for any numbers. He picked out 10 months, the salary figure, the figure that Newcastle were willing to pay Darlington and at the bottom, another handsome figure to be paid for agent fees.

Jarrod placed the document on the table.

"So, if I said that I wanted to leave Darlington, and sign for Newcastle on a week-to-week contract," asked Jarrod, lowering his voice at the mention of the real players in this conversation.

"You don't want that though," said Duddy, calling his bluff with ease. "You want the best of both worlds. You want to stay at Darlington, but you want to have that chance to play at Newcastle."

"Okay," said Jarrod, immediately conceding defeat and moving on, "what about my contract at Darlington?"

"You still have two years to run on that contract," said Duddy.

"Two years?" asked Jarrod, genuinely surprised.

"Yes," said Duddy, producing his current contract, turning to the relevant page. He slid the document into Jarrod's hands. It said three years. Jarrod could have sworn it was only for two, he would have been happy with two, but in the excitement of signing the document last year he must have missed that.

"Oh right," said Jarrod, suddenly no longer feeling in control of his own career.

"June is happy to increase that by a year," said Duddy, "should you wish to have the safety of a longer contract when you return to Darlington."

"No, no," said Jarrod, a little distant this time, as if he was still in denial about the length of the contract.

"Okay," said Duddy, bashing his hand on the table for effect. "What are your movements today?"

"Right," said Jarrod, jolted back into the conversation, "back to the clinic, probably home to Darlington by one, then grab the kids from school."

"Can you make it back to Newcastle in the afternoon?" asked Duddy.

"If I bring the kids," he said, calculating in his head, "I can be here at about 5pm."

"And if you don't," said Duddy, suggesting that this was far bigger than any school run, "what time can you make it here?"

"How about three?" suggested Jarrod, a little flustered.

"Three it is," said Duddy, as the lady arrived with the two plates of food.

Jarrod tucked in straight away, taking a moment to let the steam dissipate.

"I'll confirm as soon as we've finished," said Duddy, sensing that he had maybe rattled Jarrod's cage a little. "I'll text you the details, but park your car in the main car park at the stadium and tell the attendant who you are. They'll take you in via the player's entrance to avoid any scrutiny."

"Right," said Jarrod, taking in a mouthful of delicious melted Emmental cheese.

"And remember," continued Duddy, "you're signing for Newcastle this afternoon. You should be over the moon."

Jarrod smiled. What a statement. If he stripped back all the craziness associated with this whole situation, and considered what it looked like to the onlooker, Duddy was right. He was wanted by Newcastle and he was being offered an amazing opportunity to fulfil his life-long dream of playing for the club he had supported from the moment he had entered the world. In reality, he was over the moon. It was only tempered by the fact that he was a father of two with a recovering wife who was effectively putting his life in danger to chase his dream. What a situation to be in.

Conversation turned to Marianne. Duddy softened up, telling Jarrod that he had been married to a Mediterranean lady too, a fiery Spanish lady who had kept him on his toes before they divorced a year later. He admitted to visiting her every now and again and enjoying each other's company, but that the experience had made it very unlikely that he would marry again. Jarrod felt a genuine warmth, and as they finished their meal and emptied the bottle, he felt as though he had made a new friend.

"Duddy, it has been an absolute pleasure," said Jarrod sincerely. He had to make it back to the clinic and stood up. Duddy didn't feel the need to stand up this time.

"I'll see you this afternoon," he said, and waved away Jarrod like a headmaster dismissing an errant schoolboy at the end of detention, albeit with a smile on his face.

Jarrod made a point of paying for both at the counter, the bill was more expensive than he had anticipated; Duddy had obviously been in there for breakfast too. Jarrod strode out of the café and into the glorious sunshine. He didn't care if eyes were on him or not. He skipped down the kerb and across the street, finding his way back along the winding streets to the clinic.

By the time Jarrod skipped through reception and softly landed at Marianne's side at the clinic, the bag containing the chemo drug had been replaced by the bag containing the anti-nausea medicine, and it was almost gone too. Jarrod checked his watch, barely able to believe that he had been gone for nearly two hours. He put his hand on Marianne's. She was looking sleepy, and spoke slowly and softly.

"How did you go?" she smiled.

"It went very well indeed," said Jarrod, before quickly deflecting the attention to his wife. "How's the final session been?"

Marianne exhaled through her pursed lips, suggesting it had been draining.

"To be honest, I've been dozing on and off I think," she said, maintaining the calmness that surrounded her.

"Nearly done by the look of it," said Jarrod looking at the bag that was now concave up on its metal stand.

"Indeed it is," came Anne-Charlotte's voice. She walked over and began to dismantle the cannula, taking care to distract Marianne while she pulled the needle from her hand. Marianne flinched but the nurse continued in her soothing tone, breaking into French. Marianne put her hand on hers and smiled.

Jarrod took care of the paperwork while Marianne got to her feet and steadied herself, grabbing her belongings and checking to see if she'd dropped anything down the side of the chair in her slumber. They walked hand in hand like a newly married couple walking down the aisle after the ceremony. There were well-wishes from the congregation and smiles all round.

Stepping out into the fresh air, Jarrod began to rummage for his car keys in his pocket. Marianne stopped him as they walked past the low sign at the front of the tiny front garden.

"Take a photo," she said.

"Take a photo?" replied Jarrod, startled. He was usually the goof ball who took photos of anything remotely interesting but here was Marianne, standing in front of a sign for the oncology clinic, asking for a photo. He whipped out his phone and took a shot. Marianne checked it and asked for another. He took the same shot with the same pose, which Marianne again rejected.

"Jump in the air," said Jarrod, cheekily. And she did, and the result was a great photo of a great woman who had triumphed in her personal battle with cancer.

There was little conversation in the car on the way back down the A1. Jarrod's mind was absolutely buzzing but he was keeping it to himself. He suggested to Marianne that they might go out for lunch but she was more keen to get home and crawl under the covers.

That situation would work perfectly for Jarrod, so he played along, wondering how he was going to get the kids picked up. Jarrod packed off Marianne to bed, making sure she had everything, and that she should ring him if she needed anything. She could barely move and Jarrod helped her into bed.

Pippa Robson was the first number he rang. She was more than happy to lend a hand getting the kids from school. She could drop them back home or they could come over for a few hours. It had been confirmed that Seb had a crush on their daughter Michaela, the younger daughter Gabby and Aneka were as thick as thieves. They would be delighted to have a late change of plan when school ended. Jarrod thanked Pippa for helping him out for the hundredth time. He then did the right thing and rang the school to let them know the plans.

It was not the right time to ring Dad. Jarrod had stuffed up many times and rung at four in the morning. Dad had put on his happy voice most times answering the phone at that ungodly hour, but on a couple of occasions had given his son an earful. He decided not to risk it.

He instead rang June. June answered the phone within one ring.

"Hello Jarrod," she said cheerily, "you must be so excited. Where are you now?"

"I'm just heading up to meet with Newcastle," replied Jarrod. "I should be more nervous than I am. Is there anything I need to know?"

"No," said June matter-of-factly. "We've been told to keep this as quiet as possible, but as far as we know Newcastle will be making you an offer today, and if your agent is who I think it is, he'll be getting you a very good deal."

"You could say that," said Jarrod with an air of mystery, "but what are Darlington getting out of this?"

"Don't you worry about that," said June with a laugh. "Newcastle have offered two under-21 players to us for the season, and with the money that we get for your loan deal, we're going to be doing very well indeed."

"Ah that's great," said Jarrod, relieved that Darlington would be well and truly compensated.

"We'll have quite a hole to fill in the midfield, mind," concluded June. "Keep us informed, I'll speak with you on your way back down."

"Thanks for everything, June."

Chapter 20

SIGNATURE

Jarrod glanced at his mobile. He always felt guilty for doing that when he was driving, yet struggled to see how displaying his texts on the car's console would make it any safer. There was a text from Duddy confirming the time and place. It was all part of Duddy's exemplary professional service and Jarrod got an instant sense of calm from it.

Arriving in the centre of Newcastle, with the looming structure of St James' bearing down on him, Jarrod felt a little overawed. Realising he couldn't turn right into Strawberry Place after a toot from behind, he edged up Barrack Road and found a right turn into the car park.

He was met by a familiar car park attendant, who recognised him immediately and ushered him over to a laneway that led to a gated tunnel that ran under the stadium. A second gentleman opened his door once he had gone as far as he could. Jarrod was instructed to leave his keys with him. A third man, a tall gentleman with greying hair who looked sharp in a well-fitted suit, greeted Jarrod with a warm handshake and showed him through a door and led him along a long corridor. They passed the press area, and the tunnel to the pitch, then took a lift up a few floors and came out in a breakout area next to a suite of offices.

"Here's our man," he could hear, before he walked a few feet further, seeing Duddy leaning out of one of the offices, "come on in."

Jarrod leaned in tentatively to check who was in there. It was like being a teenager back in Gateshead on his first day when he'd just arrived from Sydney. Once he'd seen that there were familiar faces in there, he felt at ease and walked in confidently and went straight in for the handshakes.

Duddy was now seated. Jarrod walked straight past him and over to the desk and offered his hand to Benito Raffaella, the flamboyant Chilean manager of Newcastle. He was perusing some data on a printed report. Mr Raffaella looked up from his papers and gave him a big smile, grabbing his hand quickly and standing up to greet him.

"Hello Jarrod," he said in his heavy South American accent, "good to see you again."

They had already met a couple of times at the North East Football Writers awards, when Mr Raffaella had made a point both times of coming over and chatting with Jarrod and Marianne. Jarrod had not thought anything of it at the time but he was now starting to think that he had been a long time target.

"You may not have met our contracts manager, Martin Penfold," he said, presenting his colleague with an open palm. "Martin has been at the club for a long time. Longer than me. He will be instrumental in rebuilding our squad, now that we are free from the constraints of the previous owner."

Jarrod shook the hand of Mr Penfold who looked like an old head on a young body. He couldn't help thinking that Mr Raffaella was having a dig at someone who wasn't in the room, and it gave him the feeling that he was already getting involved in some sort of office politics.

"Hello again Duddy," said Jarrod, making sure he was being inclusive, to which the man mountain simply nodded his head with his eyes closed.

"Now, Jarrod," said Mr Raffaella, "why are you in our plans?"

It was a question that Jarrod had no idea how to answer. He looked at Duddy for help.

"I think that's a rhetorical question," said Duddy in his smooth Scottish accent, turning to the Newcastle manager. "The fact is that you are in Newcastle United's plans and the reason for that is 'because you are.'"

Jarrod smiled. He looked at Mr Raffaella who was already smiling.

"I've been looking for a player like you," he said, "a player with skill and precision. A model professional in peak fitness ..." Jarrod was still standing and felt himself straighten up. "... someone with a calm persona on the field to complement some of the more, how should I say, 'fragile' personalities that we have at the club right now."

"Mr Raffaella needs a leader," said Duddy in his uncompromising and forthright manner. "He's got way too many pansies in the squad."

Jarrod felt that last comment was a little unnecessary, but the first part made complete sense. Jarrod had been captain of Gateshead for a long while. He had gone into last season as captain of Darlington and had even tasted some managerial duties when manager Gary Hollister had been absent. He was definitely a leader, even though in his head he couldn't quite see what it was that made the people around him respect him.

He wasn't outspoken. He didn't rush in to defend his teammates if they were acting like buffoons. He didn't go over the top with crude challenges. What he did do though was lead by example. When the going was difficult, he would always stay positive. When the team needed a lift, he would always be there with an uplifting word and he didn't take himself too seriously. He could be the butt of the joke and he would make it fun for the whole team. And of course he was personable, able to let people talk and feel good about themselves instead of making it all about him.

"Thank you Duddy," said Mr Raffaella, staring at the huge Scotsman in disdain. "As you know we lost our star midfield man recently, and although you are not the same type of player, I think you will fit in to our plans even better than he did."

"Stepping into a dead man's shoes," said Jarrod, without thinking too much about how insensitive it sounded so soon after the event.

"I wouldn't look at it that way," said Mr Penfold as Mr Raffaella and Duddy both rocked back in their chairs. There was a long and awkward silence.

"So, Jarrod," said Duddy eventually, "your current club have agreed to the terms of the loan arrangement. Newcastle United have agreed to the terms of the contract that we looked at this morning. All we need is your signature. Of course this contract does not start until you return from your holiday."

Mr Penfold took a document from a manila folder on Mr Raffaella's desk and beckoned Jarrod to take the seat opposite the manager. Duddy was sitting well away by the door, as if he had nothing to do or say at this point. Mr Raffaella stared at Jarrod as he sat down. Jarrod was starting to feel a little uneasy but he had probably brought that upon himself. He took the document in both hands and pretended to read it. In reality his mind was racing.

Thoughts of Dad, of 2am wake up calls growing up, of hand-me-down football shirts that came in the post, of the posters on his wall, of the heartache and disappointment that came with season after season of being soundly beaten by the bigger clubs, but also of the pride and the love that he felt for this club that he had been born into. He dropped the document back onto the table as though he was going to swish it away and storm out, but instead picked up the pen quickly.

"Where do I sign?" he asked.

Mr Penfold showed him the way as Duddy stood up and towered almost menacingly over his shoulder.

"Welcome to Newcastle United," said Mr Penfold while Mr Raffaella stood up and offered his hand. One round of congratulatory handshakes, a pat on the back from Duddy and it was all over.

"Now excuse me, Jarrod," said Mr Raffaella, "but I have an important call to make. Thank you for joining us. Martin will take you to the contracts office with Duddy and we will give you a copy of the contract and some further information that you will need. See you in two weeks."

Chapter 21

ROOS

Jarrod had never been to Prague despite all his years in Europe, and despite it being a popular destination for a stag night or a boys' weekend. The team hotel was near the castle, up on a hill overlooking the city and it was absolutely breathtaking. After arriving in the late afternoon and checking in, the team was instructed to meet at an address on Wenceslas Square for a team meeting and dinner.

The players were to get there by foot, and Jarrod was excited to be able to walk through the streets unhindered in the balmy evening sunshine. Dressed in dark blue team shirt and khaki shorts, thankfully not the conspicuous yellow that they often wore, they looked very sharp. It wasn't long before some of the locals and some eager Aussie fans cottoned on and they had an entourage of interested onlookers.

They eventually spread out in twos and threes, and Jarrod took an age getting some quirky photos on the Charles Bridge with his teammate Jan Haratounan. The walk took much longer than they thought with many photo opportunities and they caught up with Dane Radzinski who had been drawn in to a stall selling paintings. A wild scream suddenly broke the mood, an ear-piercing high pitched male scream. Everyone stopped momentarily in their tracks.

Thoughts of Rambouillet being murdered in the street, memories of the London Bridge knife attacks and other horrible terrorist acts ran through Jarrod's mind for that split second. He could feel his senses heighten and the hairs on his arms bristle. He already had his hand on Jan's arm as if ready to pull him away from danger. His heart instantly pumped harder. For a split second, this was going to be a scene replayed on every news bulletin around the world.

That was until teenage Socceroo Miles Carter stepped out from around a market stall, thrashing away trying to karate chop an aggressive wasp. Everyone on the bridge had stopped and the mood lifted immediately, relief flooding through the throng and a sense of elation at the entertaining scene that was unfolding in front of them.

Miles was red in the face, cursing. Jarrod knew how those total bastard wasps operated, and felt a little guilty laughing with the crowd. He grabbed the young star around the shoulder as he walked past. Rescuing Dane from a deep conversation with another stall holder, they made their way through the Old Town Square and eventually on to Wenceslas Square.

The square was more like a grand avenue, by now the street lights had come on to illuminate the impending darkness and a plume of moths were dancing around the floodlights in the distance at the far end of the street. They found the venue and made their way in. The proceedings got underway as soon as they arrived, suggesting that they had taken a rather long and rambling route.

There was an introduction of the coaches and the players,

Jarrod getting a little mention for being the only player to have won promotion this season. That was fairly insignificant compared to the two Adelaide United players who had just wrapped up a Grand Final victory to go alongside their Premiers' Plate, but he was taking it all the same.

A fantastic buffet meal followed, the players had time to chat before being given loose instructions to be back at the hotel by midnight, and down for breakfast at 7.30am. Jarrod chuckled as the younger players moaned about the early start. The opportunity for shenanigans on the other hand was not lost on Jarrod, with a few of the players tucking in to the tall glasses of beer. It was inevitable that it would be quite a colourful walk back to the hotel. The team manager Rhett handed out a card with the hotel address to each player and let them know that he would be waiting to do a head count in the lobby at the other end.

Thursday consisted of three light training sessions, before Friday night's game at local team Sparta Prague's stadium nearby. Continuing the theme of their stay in Prague, the players were encouraged to walk to the stadium. Despite it being way before kick-off, there were still plenty of fans around the stadium. The meet and greets with the numerous Aussie fans was a great way to start the night. A group of the players made the call to take the metro the one stop to the station nearest the stadium, just for the experience. This was definitely the most relaxed international camp that he could have imagined.

Jarrod was named as a substitute for this one and despite an early injury to defensive midfielder Marley South, the like-for-like swap didn't eventuate. Jarrod remained an unused substitute, but played the role of motivator and teammate very enthusiastically.

The game had been quiet up until the 60th minute before a

Czech defender lunged in on Jan and received the night's first card, a straight red, sending the crowd into a spin. From then on it was an absolute mad-house, with over-the-top challenges and on-field confrontations between the players and coaching staff of both teams.

What was meant to be a friendly was anything but, and in the final third of the game there were two more red cards, one for each team, and at least five yellows. The goals had not come though, and the final whistle sounded to a chorus of boos from the home fans. The pocket of Australian fans housed safely away on their own in one corner gave their players a rousing send-off as they walked past to the tunnel. Jarrod had been quite pleased to have missed out on the carnage, the dugout was fierce enough.

There was no walking home after the game, the team coach being rocked by a small mob of Czech fans as it edged through the gates of the stadium after a rather hurried post-match conference. The Socceroos had just made their latest arch-enemy, and the Australian press the following morning was scathing of the Czech players' conduct.

Jarrod had caught the bug – he knew that playing for his country was always an honour, but given his age and his club's standing in World football, he found it amazing that he was involved, let alone on the bench.

Chapter 22

PERUVIAN

A short flight to Geneva at lunchtime on the Saturday saw the team board a coach; the drive along Lake Geneva was incredibly picturesque. Jarrod took it all in through the rain soaked windows – after all he was due back in a week's time with Marianne and the kids for a short holiday. He was keen to get some inside knowledge to impress the family.

They arrived in Lausanne and checked into an absolutely beautiful hotel high up from the edge of the lake with what would be an amazing view if the weather cleared. Jarrod made a point of asking Rhett who the genius was who booked these hotels, the team manager giving him a look as if to imply it was him. Jarrod was almost 99.9 per cent sure it wasn't Rhett though, and whoever made these calls was someone he should get to know better.

The players had half-day training on the Sunday and Monday mornings ahead of the second game, and were encouraged to make the most of the area. Jarrod was on to it straight away on the Sunday morning before breakfast, collaring the night receptionist for a good half an hour to find out where he should visit and where the best places were for night time dining.

He managed to persuade Jan to come with him on a bit of a train journey to the magnificent Château de Chillon, a castle built in the lake with a wild history of invasions and battles. The two of them enjoyed the experience and stopped off in Montreux for an early dinner on the way back. They eventually returned to Lausanne at ten, a few of the players were still up and about in the hotel bar, exchanging stories about their days.

It turned out that Miles and the three other youngsters in the squad had spent the least productive afternoon, hooking up a Playstation in one of their rooms and playing an epic FIFA tournament. Jarrod felt good to have made it out to discover his future holiday destination, but was pretty sure he would have been in that FIFA tournament if he had been in his teens.

A boat trip on the Monday afternoon confirmed that Lake Geneva was going to be a fantastic holiday destination, the warm sunshine and calm waters making for a fabulous tour.

Tuesday came though to interrupt the sightseeing, the players clicked in to game mode as soon as breakfast was over. They were playing Peru, a strange team to be playing in Switzerland of all places, but the central European destination for at least half of both squads was a good fit. Mike collared Jarrod as he was walking out of the dining room. Jarrod was going to start the game and he was going to play in a back three. He felt like he did when he'd been thrown in the deep end at Brunton Park all those years ago, and he could feel his chest puffing out with pride.

The team bus took forever to get through the tight streets around the hotel, the driver cursing away in French for what would be a winding route of only about two kilometres. His agitation got to the coaching staff and Jim Grant eventually walked up to the front and distracted the driver with a few questions in his rusty school French.

The mood seemed to flow on to the players, who were craning

their necks and wondering what was going on. When they arrived, they were only fifteen minutes later than planned, but the rush to get off the bus and the impatience of waiting for their bags to come out of the luggage storage all made for a strangely tense atmosphere.

The changing facilities at La Pontaise Stadium were basic, but when the green, gold and blue filled the barren concrete space, there was a home changing room feel about it. The mood began to lift. Jarrod went through his familiar routine, getting changed quickly, but taking his time to line up the laces on his ankle brace. He was one of the last out as a result, and the warm evening air hit him as he jogged over the running track and onto the field. A smattering of applause came from behind him. He looked back and realised that it was for the two Peruvian players coming out of the tunnel behind him and he smirked.

The warm up started almost immediately with Jim and captain Nikos Galanos leading the players through a routine of jogging and stretching, before they went in to two circles and did the old keep-ball game, one touch, first touch is free. Jarrod was in the middle to start with and could feel the power in his legs. He was in very good condition physically after a long season and could sense that the occasion was giving him an extra buzz.

Goalkeeper Kareem Al-Hussain, A-League winner with Adelaide United that season, slipped the ball through Jarrod's legs. That drew cheers from the circle and ramped up Jarrod even more until he lunged and intercepted and managed to free himself from the centre. He was game ready. His teammates appeared focused. There were a noisy group of Peru fans banging away at their drums at the far end, while the Australian section was finally starting to fill up with green and gold jerseys, inflatable kangaroos and Aussie flags.

The players retreated to the changing rooms for the final talk, and Mike embellished the instructions that they had worked on over the past three training sessions. They were coming to win this game, to play attractive football and to make the opposition do all the running. That was the plan. The execution though was down to the players. Jarrod could feel a resolve in the changing room, and almost a relief that they were going all-out for the win.

The players assembled in the tunnel and were matched up with their miniature mascots. Jarrod shook hands with a few of the Peru players, not offering any of his limited Spanish, but having a sideways look at Miles who was greeting each perplexed player with a cheery 'buongiorno'.

The music started as they walked out again into what was now a fairly full stadium, Lausanne having turned out in good numbers for a totally meaningless Tuesday night international friendly. The drawcard was clearly the Peru number 9, Jojo Bustamante, who had started his European career with nearby Servette FC before moving on to giants Paris St Germain and lighting up Ligue 1 with his electrifying pace.

The players paused at the side of the field before starting the march towards the centre circle, where the referee and his assistants stopped and the players fanned out either side in the well-practised FIFA tradition. The Peru anthem played, the players all linking arms and belting out their national song before a rousing cheer from the crowd.

Jarrod felt his heart beating fast as the Australian anthem was announced and the trumpets heralded the intro. The players all stood at a slight angle, facing the tunnel, with their hands on their hearts, and they absolutely roared the lyrics, making sure that they all got the tempo right at the end when it reached its climax. Jarrod could feel a tear forming. His mouth started to waver as he delivered the last line and the roar from the Green and Gold Army was bigger than expected. The fans had eventually turned up from their pre-match drinking holes.

A late fitness test saw Marley South given his defensive midfield spot, playing just in front of Jarrod, who was in the middle of a flat back three with two other 'experienced' players in captain Nikos and Stef Rodovic. This was going to be some test up against the megastar JoJo. Jarrod was relishing the challenge. A moment of quiet came over the stadium before a big noise greeted the opening whistle.

The green and gold-clad Socceroos made a point of circulating the ball though the whole team and drawing the Peru team into their half to set the scene for an absorbing first half. Jarrod's early contribution was below par by his standards, a stray pass was intercepted which got the Peru fans excited, then he was caught in possession on halfway and gifted the ball to the winger who galloped down the line before greedily firing into the crowd.

Jarrod knew that he had to get some better touches under his belt, and made a point of doing the simple things properly for a fifteen minute period. This steadied the defence and in turn, his own nerves. A crunching double-barrelled tackle on two Peru players then got his adrenaline going, firstly sliding in as last man to dispossess the striker who would have been through on goal. Then, when JoJo looked to pick up the crumbs and bear down on goal, Jarrod scrambled to find another stretch to toe the ball away for a corner. His fellow defenders both patted him on the back as they raced past to get into position.

The game was becoming very open, the three-man defence of

the Socceroos exposed to the ball in behind. It was from another intercept, this time Nikos reading the intended through ball before it had been kicked, that Australia fashioned their first meaningful assault on goal. The long ball out wide to Jan fell perfectly into his stride and he raced around his marker to the byline. A slightly miss-hit cross then ballooned all the way to the far side of the penalty area where Dane had found acres of space and let fly with the most ferocious volley.

The ball veered violently towards the top corner in a split second and crashed off the corner of post and bar. Jarrod wondered if he'd ever seen a ball hit so hard. The ball ended up almost at the halfway line where Stef controlled the ball, shaking his head in disbelief.

That moment gave the Aussies a lift, and any lingering doubts about the system they were playing were dispelled as they finished the half on top. Peru had lost the midfield, chasing the ball while the Socceroos knocked the ball confidently and competently around the back and the middle of midfield. The fans seemed genuinely impressed and gave the players huge applause as they jogged off down the tunnel. Manager Mike Jerszek was keen to make a change as soon as they walked into the changing room.

"Zach, get stripped off," he said pointing at Zach Everett. "Mitchell, well done, thanks for playing through the pain."

Jarrod hadn't noticed that Mitchell Moore's sock was covered in blood and he got the physio Alex Covac to help him remove his boot and peel off the sock. It revealed a gash that would surely require a fair few stitches, the dark red wound contrasting against his milky white skin.

"Jarrod," said Mike, turning 360 degrees before spotting him on the second rotation, "Jarrod, you move into the holding role in front of the back three, Zach is coming on as centre-back."

Jarrod could feel his eyebrows lift – this was quite a move. Zach had only figured sporadically over the last two years and was seen more as a wing-back, but had played the role on a few occasions at club level to much acclaim. The thought of reverting to his most comfortable position on the field gave Jarrod a boost. This was going to be some half.

With barely three minutes gone in the second half, and with Jarrod already getting more of the ball as the go-to midfielder, Australia found a way through. Peru's staunch defence was dragged over to deal with Jan who had broken clear into the corner down the left. Coming almost to a stop and turning back towards his own half, a sudden pirouette and a burst of pace saw him leave two defenders in his wake and he clipped the ball into the middle where the towering Ed Charrah leapt with his man and powered a header beyond the outstretched palm of the keeper and into the net. Ed raced over to Jan to congratulate him on the impeccable service, the rest of the team soon caught up to join them to salute a very well-worked goal. This was more like it.

Jarrod found himself shoulder to shoulder with his midfield adversary soon after, but lost out in the physical dual. His opponent slipped the ball to danger man JoJo, and he raced into the box. Zach however, raced across to get a leg in front of the shot, the ball ricocheting into the Peru striker's face and out for a goal kick.

That missed opportunity seemed to knock the fizz out of his game from then on, and the Peru number 9 looked a little jaded whenever the ball came to him. The board going up showing his number was a blessed relief to the Australia players, and Peru reverted to a sturdy 4-4-2. This was Jarrod's chance to carve out some opportunities as the South Americans struggled to transition between formations.

There were 10 minutes left on the clock when Nikos floated a long ball to the right hand side for Dane to control. A first time pass to Jarrod found him moving forward into space, and with options either side and in front, he kept running straight at the defence, waiting to offload when the tackle loomed. The expert running of the Socceroos players in front of him pulled the defenders away, and a communication breakdown saw both Peru midfielders leave the challenge to each other.

Jarrod simply steamed past the static defensive line, reached the byline and slotted a simple ball behind the in-rushing players. Jan got there first to sweep the ball unhindered past the Peru goalkeeper and punch the air with excitement as the ball brushed the inside of the roof of the net with that satisfying bristling noise.

Australia were in total command now, and Jarrod found himself at the centre of everything good that his team produced. Mike urged them on to get a third, and had a go at keeper Kareem when he was booked for unnecessary time-wasting. The final whistle was greeted with a huge cheer from the Australian bench and from the fans behind the goal. Jarrod was collared immediately by the Fox Sports crew who ushered him over to the waiting camera, he didn't have time to even rub the dried spit from the corners of his mouth.

"Jarrod Black," said the presenter Caleb Powell, "a very solid performance from you in a very professional second half. What was the difference in the second 45 minutes?"

Jarrod though for a second, remembering the media coaching that urged him to take a moment to think before talking, especially when emotions were high straight after the final whistle.

"We worked so hard all game," he said, trying to be diplomatic and inclusive, "and across the board we stuck to our game plan. This was a very attack-minded display and we showed that we have the personnel to adapt to any type of situation."

That was very well worded.

"You enjoyed that second goal?" asked the reporter.

"Ha haaa," he said trying to stop smiling, "they didn't want to tackle me did they? It just opened up beautifully for me and when I got to the byline the hard work was done. Jan just seems to know exactly where I'm going to play the ball. It's like we're identical twins!"

Jan walked past at this point and ruffled Jarrod's hair playfully, which was a really nice thing to see on screen, a show of a well-bonded team and that the players all respected each other. Jarrod cut the interview right there.

"Thanks Caleb," he said, leaving the reporter prematurely. "Got to go and see the supporters."

He strode up behind Jan and reached down to tug at his shorts, as if he was going to pull them right down, before tugging them down a centimetre or two. Jan turned and they put their arms around each other and joined the rest of the squad who were lined up in front of the fans. The roar they received when their interlinked hands went up in the air was a moment that would surely be seared into Jarrod's memory forever.

Jarrod knew he'd been part of something a bit special the night before as they assembled down in reception. The mood was especially positive and there were some journalists and a few Socceroos fans there. Hopefully those fans had been to bed that night. The players were instructed to meet down at the Olympic Museum on the shores of the lake, and in common with the theme of giving them free rein, they were to do that on foot.

Jarrod was quickly becoming used to this. It was something that he had never been allowed to do, especially for overseas games, the fear of security and welfare of the players having the trump card over cultural experience. Perhaps this was the beginning of a new era. Maybe it was just the Australian way and Jarrod had been a little removed from it.

Jarrod absolutely loved the morning. There were loads of interactive displays and plenty of Australian references throughout. The players took in as much as they could in the three-hour visit. A team photo in front of an Olympic flower display was professionally done. Jarrod sensed that this was being done with one eye on the Olympic qualifiers in the autumn, or even a potential Australian bid for the Olympic Games.

The sculptures in the garden were magnificent, the vista over the lake made it a magical visit, it was such a shame to have to leave. A coach picked them up this time. As they waited to board, a group of school children filed past and one of them noticed the badge and came up to Jarrod asking for a photo in French. Jarrod knew enough to cotton on to what was happening – this young one had obviously put two and two together and realised who they were – and the players all got into formation around the young boy, a Socceroos cap placed on his head as they posed for a quick photo. That must have made the boy's day.

The checkout from the hotel was quick and efficient, the coach loaded back up with players and officials, and it was off to Geneva airport for the flight back to London. All the players were travelling back there. Some were continuing on to other destinations, others were heading back to Australia. A handful of UK-based players caught the train into London and eventually split up to go to their respective train stations.

Jarrod and Jan caught the same train up from Kings Cross and sat chatting until a warm embrace at Darlington saw the journey conclude for Jarrod. Jarrod commandeered the lone taxi at the station and he was home just before midnight, gently lifting the covers and snuggling with Marianne. What a trip, and there was more travelling to come yet.

Jarrod had been due to meet Marcus and Dennis, the detective team, in Newcastle the next day. The transfer window had officially opened and they were keen to make it known to the world that Jarrod had signed for Newcastle. A subsequent decision though had been made while Jarrod was returning to Darlington. Given that Jarrod was heading away on holiday that week, they would continue to wait until his return to announce the move. Marianne had also changed plans.

She would continue on from their holiday, taking the kids to her parents' place in the Pyrenees. With them safely out of the country, Jarrod could accelerate the process of integrating himself into Newcastle United with no distractions. Jarrod was also relieved that they would be out of harm's way. He just had the feeling that he was walking into the lion's den and there was going to be bloodshed.

A day of packing then and getting ready for holiday. Jarrod was ready for down time.

Chapter 23

RETURN

Jarrod arrived back at Newcastle airport after leaving Marianne, Sebastian and Aneka at Geneva airport. They had enjoyed the most amazing week. It had been made all the more amazing after Jarrod announced that he was joining Newcastle. He had even booked a table at a high-end restaurant in Évian-les-Bains and chartered a speedboat to take them from their hotel on the Swiss side of Lake Geneva, using his knowledge picked up the week before. Marianne was very excited. Aneka was amazed. Even Sebastian showed some emotion and was so proud that his dad was moving to the Premier League.

Jarrod did have to calm Marianne though, especially when he explained that he was going to be on a much higher salary. He asked Marianne not to tell anyone yet as there was going to be an official announcement when he returned. He knew that she would keep it to herself but she would be burning inside.

He also made sure that the kids knew the situation too and that they needed to refrain from telling anyone or posting anything on social media. They talked excitedly through their dinner, Jarrod convincing Marianne that they should stay in Darlington as he didn't know the length of the loan deal, and Marianne convincing Jarrod that they should start thinking about life after football; and to perhaps look to buy another property, this time in Newcastle. Jarrod was happy that the announcement was well received.

The rest of the week had been very relaxed. Jarrod had pre-organised as much as he could and was sitting back and enjoying the fruits of that preparation. It was with a twinge of sadness that the eight days had to come to an end, and he felt a little lost on the flight back via Amsterdam after leaving the rest of the family in Geneva Airport. By the time he had arrived into Newcastle airport though his mood and demeanour had changed from relaxed to focused. It was Thursday afternoon.

After checking in with D.I. Allison while waiting at Schipol Airport, and with Jarrod now flying solo for two weeks, it was decided that they would strike quickly, Duddy would organise a press conference for early evening at St James' Park. Jarrod took cue from the Socceroos policy of giving their players free rein and hopped on the metro at Newcastle airport, rolling into Jesmond and finding the functional hotel that had been hastily booked for him.

Within ten minutes he was off again, this time in a taxi and straight to St James' Park where he instructed the driver to drop him in the same spot that he had come in previously, away from prying eyes. Again, the car park attendants seemed to know what was happening and ushered him through that same door and through to the inner workings of the stadium.

Jarrod met the medical team and went through a series of simple yet thorough tests and a barrage of questions, ranging from alcohol consumption to dental hygiene. He got the feeling that time was pressing, especially when he was asked not to get changed straight away after the final physical examination and was instead handed a pile of club training gear in his range of sizes.

He was asked to get ready in the right sizes, eventually appearing from the medical suite to a waiting media pack. The club photographer Renée sent him straight back in to go for the smaller sizes, which gave everyone a giggle. He reappeared looking very sleek in the club's new training shirts, shorts and socks. Renée gave him a wink as he walked past her, still smiling.

Jarrod was ushered up in the lift to meet up with manager Mr Raffaella. It was like a rerun of the previous meeting, Duddy sitting at the doorway and Mr Penfold to the side of the manager's desk.

"Great to see you again," said Mr Raffaella. "You look very relaxed."

"Well, I was until I arrived at the airport," said Jarrod truthfully. "This is all a bit crazy."

"I'd like to think that we're efficient in our operations, Jarrod," said the manager.

"There's no doubt about that," said Jarrod glancing at the clock near Duddy's head that let him know that he'd been in the country for barely two hours.

"Jarrod," said Mr Penfold, standing up again from his seat, "we've assembled the media downstairs and we are going to announce you as our new signing."

"Right," said Jarrod with no suggestion of emotion.

"We would like your angle to be that of a life-changing opportunity," continued Mr Penfold, "that this is the club you have supported all your life, of the pride in pulling on the black and white shirt."

"Of course," said Jarrod, "that's pretty much the truth."

"And feel free to mention your international call up too," said Mr Raffaella. "By all accounts, that went very well."

Before Jarrod could speak, Mr Raffaella stood up.

"Right, let's go," he said. The three of them left the room, Duddy ducking as he made his way through the door, and putting his arm around Jarrod as the others walked in front.

"Bloody well done, son," said Duddy. Jarrod didn't know whether he was alluding to him signing for Newcastle or playing well for Australia, or if it was simply a general congratulations for everything.

Chapter 24

MEDIA

The media room was a space strangely divided in two by a partition, not big enough to make two rooms, but big enough to be a token divider between two distinct spaces. On one side was a breakout room with tea and coffee laid out, and on the other, seating for journalists, a fixed camera and a stage. It was absolutely packed when they walked in from around the back of the signage at the rear of the stage.

Mr Penfold and Jarrod walked in first, with Mr Raffaella leaving a dramatic pause before entering. Duddy found his way to the media seating and found a vacant spot. After trying twice to shoehorn his enormous frame into the small chair and desk combo, he chuckled and gave up to stand at the back, the scene giving all the attendees, Jarrod included, a good laugh.

"Ladies and gentlemen," said Mr Penfold, "we would like to announce the signature of Jarrod Black on a one year loan deal from Darlington FC."

He wasn't reading from any notes, which Jarrod found very impressive.

"Jarrod has played in the North East of England for his entire career," he continued, "and it is with great pleasure that we finally welcome him to the club for the forthcoming season. His leadership qualities, fitness and talent will be an asset to our team, and we look forward to seeing him in the black and white of Newcastle United."

There was a spontaneous round of applause. Jarrod smiled nervously.

"We now invite questions from the floor."

There was a delay. It seemed that no-one wanted to be the first, then a booming Australian accent broke the silence.

"Caleb Powell, Fox Sports."

Jarrod remembered how he had cut him short on TV ten days earlier and immediately felt a little uncomfortable.

"Jarrod, congratulations on your move. Did this come as a surprise?"

Jarrod thought for a moment, and was again feeling the guilt after spending a couple of nights at the hotel with Caleb in a group situation and not once offering any inkling that this was about to happen.

"Yes, it was definitely a surprise," he said. "After spending the last season in League Two, it was a huge surprise to get a call up for Australia, let alone get a call from Newcastle United. This has been a very big year so far."

"What do you feel you bring to the club?" asked Caleb before anyone could interrupt.

"I hope I bring a lot of experience," he replied, "but mainly the desire and passion that growing up a Toon fan will give me when I pull on the shirt and walk out to *Local Hero* playing in a packed St James' Park."

Jarrod felt relieved that he remembered the name of the song they played, and felt as if he should be shifting pebbles from one pocket to another like a cricket umpire as he ticked comments off the list in his head.

"What an honour to be playing in the stadium once graced by Alan Shearer, Kevin Keegan and Malcolm Macdonald."

He could feel himself warming to this task.

"And what a privilege to be playing in front of the most passionate fans in Europe."

There, job done. But there was more.

"Doug Hardy, *Chronicle*," came the next question. "Are you ready to play at the top level of English football? After all, you've never played in the Premier League."

Mr Raffaella chose to answer this one.

"Jarrod Black is a very talented player," he said, turning and smiling at Jarrod. "He has been a long-term target of this club, even before my arrival, but his age was seen as a barrier. Now that we can use our judgement on such matters, we are finally bringing in a player that will perfectly fit in with the culture and tactics that we are trying to create."

Mr Raffaella definitely had a way with words, even in his non-native tongue, and again there seemed to be a carefully managed dig at someone hidden in his sentence.

Jarrod took the pause as an invitation to speak, and looked at Mr Raffaella to confirm he could go on.

"Thank you," he said. "It is true that I have never played in the Premier League, and I make no secret that I was gutted not to get there with Gateshead. Who knows how that would have gone. But, I have always felt ready and capable of playing at the top level."

"Kieran Prendergast, Radio Teesside," came the next voice. Jarrod recognised that name, and immediately felt his temperature go up a degree or two. Jarrod had given Kieran a hard time in an interview towards the end of the season, and he knew that he was going to get some payback. He stared at the reporter, noticing the smug face of photographer Shorty just behind him, thoroughly enjoying this unexpectedly awkward moment.

"Do you feel as though you are letting the Darlington fans down, given that you were their marquee signing only 12 months ago?"

Boom. That was a tough one. Jarrod stared straight at Kieran, looking for inspiration. He found it, just as he started to speak. He remembered previous press conferences when he was instructed to turn the conversation towards the new club, not the old.

"Darlington has given me a new lease of life," he said, "and I am very grateful to everyone involved at Darlington FC. They are building something very special and I have been part of an amazing season. However, this opportunity has come up and Darlington have been fully supportive of making this dream a reality. Remember this is a loan deal. It's not over yet."

He stopped short of finishing with 'So don't worry' but felt that would have been condescending.

There were a number of other questions that Jarrod attended to, leaving Mr Penfold to answer all the financial questions. As the press conference began to veer off-topic and the first Rambouillet question arose, Mr Raffaella stood up to signify the end and thanked everyone for coming. Photos would be taking place by the pitchside, and all photographers who were invited were already there. Renée had produced a selection of football boots that Jarrod quickly sized up and changed into, his low sneakers not fitting the bill.

Jarrod was told to walk past the 'Keep off the grass' sign and to stand with the ball under his bent arm, giving the impression of a hard-working local lad. After a barrage of shots, and some slight adjustments to his pose, he was asked to do some ball juggling. This was definitely not his forte, and he had visions of old footage of Diego Maradona and Jimmy Greaves that he had seen when they signed for their respective clubs - simply amazing.

He did a few juggles and trapped the ball between his calf and the back of his thigh, and gave a big smile after realising he'd actually succeeded. That was the shot that would make the news, despite some further tricks of a similarly low level of difficulty. He signed the ball and held up a Newcastle United scarf with the sponsors' names behind them in the East Stand. Mr Raffaella arrived in time to get in a shot of them shaking hands.

The photographers and journalists then stopped snapping, a number of them offered to shake hands with Jarrod. That was a really nice touch, especially as Jarrod had seen a lot of them at various points over the years. It was good to see them all in one place. He got the feeling that they were all in this together.

Even Shorty showed no hard feelings for the airport incident that was clearly fresh in his mind. In fact, in retrospect, Jarrod was either feeling a little self-aware, or he sensed that they all knew something about this whole situation. Duddy was watching on, smiling through his four-day growth, and eventually joined the throng to shake Jarrod's hand.

"Got to head off," he said. "Signings all over the place."

"Thanks for your help Duddy," said Jarrod placing his left hand over Duddy's handshake.

"Good luck," said the Scotsman as he quickly turned and strode through the tunnel and out of sight.

Jarrod grinned through another few congratulatory handshakes, posed for a couple of selfies, before the crowd thinned out and he was left with Mr Penfold and Renée.

"Welcome to Newcastle," said Renée, "and well done on a quick and efficient press conference."

"Thanks, Renée," he replied, "you don't know how much of a whirlwind this has been."

"Oh, I think I've got a good idea," she replied. She put her arm around him and guided him back through the tunnel with the rest of the departing bodies.

Chapter 25

RAILWAY

Jarrod Black was now a Newcastle United player. He was also staying in a hotel, he was due at the first day of pre-season training in the morning but didn't have any football kit with him. He was also very hungry, starting to flail after an adrenaline high and could feel his eyes misting over.

He sat on the edge of the bed for five minutes, resisting the urge to flop back onto the immaculately made bed and pondered. He leapt to his feet a moment later, grabbed his 'man bag' and was just about to burst out of the door, destination Darlington by quickest method, when he stopped. His mind started to rewind and he retreated to the bed.

The club would have some gear for him. He had plenty of clothes on him, some of it even clean after he made use of the laundry facilities in their apartment in Switzerland. He had everything he needed. A quick bite to eat was all he would need, but it felt a little odd to be eating alone. He took out his phone and sat thinking for a moment.

"Dan speaking," came the voice when he finally made up his mind who to start with. It was Dan Collier, a young Darlington player who lived in Newcastle and someone he had shared a lift with a few weeks ago.

"Hey Dan, Jarrod Black here," said Jarrod, unsure as to whether or not to use his full name to distinguish between all the other Jarrods he would know.

"Heyyyy, Jarrod, I was just talking about you!" exclaimed the excitable voice. "You've signed for Newcastle? Am I hearing that right?"

"I'll tell you all about it over a curry, if you're free," said Jarrod.

"That would be right, you're in Newcastle," replied Dan, cottoning on. "Where are you?"

"I'm in Jesmond," said Jarrod, not giving away his exact location.

"No way! You'll be at the Holiday Inn then," deduced Dan, "I'm just a few blocks away at me Mam's."

There was a short muffled exchange with his mum.

"Yep, I'm good," he said. "Let's do that railway carriage restaurant – it's been there for a few years now and I've never been."

"What's the name?" asked Jarrod.

"Ah I forget, just type in railway carriage curry and you'll find it. See you there in half an hour. I doubt we'll need to book during the week."

And he was right. As soon as they'd finished the call, Jarrod tapped a quick search in his phone and found it straight away. This was great. He had found himself at a loose end in Newcastle during the week and now he was going out for dinner with his now ex-teammate who had once given him a lift up from Darlington after training. They hit it off last time, Jarrod being the interviewer and Dan being the centre of the conversation as they drove up the A1, Jarrod had felt a connection with him. Jarrod was very keen to talk with someone and Dan seemed just the man.

Jarrod found the restaurant easily and as he walked up the

steps and opened the door, he spied Dan coming around the corner a few seconds behind. They clasped hands and made their way in. They were shown to a spot amongst the cluster of small tables in the long thin restaurant. Dan ordered a half pint of lager as soon as they sat down, Jarrod got his customary bottle of sparkling water and they got straight down to the matter in hand.

"So what … happened Jarrod?" asked Dan tentatively.

"Ah, man," started Jarrod as if he was going to launch into a tale of despair and angst, but instead continued, "I've finally made it to the Premier League. I'm absolutely buzzing. Thanks for coming out on a school night, I'm sure you've got an early start."

Dan would have to leave at 7.30am to get to training by 9.30am through the heavy morning traffic, but he was very keen to meet up with someone who he felt had become a mentor to him.

"Yes, you know what it's like here in the mornings," he agreed, "but I'm getting the inside scoop here, aren't I?"

"I guess you are the first person I've spoken to since the announcement this afternoon," said Jarrod, "and I feel that I owe my Darlington teammates an explanation. This was very unexpected."

"They've been after you for years though," said Dan, showing his inner knowledge of the news from Newcastle United through simply living in the city and being a fan. "They're taking a risk I guess, because you're getting on …"

Jarrod coughed comically.

"… well you are, admit it," he continued. "You're in your mid-thirties. A lot of players your age are giving up the game or moving into coaching roles. Not you though, you're making the biggest move of your career. It's mental!"

Jarrod went on to pour his thoughts out, keeping well away

from the other reason he had accepted the move, even though Rambouillet's name came up a number of times. Dan was playing the role of interviewer, devil's advocate and agony uncle to perfection, and he showed that he was mature beyond his years.

They ordered food, Dan had another beer and Jarrod ordered a glass of white wine to go with the spicy curry he'd chosen. They were absolutely wrapped up in this totally unexpected and enjoyable conversation. As the waiter came with the bill at the end of the meal, the conversation came to a head.

"So, are we going to see you back in a Darlington shirt at some point?" asked Dan. Good question.

"I sincerely hope so," said Jarrod. "I'm not done yet. Hopefully we'll be in the Championship and we can go on to push for promotion to the Premier League together. What a story that would be."

"Would you like me to pass on anything to the lads tomorrow at training?" asked Dan.

Jarrod thought for a few seconds.

"Let them know that I'll be coming down in the next few days to say hello. Hopefully I'm still welcome."

"Of course you're welcome," said Dan with his arms out wide. "You've just grabbed the most amazing opportunity of your life. We're all rooting for you. I had loads of texts tonight just before coming here, not one of them critical. Everyone wants to see you play where you belong. In the Premier League. Gives us an extra reason to watch Match of the Day."

That was enough for Jarrod. He slapped a fifty pound note on the table, after first slapping down a fifty Euro note that was still in his wallet from his holidays. Dan was more than happy to let Jarrod pay.

"My shout next time," said Dan.

"It'll be at the Ritz, mind," joked Jarrod.

They left each other at the door. It was still quite early, but they both had heavy schedules in the morning. Jarrod was due at training at 9am and he had a lot on his mind. He would check in with Marianne tonight to see how they went with their journey. He'd also check in with D.I. Allison to get some coaching about what his responsibilities were from hereon. The Detective Inspector decided that a get together at the hotel would be best and organised a breakfast meet, at 6.45am in the dining room.

Jarrod was exhausted. He reflected on an eventful day that started in Geneva and ended in Newcastle. He had been presented to the world as a United player, it was the beginning of a new chapter in his career. He had absolutely no problem sleeping that night and happily left a barrage of text messages unanswered.

Chapter 26

BRIEFING

"Good to see you Jarrod," said Marcus, or D.I. Allison as Jarrod still chose to call him. "First day on the new job, you must be excited."

"Filled with anxiety," replied Jarrod, offering his hand to the Detective Inspector, who was already down to the end of his coffee. He had clearly been there for some time already. They shook hands and Jarrod sat down in the seat opposite. "It's like the first day at high school. I've got butterflies."

"Okay," said D.I. Allison, beckoning the waiter over. Jarrod ordered a long black coffee, the Detective Inspector ordered another macchiato for himself. As the waiter left them he continued: "So today, and for the next two or three days, you simply need to get to know everyone at the club. I'm sure you'll have no problem doing that as you'll be in testing and analysis today."

"So am I expecting something to happen … or do I have to go looking for it?" asked Jarrod. That was an interesting question. Jarrod had no training at being a supersleuth, but he was very social. He was used to being surrounded by people and had become accustomed to being in a leadership role. He was naturally inquisitive and was good at getting people to talk. The Detective

Inspector knew this about Jarrod. They had done their homework on him.

"No, you shouldn't expect anything to happen, and no, you don't need to go looking for it," said D.I. Allison. "I would expect someone to eventually reach out to you, but not on day one. Maybe not even in week one. But soon, you will find yourself in an unusual conversation and you'll know at that point. That's when you need to start to talk to us regularly."

"And how do I communicate with you?" asked Jarrod. "Do I just use my phone? Text and you'll call? Only call at a certain time?"

"Good question," said D.I. Allison, pulling out his wallet. "Take this card. Add the phone number to your contacts list under Nana. Assuming you don't have a contact for Nana already that is."

Jarrod took the card, placed it in front of him and took out his mobile phone. He flicked through his contacts. He was pretty sure that he didn't have anyone with that name. Neither of his grandmothers had been given the moniker Nana and there were no players of that name. He added the contact and saved.

"Now, make sure your phone is backed up," continued D.I. Allison. "You may need to lose the phone at any given time. Oh, and make sure you have a good PIN number, not 1-2-3-4 or your birthday."

Jarrod had never put a PIN on his phone and felt a little uneasy. He didn't share that information with the Detective Inspector. He'd probably worked that out already by watching him open his phone. The Detective Inspector could see that Jarrod was ready for his next instruction.

"Now, download the app Signal 7 on your phone and add that number to it," he continued. "It's an encrypted message system that I use. Nothing fancy, it's not something that the police force use by default."

Jarrod downloaded the app and started it up, found the option to add a number and skipped over all the options for customising his settings.

"Good," said D.I. Allison. "Now, use Signal 7 to contact me. You can use voice calls on there too if it's urgent. Do you have any other questions?"

The waiter returned with their coffees and offered breakfast.

"Jarrod, you'll be taking breakfast, I imagine," said D.I. Allison. "So yes, I'll be getting something from the buffet."

"Oh, yes, I'll be doing the same," said Jarrod. The waiter pointed them the way, the two of them catching a glimpse of the sumptuous buffet that had been assembled as they had talked.

They returned with their spoils, Jarrod's fruit-heavy diet putting the Detective Inspector's attempt at a Full English breakfast to shame. They didn't talk any further about the situation, and instead talk turned to football. Jarrod knew that the Detective Inspector was a full-on supporter, and felt that it was a good time to fill in some gaps in his knowledge about the goings on at the club.

There had been enormous upheaval at the club recently. The long-term owner of the club had finally relinquished his iron fist and had been bought out by a consortium of businessmen brought together by the supporters' trust. This was timed perfectly with the end of their former manager Mr Raffaella's contract expiry, and they had offered him a return to the club to work with the new owners.

It was relief all round, and the Detective Inspector filled in Jarrod with the details of the previous season and how the buy-out unfolded. Jarrod found it fascinating, and was grateful to be given the run-down by a true Newcastle fan. He could feel his butterflies disappear, replaced by a warm feeling of pride and excitement. He was stepping in to a new era of positivity at a club that had been swathed in disappointment for years. This was going to be fantastic.

The two men realised that they had been chatting for way too long, it was time for Jarrod to start making his way to Little Benton. Jarrod still had half an hour to get ready and they left the dining room like two mates after a long-awaited catch-up.

It was a short hop to the training ground. He received a text that he would be picked up by one of the other players in the hotel car park, which put his mind at ease. He sat again in the same spot on the edge of the bed where he had sat yesterday evening and gave himself five minutes to think. His head rested on the ends of his fingers, his thumbs rolling around the muscles of his jaw.

As if shot by a bolt of electricity, he was up. He put his thoughts into action, rifling through his suitcase to find some training gear, and lifted his trainers out of a plastic bag – they were still wet after he ran through a few puddles on a jog two days earlier. He wasn't going to be the most appropriately dressed today, but he wasn't going to be far off.

Chapter 27

INTRO

Rodhri Callaghan, Irish central defender, had picked Jarrod up from the hotel and ten minutes later they rolled in to the car park at the training ground for the first day of pre-season. It was only twelve months since he'd done the same thing at Gateshead. So much had happened since then.

After meeting a large majority of the players, some of them he knew from TV, some he had even played against in the past and after trying to process all the names of the players and the staff, the morning took on a very familiar pattern. They had a welcome back speech from Mr Raffaella including a brief introduction to the new staff and players. They were invited to try on the latest training gear to make sure they had the right sizes. They also were given the opportunity to get acquainted with the new football for the new EPL season.

It was time for the first of the testing processes, with a weigh-in, a blood sample and a one-on-one chat with one of three medical staff for a series of questions. Jarrod already had a file, created the day before at his medical. The questions were so similar that the doctor could have copied the answers from the previous day, but chose instead to go through them again. It had after all been quite a rush yesterday.

The players assembled outside again in the warm sunshine for a warm up of jogging and stretching. Jarrod had been offered boots, socks and shin pads by the guy in charge of the training kit. He was now looking the part. Club photographer Renée was there, getting some snaps to show the world that pre-season had started and that their new signing, Jarrod, denoted a new chapter for the club. Jarrod felt himself smiling whenever he sensed the cameras were close, quite different to the same time last year at Gateshead. In fact he couldn't help himself. He was so proud and still so amazed at being signed by Newcastle at such a mature age.

Jarrod found a flood of text messages on his mobile phone after he'd showered and got dressed back into his civilian clothes. He was astonished to find three invites to upcoming events in Newcastle, one of them tomorrow night. The terrain had definitely changed, and he felt as though he'd stepped up a notch and become a tradable commodity again with lots of brokers fighting to get a piece of him.

He'd taken on board the Detective Inspector's words of wisdom and not even thought about his real agenda, but a flashback moment whilst having a tour of the facilities from one of the medical staff at the end of the day caught him by surprise. They had walked by the rehabilitation gym and opened the door. Choosing not to disturb the four staff who were going through serious sessions with two badly injured players, they simply watched for a moment from the doorway.

Two of the staff members looked like assistants – they were the ones doing the heavy lifting as their patients were helped into position for exercises – the others might have been the physiotherapists, watching and giving instructions. Jarrod had a moment of déjà vu as the taller of the two assistants glanced his way and caught his eye, staring until Jarrod was compelled to look away.

He'd seen him before. When he looked back, the assistant smiled at him and nodded. It was from the end of season party, one of the two Eastern European guys who had stumbled in towards the end of the night. He looked at the other assistant who was busy with his player and recognised him too. Ivan and Dimitri. That was it. He remembered them. He had been talking to Jack Thomas. They were on the dancefloor and Ivan introduced himself and his friend Dimitri. Jarrod remembered drugs. He stopped himself from staring, his tour guide let go of the door and they walked off to the next destination.

That moment was lodged in Jarrod's mind, and whilst it didn't consume his thoughts, it was definitely lodged. In fact, while he vaguely recognised both of the players receiving treatment, he placed the one with the knee brace somewhere else. He couldn't figure out where though.

Chapter 28

LISTEN

Jarrod had been in Newcastle for three days. He hadn't been back to Darlington to sort out his clothes and had even made an early morning dash to Eldon Square to stock up on shirts and trousers. He was aware of the risks of heading out into town, but knew that his face would not be as recognisable as his name. This might be the last chance for a while to head out incognito.

Training was such a polished experience. Even when it rained hard for a five minute period this morning, the training fields remained pristine and there seemed to be no mud or dirt around. It felt like all the players were a step higher than Jarrod in their physical fitness and overall athleticism. That gave Jarrod mixed feelings – he knew that playing in the Premiership would be very demanding and the speed of the game would be that little bit more intense, but he was also revelling in training with players that he considered to be at his level or above.

When training was over, the players seemed to have lots to do. Most players stayed behind to continue in the gym, meet up and chat with the physio team or even have one-on-one personal training sessions. Jarrod took the opportunity to have a media training session where he worked on delivery, eye contact and other interview skills that would surely come in handy.

The players all ate together in the hotel-like restaurant in between training sessions. At the chef's insistence, Jarrod plucked up the courage on the third day to ask for a special meal of fried lardons, a fatty bacon cut into thin strips, with short cut pasta and a thin mayonnaise. It was something he'd had a couple of times on trips to the continent; it was a great way to use up leftover pasta for the following day's lunch. He was amazed that chef Bruno knew the dish, he even added some thinly sliced shallots as if he was trying to impress the new signing. Jarrod was indeed very impressed.

Jarrod was enjoying the experience, even taking in some quiet time reading the newspapers in the lounge room, something he had never got the chance to do in the past. It was here that he could half read, half observe, and he started to think about the sort of things he should be noticing, the everyday mundane things that D.I. Allison would be interested to hear about. He found himself listening in on conversations that he wouldn't normally care about and made himself more approachable to his teammates and all the staff so he could simply get people talking about themselves.

He sparked up a conversation with Alain Ventoux, a young Belgian player on the fringe of the national team, who had been with the club for a few years. Jarrod made sure there were a few people in the lounge room, to have a bigger audience and to make it feel like an open discussion. He turned the subject to the matter in hand.

"So, Rambouillet," he said in his best accent, appreciating that he was talking with a French speaker, "how did that affect everyone?"

"You know," replied Alain, "the season had ended, and we were all ready for some time off. André was not one of the most popular players at the club, despite his obvious talent."

Alain was being very direct.

"We were all brought in here the next day," he continued, "those of us who had not gone away on holiday. So there were maybe just over half of the first team squad. We were all asked questions individually by a few policemen, and then the club offered us counselling. They gave us an official line to follow if we were contacted by the media or had pre-booked interviews lined up."

Jarrod wondered what the official line was, but wasn't going to ask. He didn't need to, as Alain continued.

"We were asked to give no comment and refer any questions back to the club. We were told that André had been shot by a lone-wolf gunman, and that it was perhaps a case of mistaken identity."

"I remember seeing it on TV that night," said Jarrod, "It was graphic."

"Yes," said Alain, "horrible. We haven't seen Yannick since either."

Jarrod raised his eyebrow to suggest that he didn't know who Yannick was.

"Yannick was the guy he was with that night," he continued. "He was like his translator. Nothing official though, just seemed like a good friend of his and he was here sometimes when André had media duties."

David Ponte was leaning against the doorway, having stopped to take in the conversation. He was another French speaker, a Canadian-born player now with a Geordie accent.

"Now, he was a dodgy bloke," he said, joining the conversation.

He walked in and sat down in one of the comfortable seats. "I overheard him talking to André a couple of times and he was being a real ball-breaker."

"What do you mean?" asked Alain.

"He'd be giving André a hard time," he said. "Talking about how the family would be disappointed with him if he didn't raise his game."

"That's strange," said Alain, "I thought they were just mates."

"Must have been family of some kind," said David. "But I never really talked to Yannick after that. I thought he was a bit of a loser. A hanger-on."

Jarrod listened intently to the conversation. He had no idea if this was something of interest to the Detective Inspector or not, but he kept the discussion going. In the end he didn't get much further than Rambouillet having a family member or a good friend called Yannick who used to give him a hard time. Still, it was something.

Jarrod had another one of those moments when Rambouillet's name came up when he was in the club superstore. There were a few shirts on the rack with Rambouillet's name on the back and he asked the assistant if they should really be in there. The assistant agreed and took them off the rack and took them out into the store room with Jarrod and showed him a large plastic tub that was overflowing with Rambouillet gear.

He told Jarrod that they had been given the directive to remove anything with his name, but had obviously not done a very thorough job. When Jarrod asked the assistant about the French international, he seemed to stop at giving him any praise. It turned out that Rambouillet had been in the club shop a few times and had demanded on more than one occasion to take a whole load of brand new gear. He hadn't left a good impression, and he was thought of in the shop as a bit of a prima donna.

Jarrod was getting a picture of how Rambouillet was regarded by his teammates, and had managed to get people talking about him even without prompting. Nigerian forward Nixon Ebutu and David had been in conversation at training one time, and Jarrod found himself tuning in, moving closer to the pair as they did their stretching exercises.

On the pretence of finding a spot with more space, he got within earshot and heard Nixon complaining about being owed '50 grand' by Rambouillet and that he'd never get it back. Whilst that wasn't enormous money in the scheme of a professional football player's salary, it owas still a good year's wage to most supporters. It made Jarrod blow out his cheeks in disbelief when he heard it.

Chapter 29

ACCOMPLISH

On day five, with a trip to Ireland coming up and a friendly game in Dublin, Jarrod decided it was time to head home and replenish his clothing options, check on the house, and also spend an hour or two in the company of D.I. Allison.

D.I. Allison's car was in the driveway when he showed up at home. The Detective Inspector, standing by the door, looked as though he'd been there for some time, but the ticking engine of his car meant he'd only just arrived himself. Jarrod had a sense of empathy with the Detective Inspector, a fellow football man and a proud North-Easterner. He likened him to Dad's brother Craig who he saw every few months. After a warm greeting, the Detective Inspector offered to take in some bags from the taxi. They made their way in. D.I. Allison sat at the bench, Jarrod taking his usual spot at the other side and filling up the kettle.

"Thanks for coming, Marcus," said Jarrod, using the Detective Inspector's first name to suggest familiarity.

"It was definitely time to check in," said D.I. Allison. "We're making in-roads in the Rambouillet case and we're keen to hear what you have. How has the first week been?"

"I'm getting pretty tired of being fake," replied Jarrod. "Even though I'm just being myself, the additional agenda means I have to concentrate all the time when I'm around people. I don't feel as if I've relaxed once since I've been back from our holidays. Plus the training is intense!"

"Aye, straight from frolicking on the water in Switzerland to pre-season," said D.I. Allison, "I'd imagine it's a shock to the body."

"Aching, I am. It's a step up for me," said Jarrod. "Now, what can I tell you about Rambouillet?"

"So," he said, pausing to remember the details, "Rambouillet owed money to one of the players, Nixon Ebutu. He was having a grumble to David Ponte yesterday. Rambouillet wasn't very popular either. I'm hearing that he could be a bit of a dickhead. You know, big headed. As if he owned the place."

D.I. Allison had taken out his notepad and began to write. He kept his eyes on Jarrod, only glancing down briefly.

"He had a friend. Yannick," continued Jarrod.

"Yes," interrupted D.I. Allison, "Yannick Lefevre. He was with Rambouillet when he died. We interviewed him a number of times before he went back to France."

"Yes," said Jarrod, "the players were wondering where he had been."

"Oh?" said D.I.Allison. "They knew him?"

"He was the unofficial translator," said Jarrod. "No one really knew why he was always with Rambouillet. They just assumed he was a family friend acting as translator."

"Interesting," said the D.I., quickly adding some detail to his notes.

"I'm guessing that's news to you," said Jarrod.

"It is. It is," said D.I. Allison. "We knew he came over frequently from his home in France, but we didn't realise that he spent a lot of time around the rest of the players. No, that's very interesting."

Jarrod got a rush of accomplishment. He knew something the police hadn't known. He went on to fill in the Detective Inspector about everything he could think of, from the way Yannick had given Rambouillet a hard time, to the way his teammates talked about him with disdain. They had all agreed though that he was a fantastic footballer, and a great player to play with.

He mentioned the two guys Ivan and Dimitri, and how he recognised one of the injured players being treated. The day was quickly getting away from both men and when Jarrod realised the time, he was quick to ask if the Detective Inspector had somewhere to be. Jarrod had to be at training later that afternoon. He had achieved absolutely nothing of what he had come to do.

"Thanks for your input, Jarrod," said D.I. Allison.

"Thanks for coming to see me at home," said Jarrod, who was glad to be on home turf in the comfort of his own home.

"Now, don't be surprised if you get some sort of contact this week," said D.I. Allison. "The new season is upon us, the first pre-season fixtures are happening. There's money to be made on insider knowledge being shared. It's often prime time for betting irregularities."

"I see," said Jarrod. "I don't suppose you know who will be contacting me?"

"No," said D.I. Allison, "that's for you to find out."

With that, he bid Jarrod a good day. Jarrod showed him out and then got frantic, unzipping his suitcase and making two colour-coordinated piles of washing on the floor of the lounge room. He repacked some items back into one of the suitcases and headed off to his bedroom to find some fresh clothes. After checking twice to see if he had put his dress shoes in, and having rifled through the bare cupboards for something for lunch, he locked up and was on the road back to Newcastle.

"Dad!" exclaimed Jarrod excitedly.

"Jarrod," said Dad with a croak in his voice. "You were counting on me being up. Gone eleven o'clock here."

"Just checking in, see how you're doing," said Jarrod.

"Ah, all good here," said Dad. "More importantly though, how's my little laddie going at St James' Park? You'll be off to Ireland today."

Jarrod was impressed with his dad's knowledge of his movements, although he didn't get the right day. He proceeded to tell Dad all about his first week at Newcastle, he knew that he would be wanting to hear all about that first. When Mum excitedly grabbed the phone, she wanted to know all about their holiday in Switzerland, and how the kids were, how was Marianne, and was he sleeping well. He may have been away from home for nearly 20 years but he was still his mother's little boy.

"Remember to wish your sister good luck," said Dad. "The World Cup starts tomorrow and it's all happening here. Who would have thought – a son at Newcastle and a daughter at the World Cup!"

"Shit, yes!" exclaimed Jarrod, having totally forgotten that Anna had been selected for the Matildas and that she was going to be playing in the World Cup on home soil. He had made a point of writing on the blackboard a few weeks ago in the kitchen in big letters, 'Anna World Cup!' but he wasn't in the house much at the moment and it had slipped his mind.

Jarrod had found solace amidst the madness, the familiar car journey back to Newcastle for training went very quickly. Mum filled him in on the people in the street, the boys he grew up with and the extended family. Jarrod loved hearing all about it. About what it could have been like if he still lived in Sydney.

There was an extra skip in his step as he ran out onto the training field at Little Benton. The fatigue had gone, he was ready for anything.

Chapter 30

JOURNO

The players had all assembled at St James' Park for a team meeting. Jarrod had arrived very early on the metro and after a glance at his watch he decided to head down the hill to Eldon Square to have a quick browse of the shops. It was just after the early morning rush and just after the shops opened, so there was barely a soul as he walked around the clothes stores upstairs, trailing his wheelie case behind him. He looked every bit the footballer, a lean figure dressed in smart sport casual clothing and well-coiffed after a recent visit to the barber.

He made his way into a very dark shop playing funky music and instantly became aware that eyes were trained on him. He had a casual glance at a rack of jackets, some really good stuff on show, but he couldn't help feeling that he was being watched. It seemed as though people were deliberately walking past him as he browsed, as if they were keen to get close to him.

He quickly turned and made his way out of the dark shop and back into the bright lights of the shopping centre. The feeling of paranoia lifted when he looked around and realised that there was no one within 20 metres. He hurried back along the walkway over Percy Street and back down the other side. He'd been spooked. It might have been a panic attack. Whatever it was, it had absolutely freaked Jarrod, and he was very keen to get away from it.

He arrived up at St James' Park with beads of sweat running down his forehead. He made his way into the lift at reception, up to the mezzanine level where the players had been asked to meet. He was still one of the first ones there despite his unsuccessful foray into town.

His mania had gone, he was now feeling relief and comfort as he saw his teammates and was greeted warmly. They were off to Ireland today and they were going to stay in very posh accommodation, making the trip seem like a holiday.

They were due to meet Mr Raffaella and his team for a team briefing in ten minutes; players continued to arrive, the buzz growing louder as the group grew in numbers. Jarrod got a tap on the shoulder. It was Iain Merritt, one of the two physios who had been hard at work the other day when Jarrod was getting his guided tour of the training facilities.

"Hello Jarrod, how are you doing?" asked Iain. Without waiting for an answer he continued. "I've got a reporter downstairs looking for a few words from you. Do you mind coming down afterwards and popping your head in next to reception to have a quick chat?"

"Sure, no problem," said Jarrod. He was confused as to why it would be physio Iain Merritt setting up interviews with reporters instead of one of the three media people at the club who were actually responsible for that sort of thing.

"Great, I'll see you afterwards," Iain said, almost whispering. Jarrod had been introduced to Iain a couple of days before. Jarrod, being a good judge of character, had earmarked the straight-laced physiotherapist as one of the good guys. He had no reason to think otherwise now, but still it was an odd request. Perhaps it was a reporter from a fitness magazine, or perhaps he was a friend of his and he was doing him a favour.

Mr Raffaella and his three assistants arrived through the double doors. A blast of smoke and some spotlights would not have been out of place, such was the sense of occasion. The players were ushered into a meeting room, where they were invited to take a seat or find a place to stand. The majority of the players opted to stand and it wasn't until one of the older players sat down that a few others took the comfy seats and made themselves at home.

This was a tactics meeting. One of the assistants, Antonio, wheeled in a huge whiteboard that still had the remnants of a previous meeting scribbled all over it. He rubbed off the mess and handed the marker pen to the boss.

"Good morning lads," said Mr Raffaella. "I would just like five minutes of your time to announce the team for this evening's game."

This was classic Raffaella. Sometimes he'd keep the team to himself until ten minutes before kick-off. The one thing that was consistent about his methods was the unpredictability. This time he was announcing the line up before they'd even set foot in the country. It was probably to give the players who were in the starting line-up a chance to start forming relationships on the journey across, to invite some camaraderie to develop. Jarrod wasn't too sure if this was a good idea though. Perhaps a little exclusive.

As it turned out, Jarrod was in the starting line-up. Once his name had been read out and written up on the board in a midfield position, he listened intently as the remainder of the team was read out and scribed in positions next to his name. It was a 3-5-2 formation with Jarrod playing a deep central midfield role – it was effectively 4-4-2 when defending, Jarrod felt naturally very comfortable in that position.

Mr Raffaella ran through the set piece responsibilities. He earmarked another new signing Sammy N'Djame as the free kick taker anywhere around the edge of the box. Jarrod was given corners from the left, Willem Leeuwin from the right. Inswinging corners obviously the requirement today, probably some weakness that the boss wanted to exploit.

There was youth in goal with 18-year-old Ollie Sheen set to make his debut. Jarrod had seen him in action in training. He was an amazing shot stopper but his slight frame made him look a little shy when the ball came in high when he was surrounded by players.

Mr Raffaella and his crew left and team manager Russ Bernall took their spot at the whiteboard. He didn't write anything, but read some key timings from a clipboard – ten minutes to boarding on the coach downstairs, when they were expected at the gate at the airport and a 4pm arrival at Carton House. Jarrod loved this part of the season, going on away trips to places he'd never been. Newcastle United was on another level and he could sense that he was part of a very slick operation that left no detail unchecked.

The majority of the players waited for the lifts, while Jarrod made his way down the flights of stairs to the ground floor where he found Iain deep in conversation with another man.

"Gentlemen," said Jarrod confidently, "we have five minutes before the coach leaves. What can I do for you?"

"Yes, Jarrod," said Iain, a little flustered from having been interrupted from what looked like an intense discussion. "Meet Aram, a journalist all the way from Armenia."

The diminutive Aram held out his hand and smiled. Jarrod shook his hand. Iain directed them over to an area behind the lifts where there was a table and chairs, recently vacated with some rubbish left strewn on the table. They sat down, Aram casually picking up the rubbish before looking around for a non-existent bin and placing it on the floor.

"Thanks for meeting with me," he said in very good English albeit with a strong accent. "I am here for research into today's game and I have a few questions."

Jarrod looked at Iain, as if for advice. Iain simply nodded his head and turned to Aram. Jarrod took that as affirmation that this was okay.

"Fire away," said Jarrod chirpily, raising his voice as though he wanted someone to hear.

"Thank you," said Aram, "Firstly, can you confirm the starting line-up for today's game? I believe it will be a 3-5-2 formation …"

Jarrod was instantly impressed. Must be a very knowledgeable journalist. He went through the team line-up as much as he could remember, going back to correct a couple of positions. He then went through pretty much the whole briefing that they had just sat in with the boss, from the corner takers, the free-kick taker, who was on penalty duty and finally finishing with Ollie Sheen's debut in goal. Aram wrote furiously on a notepad in what was obviously his native language, flipping the page and continuing even when Jarrod had eventually stopped talking. Conscious that he would not have much time, Aram asked one last question.

"Are the players up for a battle tonight, or are you treating this game as a practice game?"

Jarrod thought for a second, standing up and grabbing his small backpack.

"I can say that I'm fired up for this one," said Jarrod truthfully. "I can't speak for anyone else, but hopefully if we can demonstrate that we're taking it seriously in the first fifteen minutes, that'll be infectious. I expect the second half to have a lot of substitutions, but you'd expect that anyway from a pre-season game."

Aram stood up and was beaming.

"Thank you so much, Jarrod," he said, and put his hand on his shoulder, quite a reach for his small stature. "I hope to speak with you again soon, and good luck." He gave Jarrod a slightly uncomfortable double slap on both cheeks.

"Thanks," said Jarrod, having forgotten his name for an instant, before remembering. "Enjoy the game Aram, and I'll see you next week Iain."

The coach doors closed as soon as Jarrod got on and he found a seat at the front, next to Antonio. Jarrod glanced at his watch and gave him the 'eek' face, to which Antonio smiled and shrugged his shoulders. The trip was underway.

Chapter 31

DUBLIN

After a very short hop over to Dublin on their chartered flight, the accommodation, about 30 minutes out of town, took Jarrod's breath away. The place was palatial.

The warm afternoon had golfers out in their short sleeved shirts, there was a relaxed buzz about the place, the property itself was as close to a palace as Jarrod had ever stayed in. The temptation was to go on a wander and take in all the gardens and ornate garden furniture but the players were on a strict timeline. They only had 15 minutes before a light meal in one of the many banquet rooms.

A buffet had been prepared with light food, no bread, no potatoes, lots of seafood and a selection of rice dishes. Jarrod sensed some sport science had gone into the meal selection. There were servers on hand to advise the players and staff as to what they were eating and how much they should be having. Jarrod loaded up on smoked salmon and rice and made a garnish of cornichons to make out he was having some greens.

He found himself at a table with the three goalkeepers and two of the coaches. The temptation was there to turn the conversation to their late teammate, but Jarrod knew that he couldn't bring up the subject at every occasion. No, he had to stay cool, and instead quizzed Ollie Sheen about how he had come to Newcastle, trying to pump him up about his debut without making him more nervous than he was. Jarrod loved to make the younger players feel special. He had done it a great deal in his last two seasons, and the coaches seemed to be impressed with his line of questioning.

The players were given a briefing again by the meticulous Russ and given five minutes to go and do any last minute bathroom breaks and collect what they needed from their rooms. Jarrod only needed his small bag for afterwards, with comb and gel and various other items for preening, nail scissors for any unwanted jagged edges on the toenails and such like. Everything else would be provided, towels, shower gel, shampoo, playing kit, and all the boots and shin pads had been taken away by kit man Bevil. He also grabbed a plastic bag of old stock items he'd been offered from the club shop.

The traffic was surprisingly bad, although Jarrod had no idea what traffic was normally like in Dublin. The peak hour was in full swing and there was huge interest in the game against St Patrick's Athletic. The roads began to clog heavily with cars the closer they got to the stadium.

The stadium entrance was very olde worlde, everything painted a bright red and there were a few interested onlookers, mainly parents with kids, looking to see or even meet their idols. Jarrod made a point of handing out everything he had in his goodie bag when he had got off the bus and stretched his legs. He happily posed for a selfie with a boy who was about Seb's age. That gave him a twinge of longing, a reminder that in the midst of this crazy journey he was on, he had a family and was still a family man at heart.

A steely resolve had come over Jarrod. With the stadium at

capacity for what was billed as a testimonial match for one of the longstanding St Pat's players, the atmosphere was jovial and keen. There had after all been a whole six weeks without competitive football, so the appetite was there. This was the first chance that anyone would have to see the new signings.

Jarrod was keen to get out there and get some minutes under his belt to start the pre-season in the right manner. The first ten minutes in the bright sunshine lived up to expectations of a first pre-season game, the players looking to get the maximum of touches and passes away before even thinking about attacking. Jarrod could sense an underlying lethargy, so decided to make his presence felt and teed up a meaty challenge with his opposing central midfielder, bouncing to his feet while the St Pat's player remained on the ground. The oohs from the crowd and the speed at which Jarrod got up and continued had the desired effect. Newcastle stepped up a gear and took the game completely into their opponents' half.

A couple of corners from the left allowed Jarrod to take aim to perfect his set piece taking, the second one being met full on by the in-rushing Edgar Stefanovic but bouncing onto the bar and behind. The breakthrough came when Sammy N'Djame was up-ended right next to the 'D'. The referee thought hard and allowed himself to catch up to play and assess the exact position where the foul had taken place before ruling it to be outside the box.

A two-minute charade involving the setting of the wall and some pushing on the keeper saw N'Djame step up casually and bend the ball expertly around the wall and off the underside of the bar for a magnificent opening goal. That was the cue for an onslaught from the visitors, streaming through challenges and brushing aside players to tee up a series of chances. Stefa got a goal, powering from his fullback spot to slam the ball home from well outside the box.

Then N'Djame got the third goal, almost apologetically taking the ball past the keeper after springing the offside trap. Three goals to the good then at the break, Newcastle were cruising. The game had gone exactly to plan, and Jarrod had been involved in everything that they created. Some of the football they played was fabulous – at least Jarrod thought so – and the step up in class to Premier League was very clear.

Mr Raffaella surprised everyone by announcing no changes at the break, but let everyone know that they had ten minutes to play at 100 per cent before he would make the first of many. Jarrod could see that this was designed to stimulate the players to keep the intensity up for the sometimes slow start to the second half, and he was spot on.

The players began the second forty-five like a pack of wolves stalking their prey. It wasn't long before a midfielder coughed up possession and a rampant Newcastle forward line played triangles around their opponents. That allowed N'Djame to lash in his third, running away to salute the Newcastle fans who were clearly loving the free-scoring performance.

A five player substitution then halted play for two minutes. Jarrod half expected to be one of the players making way, but it was five of the big established names making way for the players of tomorrow to come on for a thirty five minute introduction to first team football. Marco Vetere drew a large cheer – a local lad from Fenham, despite his Italian-sounding name. He had captained the Under-18s to a youth cup final victory and was quickly becoming a cult hero. He slotted into midfield alongside Jarrod.

The first opportunity he got, Jarrod passed the ball to Marco. The youngster drew a challenge and swerved past his man with little effort, drawing applause from the crowd. His swaggering style, after being on the field for barely two minutes, was captivating to both his teammates and his opponents. The fans absolutely lapped it up. Jarrod felt as though he was witnessing the birth of a true superstar, a George Best or a Diego Maradona.

The next wave of four substitutions included a youthful replacement for Jarrod, ending the game as a one-way affair. The home side began to get more possession, and finally gave their fans some cheer. A looping ball from the right seemed to hang in the air while Ollie Sheen positioned himself to pluck it out of the air. He had already started to come back down from his leap by the time the ball arrived in his hands, causing him to fumble it as he landed. The ball bounced off his knee and away from his grasp and the St Pat's player couldn't believe his luck as he prodded the ball into the empty net from five yards out.

The young keeper had his head in his hands as the crowd saluted the goal. His defenders were quick to rally around him and give him encouragement, but in truth that was a bad mistake.

A fifth goal in injury time gave the score a more realistic look. The final whistle was greeted with cheers from the Newcastle end and applause from the rest. It had been a thoroughly entertaining game, and it had gone as expected for Mr Raffaella and his Newcastle team. Jarrod made sure no autograph or selfie hunter was left unsatisfied post-match. As other players were collared for TV and radio interviews, Jarrod enjoyed photos and chit chat with the Newcastle fans. He would have normally been the first person up for an interview after a game, but here he was way down the pecking order.

The next morning, after breakfast, Jarrod received a call from the physio, Iain.

"Good morning Jarrod," came the unusually cheery voice, "well done on a fantastic performance last night."

"Thanks, Iain," said Jarrod, trying to hide his surprise at the upbeat nature of the normally unemotional and perhaps over-professional physio. "What can I do for you?"

"Oh, nothing, nothing," he said. "Just checking in. Aram was absolutely delighted with the insight you gave him yesterday. He passes on his gratitude for your expert preview of the game and your valuable insight."

"That's kind," said Jarrod, if slightly puzzled. "I'm glad I could be of use."

"Aram would like to make a personal donation for the information received," said Iain, leaving a long pause before continuing. Jarrod's heart started pounding. He couldn't believe this conversation was actually taking place. This was completely illegal and flew totally in the face of Jarrod's moral and ethical stance on cheating and deception. Jarrod felt hot, and despite the cool of the lounge room he was in, he could feel his face reddening. He tried to compose himself and make the next words from his mouth disguise his nerves.

"That's even kinder," said Jarrod. "What do you need from me?"

"Flick me a text with your bank details," he said. "I'll pass it on to Aram. Check for activity in your bank account in the next two days."

Jarrod could feel his mouth was open, his eyebrows knitting together creating deep furrows in his forehead.

"Sure," said Jarrod, finally acknowledging his physio, "I'll get that to you as soon as I can."

"Well done, Jarrod," said Iain, reverting to his more normal monotone voice. "We'll do this again. See you when you get back."

The players were due to assemble in 15 minutes for a training session, so Jarrod knew he had to be efficient with his time. He was alone in the room he was sharing with Willem, but still made sure he was out of earshot and sat on the toilet in the bathroom, the door locked.

"Hello Jarrod," said D.I. Allison when he answered the phone, Jarrod having remembered to use the app on his phone to make the call.

"Hello Marcus," said Jarrod, "I need some guidance."

"Fire away."

"I've been offered a 'donation' by a journalist, and I need a bank account to put some money into," said Jarrod rather hurriedly. "I'm not going to use my normal details, am I?"

"Of course not," replied Marcus. "I'll text you through the bank details. We got an account set up for you already. Say, that was a good performance from the team last night. I thought you did well. N'Djame looked sharp, and what about young Marco? He can play a bit."

Jarrod's unease ebbed away, he loved the opportunity to fill in the Detective Inspector with all the footballing news. He left the bathroom, still talking casually into the phone as Willem came in to get his gear together. He wrapped up the conversation, knowing he should get on with his day.

"Thanks Marcus," he said, looking at Willem and catching his eye. "Yep, send through the details and I'll get on to it."

Jarrod's panic had eased. The scenario of having to arrange a bank account at short notice, going into a bank when he got back, raising suspicion and feeling uncomfortable, that had been nipped in the bud. Between the police and Newcastle United, Jarrod was feeling part of two extremely professional outfits.

Chapter 32

GAMBLE

The mini-tour of Ireland was now over. The players had enjoyed two days of intensive pre-season training following the comprehensive win in their first hit out. It was now back to Little Benton for training. Jarrod had arranged another breakfast meeting with the Detective Inspector at the hotel. If D.I. Allison was a family man, he must have a very patient and accommodating family.

After engaging in small talk and chatting football, D.I. Allison got down to business.

"Here's the situation," he said, squaring up his body in his seat as if the meeting had started for real. They were in the period between receiving their drinks and going to the buffet, so there would be no interruptions.

"You are out of money. You have a gambling problem. You need more money to feed that problem and you are getting heat from other people you owe money to," he continued.

"Do I look like someone in that situation?" asked Jarrod, without sounding incredulous at the suggestion.

"Jarrod," said D.I. Allison with a pause, "as you know, it is impossible to know what people are going through just by looking at them. But there are things you can do and say when in the right company that can send the right signals."

"Such as?" asked Jarrod, turning his body slightly away from the table as if being dismissive. He was clearly not feeling in control.

"Well, the physio team," said D.I. Allison. "You have identified that one physio is acting as the conduit between yourself and whoever is involved in this. You've also identified a couple of characters in there that have roused suspicion in your mind. I'd be spending a bit more time in their company."

"And how do I make that happen?" asked Jarrod, tempted to cross his arms, but knowing that he would look totally closed in that pose. All of a sudden he received a sharp kick to the shin under the table which caught him right on the pointy edge of the bone. He sat up in shock and glowered at the Detective Inspector before reaching down to feel his leg. That was hard enough to cause a bruise. He looked around to see if anyone had noticed what had just happened.

"You've taken a knock," said D.I. Allison with a hint of a smile.

"Arsehole," said Jarrod, looking at him with disgust before stopping and smiling. "That was pretty funny."

They laughed together. This was truly a most surreal situation, the Detective Inspector's dry Geordie sense of humour was winning Jarrod over.

They discussed the signs of someone with a gambling problem. Jarrod downloaded four betting apps on his phone, the Detective Inspector suggested that he keep the landing page of one of them open so the right people could notice it whenever he used his phone. He also asked what Jarrod knew about gambling, which was very little. He offered to send through a list of terms that he should get to know, phrases and words that only the betting-savvy knew. It was subtle, but every little detail could help build a picture of someone with an addiction.

Jarrod's leg throbbed when they eventually stood up to head to the buffet. He was tempted to give the Detective Inspector a kick back.

"Far out, that hurts," he said, reaching down to feel what had become a bump.

"Better see a physio about that," replied D.I. Allison.

Chapter 33

PHYSIO

Jarrod arrived at training quite early and went straight to Nelson Quinn, the physio who was always at training and who served as triage to the physio team. He explained that he had taken a knock, but couldn't remember how or when. Nelson led him to the physio table in the corner of the changing room.

"Here, let's have a look," said Nelson. Jarrod sat on the table with his hands down flat behind him to hold himself up so he could see what Nelson was doing.

"Has it been swollen for a while?" he asked.

"I've only just really noticed it this morning," said Jarrod truthfully. "It hurt a little when I put weight on it."

"Well, you've taken a bit of a hit, that's for sure," said Nelson. "Let's go and see what the guys say."

Jarrod wanted to check if Iain was there, but was pretty sure he would be. They walked along the corridor and through the double doors. The physio team had obviously heard them coming and were making their respective ways back from a table in the corner of the room to their respective stations. Iain was sat at the table and closed his laptop slowly when Nelson walked in followed by Jarrod.

"Jarrod Black," said Iain, standing up to greet him.

"Hello Iain," said Jarrod, offering his hand for a shake, which was firmly taken. "What can we do for the club's senior player?"

Nelson rather unexpectedly took control of the conversation.

"Jarrod here has a knock on his shin," he said. "Looks quite fresh, but is causing a little discomfort. I'd like you to take a look."

"With pleasure," said Iain with his eyes on Jarrod, moving slightly so that he was effectively standing in between Nelson and Jarrod. There was perhaps some power play going on in the physio team, making the situation a little awkward.

Nelson presumably got the hint.

"I'll leave you in the physio team's capable hands," he said, before turning and walking through the double doors with quite a theatrical exit.

Iain smiled at Jarrod and held his gaze just a little longer than was comfortable. He showed the way to his physio table and instructed Jarrod to take a seat. He moved across to his filing cabinet and took out the thin folder he had seen a few days earlier at the first day of pre-season training. Taking a fresh sheet of paper, he started to write on the paper, presumably name, date, symptom, that sort of thing. Presumably he'd be writing this up on a computer afterwards, but it did seem a little old school.

"Everything going well in your first weeks at Newcastle?" asked Iain as he examined the bruise on Jarrod's shin. That was a very open question, and one that broke the silence. Ivan and Dimitri were busying themselves.

"It's been an amazing introduction," said Jarrod. "And your friend Aram has made things a whole lot easier for me too."

Jarrod had toyed with this wording in his head for a while already this morning, and he felt the ambiguity was perfect for the situation.

"Ah yes, Aram is an absolute delight to work with," said Iain. "A true professional. He knows the game very well and is well connected. Thanks for taking the time to talk to him the other day."

Jarrod's phone buzzed audibly in the quiet room. He had a message. He wouldn't normally flinch in that situation, but he had an agenda. He took out his phone and flicked it on, revealing one of the betting apps, just as he had discussed with the Detective Inspector an hour earlier. He made a point of putting the phone down beside him and looking back at Iain, the bright green screen making it obvious what he was looking at. Iain didn't look, but may well have caught it in his peripheral vision.

"No problem," said Jarrod. "If you'd like me to meet with him again, I'm more than happy to help."

At that moment, there was another well-timed message on his phone. This time he took his phone and switched it off quickly, putting it back in his pocket.

"You know, Aram has a colleague who would like to meet you too," Iain said.

At this point Ivan and Dimitri had stopped what they were doing and were looking in their direction. Jarrod could sense it. Iain took a soft ice bag and placed it on the bruise.

"I'd like that," said Jarrod. "Just let me know where and when and I'll make myself available."

"Okay," said Iain smiling to himself, peering over his small glasses with raised eyebrows, "I'll be in touch."

Jarrod stayed in the room for five minutes with the ice pack on his leg. The clock on the wall suggested it was time for him to be out on the field, so he excused himself. He got down from the table and walked past Iain, who had opened his laptop and was indeed typing up the notes he had taken on the piece of paper. He placed his hand on his shoulder as he walked past.

"See you soon."

He could sense two other sets of eyes on him as he walked out and once out of sight, he could sense his heart thumping and his blood pressure elevated. The 'angry veins' on his temples would be raging.

Jarrod felt as though he had just opened a door on a whole world of badness. The light-heartedness of this ambiguous conversation was unnerving, especially with the two Russian types who had kept quiet while watching from afar. He could tell this was going to be the start of something very taxing. He was itching to get out on the field to join his teammates.

Chapter 34

RENDEZVOUS

"Say, Jarrod," said Nelson as Jarrod made his way into the changing room after the morning training session. Jarrod peeled away from his discussion with Andros Szczepanski.

"Hello Nelson," said Jarrod, unsure as to what he was going to hear.

"Iain wants to check in about your knock," said the physio. Jarrod stood for a second and then realised that he was talking about his shin that had swollen up magnificently two days back.

"Oh, that," said Jarrod dropping his shoulders noticeably. "Yes, I suppose I should check in."

"I assume it was nothing," said Nelson, part question, part statement.

Jarrod held his gaze for a second, deep in thought about what a good opportunity this was to speak again with Iain.

"Yep, getting soft in my old age," he finally said before edging away from Nelson. He was trying to give the impression of someone who was aloof and preoccupied, perhaps someone with a lot on their mind. He was actually trying to send out signals that he had a problem. It wasn't easy. He felt that the thoughts in his mind were so contrary to the character he was trying to inhabit, that it must have seemed unconvincing. He moved away from Nelson without saying anything further, not daring to look back at him and headed down the corridor to the physio room.

Iain was there alone. He was at his desk, poring over his laptop.

"You wanted to see me?" asked Jarrod.

"Ah yes," said Iain without looking up. "Yes I do."

"The lump on my shin has completely gone …" started Jarrod, keen to show his physio where the lump had been.

"Jarrod," said Iain looking straight up at him with an intense stare, "Aram has been in touch. I am of the opinion that your meeting with him last week was well received."

"The timing was exceptional," said Jarrod. "I could really do with another meeting soon."

Jarrod took a sharp intake of breath. Maybe that was too much.

"Here's an address," said Iain with the slightest hint of a smile, pushing a business card across the table to Jarrod. Jarrod took the card. It was Iain's business card, but on the back was written an address in Walker in red pen. Jarrod looked at it and then looked at Iain.

"This is Murtaka," continued Iain. "An associate of Aram's. Very interested to meet with you and discuss football. Are you interested in talking football with a good friend of Aram?"

This sounded as dodgy as hell. Jarrod felt that he was making the right move and the wrong move at the same time.

"Of course," said Jarrod, looking again at the card. This place was only about ten minutes' drive from training. "When?"

"Today," replied Iain immediately, giving a sense of urgency. "Murtaka does travel quite extensively, but is available at noon today for a chat. Keen to talk and there might not be another opportunity before next week."

"Okay, no problem," said Jarrod, looking at the clock on the wall.

"Don't worry," said Iain, "you'll be back before the afternoon session and I'm sure your meeting with Murtaka will be most beneficial."

Ugh, this is so thinly veiled, thought Jarrod. The nuances and ambiguity of the conversation was really starting to grate on him now. He had to keep calm.

"So, Murtaka," said Jarrod, pronouncing it as he had heard Iain do so, "is he a journalist too?"

Iain rocked back in his chair and thought for a moment. Jarrod felt as though he might have asked the stupidest question ever. Was his unconvincing charade making him sound too naïve? Iain would surely have expected him to cotton on by now, and Jarrod felt at that moment that he should have just said nothing.

"Murtaka, my friend," said Iain with an air of superiority, "is a very important person in football. Part agent, part football club owner, part activist. You'll be impressed with the level of knowledge of the beautiful game."

"We don't know any Murtaka," said D.I. Allison at the other end of the line when Jarrod rang in the car. "Tell me that address again."

"Burwood Road," said Jarrod, holding up the card and taking a sly glance.

"Right," said D.I. Allison, "I'll let Dennis know. We'll have someone nearby and they'll check it out beforehand."

"This is safe, right?" asked Jarrod, a little concerned.

"Like I say," said Marcus, "There'll be a presence."

Chapter 35

LOOKOUT

Jarrod was nearly there by the time he'd finished on the phone. He eventually turned off busy Walker Road and found the address. He was two minutes early. This was total suburbia, there wasn't a soul around. He stared at the address. It didn't look like a business and it didn't look as though anyone was home. He gingerly got out of the car and walked towards the front gate, picking his mobile phone from his pocket. He might need it.

"Are you looking for Murtaka?" asked a voice, startling Jarrod and making him lose grip of his phone. A comedy juggling scene ensued as Jarrod leapt down to catch the phone before it hit the ground, sending it back into the air. A slide whistle would have been the perfect sound effect as he somehow managed to catch it at the third attempt. He turned around, flustered.

It was a friendly-looking gentleman in a well-fitted suit. He offered his hand and Jarrod shook it.

"Barnes," he continued in a well-spoken nondescript London accent, "Adrian Barnes. Murtaka will see you now."

A taxi pulled up, a black one, but not quite like the black cabs Jarrod had seen around the nation's capital. A door opened and Mr Barnes stood by the door, motioning Jarrod to climb inside.

Jarrod looked around, and there was no one else around. He climbed in, and Mr Barnes opened the passenger door and climbed in the front.

Jarrod found himself in the back with a slender and obviously tall Indian lady with very short hair. Jarrod thought she might be his age or a little older. Jarrod smiled.

"Hello Jarrod," said the lady, "Murtaka Chiya."

They were sitting next to each other, so they both swivelled on their seats to be able to offer a handshake.

"Ah-ha," said Jarrod in surprise. "It's at this point that you're supposed to say that I wasn't expecting a woman. And you'd be right."

Murtaka laughed. She was intriguing and Jarrod immediately found himself very comfortable in her company.

The taxi took off and Jarrod's comfort left him. They didn't speak until they had arrived at their destination three minutes later. It was a small car park that could maybe be described as a lookout if it wasn't looking out on some of Gateshead's factories on the other side. One day this would all be beautifully landscaped and the land snapped up by savvy developers, but for now it was a slightly ragged looking park.

"Let's sit on the bench over there," said Murtaka, waiting for the driver to open her car door. Mr Barnes opened Jarrod's door and Jarrod waited for Murtaka to make the first move. Once he'd got out of the taxi and made his way around the other side, Murtaka was already making her way to sit on a rusty-looking bench that overlooked the water.

Jarrod caught her up with a jog and realised that he was a little shorter than her. She wasn't wearing any heels either. He did check and Murtaka would have surely noticed. She looked like a sprinter or a netballer. Tall, slim but powerful. And she was calling the shots.

"Thank you for coming to see me," she said as she sat down. "And I apologise for this being a slightly unusual meeting place."

Jarrod didn't find this unusual at all. It felt like the sort of place murders took place and bodies were dumped, and it fit the situation perfectly. He was still captivated by this magnificent lady next to him as he slowly sat down next to her.

"No, thank *you*, Murtaka," said Jarrod. "I'm interested to hear what you have for me."

That was quite a provocative line. It made Jarrod seem like the one with the power.

"Jarrod," said Murtaka, leaning in to him and almost touching, as if she was either going to confide in him or tell him a joke. "I want to buy Newcastle United. I have the means to buy this club. It is a club that I love."

Jarrod had forgotten to take a breath, he was so shocked. This was not what he was expecting.

"I want to make this club great again," she continued. "It has been such a long time this club has been mismanaged and abused. I want success for Newcastle and I want it at all costs."

"I thought the owner had sold up and gone?" asked Jarrod.

"Yes," she confirmed, "and that's amazing news. Now we just have to take it to the next level and get some finances into the club."

"But why?" asked Jarrod sheepishly.

"My father tried to buy the club many years ago," she said. "He had come so close and the owner simply turned around at the end of negotiations and demanded more. He was devastated but his love of football led him to another club in Spain. He did manage to buy it and he completely transformed the club."

Jarrod was listening intently.

"Since he left us," she continued, looking into the heavens, "me and my brothers have tried to walk in his footsteps. Our family business in India is one of the world's biggest companies and we have tried to achieve what he set out to do. My brothers both took over clubs in Europe, but I want to finish where he started and conquer Newcastle."

She was silent for a while, perhaps the mention of her father and family had caused her to choke up. This was extraordinary. Jarrod was processing the information that he had just heard. Here before him was someone who could turn his beloved Newcastle United into the next Man City.

"We both need money Jarrod," said Murtaka. "You need the money, I'm sure of it. I need the money to make this dream come true. My business cannot support the huge sums and we need cash. Do you think we can work together?"

Jarrod felt a twinge of guilt. He was going along with the whole story for the sake of a police investigation. As a fan though it felt difficult to jeopardise a grand plan like this, even if it was dealing with dirty money. He also felt shameful that he was going along with the lie that he needed money.

"Tell me what you need," said Jarrod, "and then I'll let you know if we can work together."

Murtaka thought for a moment and turned to Jarrod with a determined look in her eyes.

"Your next game is in two days," she said, Jarrod giving a single nod. The first team was scheduled to play at Portman Road against Ipswich Town.

"The way that injuries have worked out, there is a high chance that you will start the game. Am I right?" she continued. Again Jarrod give a single nod, waiting for the next line.

"We need a penalty to be conceded inside the first ten minutes," she said, staring at Jarrod as if she was trying to burn through his skin with some sort of laser beam from her eyes.

There was no nod. Jarrod just thought for a moment.

"And that penalty needs to result in a goal, right?" asked Jarrod.

"Not necessarily," replied Murtaka, sitting back against the bench. "I don't think we can rely on that being a certain outcome but we will budget accordingly for it."

Jarrod could just see himself launching into some sort of kamikaze tackle, slicing down a player unnecessarily and attracting the ire of teammates, manager, staff and fans alike. This was going to be difficult. Murtaka was clearly mulling over the result of the penalty kick, so there was plenty of time to think. The black taxi that they had arrived in, which had been parked across three car spots, started up with a shudder. That was probably the sign that they needed to leave. She would need an answer right now.

"What can I expect for this?" asked Jarrod, in an attempt to show that he was being motivated by money.

"You will receive a donation upon the outcome," said Murtaka. "It will be enough to keep you interested. You will not be disappointed."

She got to her feet and faced Jarrod, who looked up at her, his elbows on his thighs, his hands cradling his chin. The shadow cast over him prompted him to straighten up and then to slowly stand up, rising to almost the same height. He held out his hand instinctively and the bangled hand clinked up to his and they shook on it, staring at each other.

Jarrod could feel himself blushing. She was really very alluring in a quirky way but she showed no emotion. She turned back towards the taxi and Jarrod took that as a cue to follow. Mr Barnes opened the door for Murtaka, who climbed in. He then blocked the way for Jarrod and turned towards him.

"I apologise, dear chap," he said to Jarrod. "We're going the other way."

Jarrod wasn't going to argue. Mr Barnes closed the door and quickly climbed in the passenger side. Jarrod stood motionless as the taxi pulled away, Murtaka already engrossed in her mobile phone. At least the meeting was over and he could feel his adrenaline levels go down.

He was a good walk away from his car though, and luckily he'd been paying attention and remembered the way back. He broke into a jog when he recognised the straight road taking him slightly uphill towards Walker Road. His car was in the street off to the right just before that. He was half expecting the car to be gone, or burnt out, such was the unpredictability of the life he was living.

Chapter 36

READY

There was no further contact with Iain or Murtaka, or Aram for that matter, until the Matchday squad was meeting to head to the airport. It was 1pm on a warm sunny Wednesday in early July. There was no pre-flight pre-match briefing this time. Mr Raffaella had obviously chosen to make the most of the coach time from Stansted to Portman Road to deliver the team.

The players were all converging at the meeting spot, downstairs this time in the reception area. Iain appeared next to Jarrod as he walked through the revolving doors of the Milburn reception. He grabbed him quite firmly by the arm and led him in a slightly different direction, behind the stairs, where he sat him down at a table.

"Are you ready for today?" asked Iain. He looked a little dishevelled, not like his usual self, but tried to crack a smile.

"Yes, thanks, Iain," said Jarrod. "Fit and healthy."

"You do understand the task in hand?" said the physio. "This is an important day for a lot of people. You need to get this right."

Jarrod knew exactly what he was alluding to. He had discussed this possible meeting with the Detective Inspector and Dennis when he had checked in that morning. There had been a lot of background checking on Murtaka.

She was exactly who she said she was. She was quite a celebrity back in India. Her brothers had indeed taken control of clubs in Spain and Bulgaria, both taking lower league clubs to the top division and establishing them as contenders for a Champions League spot in a relatively short period of time. Murtaka was the youngest of the three and had been involved in a takeover bid for West Ham United by a consortium that eventually failed.

She had been seen in Newcastle, frequenting the best restaurants and being seen in business meetings and lunches over the past three years. Murtaka Chiya was definitely a noticeable character but there was no intelligence on her being involved in a bid for Newcastle United.

There was also no intelligence on Iain, and the only thing the detectives could find on Aram was that he had a sister living in Ponteland and that he was a journalist for an Armenian sport service. All thoroughly above board if not a little odd. There was no suggestion of underground activity, there were no alarm bells. Jarrod was given the instruction to continue with what was already acknowledged as 'good work', and to see how far he could take it.

"Of course, Iain," said Jarrod, choosing not to be the damaged gambling addict that he was trying to portray. "I have been given a task and I plan to execute it. Thanks for your concern."

He stood up and Iain watched him with weary eyes as he disappeared around the corner to join up with his teammates.

Chapter 37

ESPAÑA

After a routine flight to Stansted and transferring to their coach within ten minutes of landing, there was a short delay while they waited for the bags to come out. They were due to set off on the second part of the journey through rural Essex and on to Ipswich, so Jarrod took a moment to check in with Marianne and the kids.

"Daddy!" shouted Aneka at the top of her voice.

"Hi Aneka, how's your knee?" he asked. She had told him all about her knee when he rang two days ago, how she had fallen off her bike and had to go and see a doctor who put in stitches.

"Good," she replied, with little fuss. It had been a 15-minute one-way conversation last time, so Jarrod was expecting a bit more.

"Hi Dad!" came a second voice. It was Sebastian. He was chirpy.

"Hey Seb, where are you today?" asked Jarrod, hearing a lot of noise.

"We're in Lanuza!" replied Seb. Jarrod had no idea where Lanuza was, and Seb was delighting in pronouncing it like a Spaniard. "Lanuza!" It was obviously a spot near Jean-Jacques and Mireille's place in Pau, and was probably a ski resort turned tourist spot in summer.

"Es en España?" asked Jarrod in his best Spanish.

"Si, si!" replied Seb. He was loving languages at school and benefitting   from his mum's French and Spanish skills. They reverted to English, having used up all their Spanish.

"Let me speak to Mum. I'm looking forward to seeing you in six days' time," he said by way of a goodbye.

"Here she is," said Seb before some jostling of the phone, silence, then Marianne came on the phone.

"Let me just get to a quiet spot," she said. Jarrod could hear her footsteps and the din quietening down.

"We've just had the best lunch," she said. "This place is beautiful!"

"Great," said Jarrod, "the kids must be enjoying their holiday."

"They are, they are, but we're missing you. It doesn't seem right," she said.

"Make the most of it," said Jarrod, "back to school next week."

"Pah, yes, for one week," laughed Marianne, "and then they're on holiday again. What bad parents we are!"

There was a rustle, as if Marianne was moving the phone to her other ear.

"Say," she continued, "I bumped into someone you know this morning in town."

"Ah yeah?"

"He said his name was Yannick. Yannick Lefevre. Do you know him? Said he knew you."

Jarrod was immediately frozen to the spot. He had wandered away from earshot of his teammates. He could hear them goofing around before. Now he was totally gripped by the telephone conversation, he felt his temperature rising and his fist clenching. This was Rambouillet's friend. This was no coincidence.

"Er … I think he used to live in Newcastle," replied Jarrod.

"Well," interrupted Marianne, impatient at his lack of knowledge of this man who had so politely picked up one of her shopping bags and returned it to her after she had left it on the bench in the bank. "He wished you good luck in your game today. I was going to text you, but it kind of slipped my mind."

"That's good of him," said Jarrod, before changing the subject completely and catching up with how his wife was feeling after her chemotherapy, and how her parents were looking after her. The talk of his family and kids calmed him down.

There was a beep from the coach, which had roared to life. Antonio was in the doorway hollering something in Spanish, very appropriate for the phone call he'd just had. Jarrod waved apologetically and ended the conversation quickly.

"Sending my love to the family. And to my beautiful wife."

"Love you too, Jarrod. Good luck in your important game!"

Jarrod jogged over to the coach, which was all loaded up and ready to go. This was definitely not an important game. Who the hell did this Yannick guy think he was, interfering with his family. Jarrod was flushed with anger. He made his way to his seat next to Alain. He was tense. Alain glanced at him.

"You okay?" he asked.

"Sure," said Jarrod, "I thought I was going to miss the coach there!"

Chapter 38

LEGEND

They continued their journey. Mr Raffaella did the rounds and let everyone know if they were in the team, and what position he wanted them to play. Jarrod was, as expected, in the starting eleven, and was playing in front of the back three as he had done in the previous game. The coach eventually left the main road as it neared the town centre and turned into Portman Road. Time to get game ready.

Newcastle had an affinity with Ipswich through their former manager and England legend Bobby Robson. He had been in charge of Town when they had their finest moments in the early eighties, he had also been in charge of his hometown club Newcastle when they had some of their finest moments much later on. This game was to mark an anniversary. A bumper crowd was expected.

The players were relaxed, and they mixed with their Ipswich counterparts in the canteen beforehand. Some of the players took on a hearty meal, others grabbed a quick snack. Jarrod picked at a salad. His mind was completely distracted, his thoughts were with Marianne and the kids, with Yannick and with the job in hand. This was going to be difficult.

The warm up confirmed that this was indeed going to be a

balmy evening, the temperature in Newcastle always five degrees cooler than down South. Jarrod still couldn't believe that he would find it hot when the thermometer hit thirty, remembering growing up and often playing pre-season trials in 35 degree heat on a baking hot synthetic field at Christie Park.

His mind was now focused on how he was going to conjure up a penalty in the opening stages of the game and how he was going to make it look accidental. He was the last player to try to con a referee or to play for fouls. He had always prided himself on being a fair and honest player in the minds of fans, teammates and the media. This was going to test him immensely and he could feel the butterflies in his stomach. The warm up increased in intensity as the coaches signalled five minutes – time to put it in before they went back into the changing rooms to receive their last instructions.

There was a huge roar as the players emerged from the tunnel. It felt like a league game. There were ripped up newspapers and toilet roll streamers. This was clearly a big deal to Ipswich and it took Jarrod by surprise. The pressure started to weigh on Jarrod, and he felt that all eyes were on him.

After the formalities and an exchange of pennants between Andros and the Ipswich captain, the teams took their positions and the game got underway. The heat in the air dictated the first few passes, and they were backwards by Ipswich, taking the ball back to their goalkeeper, inviting the visitors to come and get the ball. Jarrod felt helpless. The ball needed to be up the other end. He shouted at Sammy N'Djame to press higher to cut off the route back to goal.

That had the desired effect and Ipswich lumped the ball forward aimlessly, Jarrod racing back to field the bouncing ball behind his back three, and in the area. A stray bounce and he might be able to conjure up a handball, but the ball bounced perfectly and he had to control and take the ball out of the area. He touched the ball to Stefa who started the first Newcastle attack.

Jarrod hadn't contemplated not being able to deliver on the required outcome in the first ten minutes. Now that three had gone already without Ipswich having any meaningful possession, he could feel himself shivering with nerves. He did have an idea.

The ball arrived at his feet in the middle of the park and he used his acceleration to glide between the two on-rushing Ipswich players. After galloping another 20 yards, he went to change direction sharply and made sure that he hadn't planted his front foot firmly. He lost grip and slid over, slightly theatrically. It was a definite skid and would have looked very convincing. He pounded the floor in mock frustration and leapt back to his feet, giving chase to the home player who had benefitted from the good fortune.

With Jarrod giving chase at full speed, and gaining on his man, the seeds of confusion were sown in the Newcastle back line. Would they go in for the tackle, or follow their player? The Ipswich player cleverly stepped in front of Jarrod, looking for the slightest touch to go to ground. Jarrod was wily enough to leap away from the player's legs so he wouldn't clip him in full flight.

The chase was still on, the player was now racing into the penalty area, pursued by Jarrod, albeit out wide on the right. The shot was possible, or more likely a cross or a square ball to pick out a teammate. Jarrod shaped his body and was completely committed now to the tackle. He leapt in the air feet first and genuinely went to block the cross, but made sure his hands were close to the ground. As the player instead feinted back on to his left, Jarrod dragged his arm close to the ball and with his momentum propelling him towards the byline, diverted the ball away from the Ipswich player with his right hand.

Jarrod hurtled for the advertising hoardings and crashed feet first into one of the electronic boards, smashing the hard plastic cover and effectively snapping the sign, which buckled. He had no thought for his own safety though and was more concerned not to be hearing a cheer or a whistle to signal a penalty. Had the referee missed it?

The Ipswich players were screaming for a penalty and for a moment their screams went unheard. As Jarrod looked up, the referee was staring at his assistant and finally pointed to the spot. The roar went up. Jarrod's knee hurt as he picked himself off the ground. Willem came over to check if he was okay. He took a couple of steps with a limp but was happy to report that he was indeed fine. He bent over for effect and flexed his knee, eventually trudging slowly towards the edge of the D, past the striker who was preparing to take the penalty.

There wasn't much he could do to influence the penalty taker or first-team goalkeeper Max Smeltz. He had thought about having a word with Max to feed him some duff information, or giving the penalty taker some cricket-style sledging as he walked past, but in the end thought he'd done enough and couldn't have asked for a better opportunity to deliver on his promise. Ten seconds later Max was picking the ball out of the net, the Ipswich forward smashing the ball into the roof of the net giving him no chance.

Jarrod held his hands up in apology to his teammates.

"Sorry, fellas," he shouted, "my fault."

"Great start, Skippy," said Max with a ruffle of his hair. It was all forgotten by the time the game kicked off again, only five minutes on the clock. Jarrod afforded himself a wry smile. Job done, the game starts now, he thought to himself.

Newcastle were on the attack immediately and maintained heavy pressure on the hosts. Jarrod played triangles with David Ponte and Andros and found himself in an advanced position. It was definitely worth a shot, and he tried to make more room on his right before cutting back in on his left. His now relaxed and even euphoric state saw him connect beautifully with a curling shot on what he considered his weaker foot. The ball sailed over and around the Ipswich goalkeeper for a fantastic equaliser.

Jarrod raced over to the Newcastle fans and punched the air. The roar that he let out was one of pure relief. Job done and first goal scored. And what a cracker.

By half time Nixon and Sammy had helped themselves to a goal a-piece and Newcastle were in total command. The mood was positive in the changing room, and no one mentioned the early penalty. In fact all the talk was of the equalising goal, an absolute gem and a great way to open his account. Jarrod lapped up the praise.

Mr Raffaella was beaming when he talked to his defensive players, asking them all if this was going to be the formation for the season. They all agreed. It worked thanks to the extra outlet in midfield in front of them and it worked because they were very fit players and could cope with the extra demands of playing a man short in a key position. Again Mr Raffaella sent out an unchanged team for the start of the second half and that had the desired effect. The intensity was high and the billing as a friendly was definitely wide of the mark.

Jarrod seemed to have found an extra gear and was putting in a lot of runs up and down the field, helping out defence and midfield in equal measure. He made a terrific run just shy of the hour mark and Willem found him with a defence-splitting through ball. Jarrod was clean through, not a position he found himself in very often. A slightly heavy touch took him close to the on-rushing goalkeeper, but he managed to get there first and touch the ball away. That sent him wide, again on his left foot. He steadied himself, tucked the ball back on his right and rolled the ball into the net just before the keeper could slide back and keep it out. Again, the celebration was vocal, more than just the goal being celebrated.

That was cue for the substitutions to start for Newcastle, with Jarrod in the first wave, his replacement Marco Vetere coming on again to loud applause. Jarrod high fived his teammates on the bench and took a seat behind the players who were yet to get the nod. His heart was still racing after scoring the goal and he could feel that he had been running on adrenaline. Now that he had stopped and his heart rate started to slow, he immediately began to feel tired. He was red in the face, such were the conditions and he was starting to settle into a very good mood indeed.

A fifth goal completed the scoring. The team all went across to the Newcastle fans and applauded for a good five minutes. Sodden shirts were tossed into the crowd and the players were as social as they had ever been with the fans. After all this was a day of celebration and the mood was more carnival than pre-season kick about.

After a buoyant coach trip back to the airport and a very late flight back to Newcastle Airport, Jarrod picked up his car at St James' and was 'home' at the hotel in ten minutes. He fumbled to find his keycard for the door and opened up to find a bottle of champagne and a note on the bedside table. Letting the door clack behind him and dropping his bag on the floor, he reached for the note and read.

'Well done Jarrod,' it read. 'Many thanks for your commitment. Please accept this token of appreciation.'

He cradled the champagne in his hand. The note wasn't signed. He had a good idea who it was from though. For someone involved in illegal dealings, Murtaka was definitely all class.

Chapter 39

MONEY

The habitual early morning debrief with the Detective Inspector got Jarrod out of bed. He was again at their usual table, newspaper in one hand and a short black coffee in the other. He was engrossed in the match report for the previous night's game and didn't notice Jarrod appearing in front of him.

"Ah good morning, Jarrod," said D.I. Allison with a smile.

"Don't tell me you were at the game," said Jarrod. "You've got no right to be here at this time if you did."

"No, no," said the D.I. "I have to pick and choose my games at this stage of the season. I was tempted, but that's a bloody long car journey. Like you say, I'd only be getting back at four or five in the morning."

They talked football as the waitress milled around. It was now a routine that they would only start talking 'work' when the waitress left them to it and they tucked in to their spoils from the buffet.

"Yannick Lefevre was in Pau yesterday," said Jarrod. "He had a 'chance' meeting with Marianne in town and wished me luck in my big game. What the hell is that about?"

The Detecive Inspector shifted in his seat.

"We're watching him," he said. "I don't think there's anything to worry about, but he's trying to spook you through your wife, that's clear."

"I can't have Marianne and the kids involved," said Jarrod pleadingly. "It's just not fair."

"They'll be back here on the weekend," said D.I. Allison, "and we've heard that Lefevre is now back in Paris."

Jarrod was relieved at this news.

"Now," he said, changing the subject, "have you checked your bank account?"

"Oh, no I haven't," replied Jarrod. "Do you want me to do that now?"

"It would be good to know the sums of money we're dealing with here," said D.I. Allison. He would probably know already, and he seemed to be prodding Jarrod to have a look. He looked up his password in the Files section of his phone and signed in to online banking, navigating the tricky security features. His eyes widened and he let out a quiet 'far out!'

"If I read it right," said D.I. Allison, "that's 150 grand."

"Jesus!" said Jarrod. "Yes it is. How much money are these people dealing with?"

"And how do they bet on these weird outcomes in games?" asked Jarrod before the Detective Inspector could speak. He genuinely didn't know anything about betting and how it worked. The players had been told in no uncertain terms over the years that betting on any football was grounds for contract termination and would lead to lengthy individual bans. He hadn't even bet on the Grand National for ten years or so, and was immune to all the betting talk that he heard in the players' suite after the game when mingling with sponsors and members.

"You should have a look at one of those apps on your phone

that you downloaded the other day," said D.I. Allison. "You can tailor any sort of bet. It's when the sums of money are large that we start to get involved. And I can tell you that there was a lot of money bet on this game, in a lot of countries. We're now following some good leads that should get us some results overseas, but not here yet."

"How long is this going to go on?" asked Jarrod. "I'm a full-time family man in five days. I won't be able to keep this up for much longer."

"Hang in there Jarrod," said D.I. Allison. "You are a very important player in this and you're doing a very good job."

Jarrod didn't know what to say to that.

"Now what's this I'm reading here," continued D.I. Allison, craning his neck to read the small print in the match report in the *Journal*. "Goal of the season contender already?"

Chapter 40

GLAMOUR

Jarrod had four full days of training ahead of him and he would be in and round the training ground constantly. The Detective Inspector had told him in a phone hook-up with Dennis towards the end of their breakfast meeting that he would definitely be expecting contact from Murtaka or someone in her circle in the lead up to the next game. That game was coming up on the Sunday at St James' Park.

Pre-season, for the previous decade at least, had always culminated in a solitary low-key home friendly right before the first weekend of the season, against some not-quite A-grade European opponent. This time however, with no concerts, rugby tournaments or major turf re-laying, there was space for at least two home fixtures.

Rumours began to swirl that manager Mr Raffaella had teed up a glamour friendly with European favourites Barcelona through his never-ending stream of contacts. It had made the papers, the *Chronicle* was adamant. The acting club owners, the Supporters Trust, were sceptical at first – surely Barcelona would be playing in the International Champions Cup – but it came to fruition that they had announced a free window in their schedule and contacted a number of clubs to help fill the void after their first opponents in the Cup had pulled out.

Even that was a bizarre tale. Turkish outfit Beşiktaş had been docked points for fielding an ineligible player after finishing second in their league. This dropped them down the final standings to only merit a qualifying round spot in the Europa League. That meant a super-early start to their season, playing some Eastern European minnow or other over two legs, which in turn ruled them out of their ICC tie with Barcelona.

Whilst that was a disaster for the Turkish club, Mr Raffaella's connections and his own club's failure to organise anything of their own for that weekend meant that it was game on. The city of Newcastle was buzzing at the news. It felt like Newcastle was being catapulted back into the big time. The first ever time Barcelona had been on Tyneside they left with their tails between their legs in a stunning 3-2 win for the Geordies. The hat-trick by Faustino Asprilla and his tumbling celebrations had become folklore. Jarrod looked at this unexpected opportunity to play the best team in Europe and had become more and more excited by the prospect.

The family was due back that day too. Jarrod was hoping for a conclusion to this whole tale before then, but couldn't help thinking that it could wait until after the game. It was Barcelona after all. The one thing that was really playing on his mind though right now was Rambouillet. Jarrod had talked to a lot of people and had been involved in detailed discussions with D.I. Allison and Dennis. He knew a lot. He even loved the way that the high ranking policemen asked loaded questions and always seemed to have a motive behind asking the most trivial of things. They always seemed to be checking facts as opposed to discovering them.

On one occasion Jarrod turned the tables and asked Dennis about the synchronised end of season parties and the coincidence between the timing of Rambouillet's death. Dennis confirmed that every professional or semi-professional club in the North East of England had been treated to an outrageously over-engineered party, and that Newcastle United were the only ones left out. The amount of money now sitting in his unregistered bank account led him to believe that throwing ten huge parties would not have been a big ticket budget item. The bottle of champagne on his bedside table the night before showed that this was someone with at least a touch of class.

Jarrod asked if they were following up on who was behind the parties. Dennis and the Detective Inspector both fell silent on their three-way phone conversation before D.I. Allison cleared his throat and told him that they were still nowhere near pinpointing the organiser. Each club had been contacted anonymously. The parties were all organised by a large scale events company in Glasgow who in turn had been instructed anonymously and paid via untraceable bank transfers.

Still, Jarrod couldn't say with any certainty that there was a link between the parties and the murder, or that Murtaka was in fact the person behind both events. What irked Jarrod more than anything was the facepaint that they had to wear that night. What was the relevance of that? The guy in the CCTV footage might have had the same. He was definitely dressed in similar fashion. But why would everyone at these parties be painted in the same way?

Jarrod had arrived at training. He was sitting at the wheel of his car, engine off, still staring out of the window as if he was driving, lost in thought. A tap on the window from Nixon gave him a fright and they both burst out laughing. At least he had looked like someone with something on his mind. That something could have been a gambling problem. Maybe he was getting good at this role.

As soon as he opened the car door though, anything other than football was off his mind.

Chapter 41

SPONGE

Training had been superb for the past three days, and Saturday was set to be a quiet day of light training, tactics and video analysis. Jarrod had stalled in his own B-licence over the past season after the move to Darlington, but had resolved to resume the process once the new season was in full swing. That was before this opportunity at Newcastle arose, so it might be delayed even further.

What it did mean though was that Jarrod was always interested in being amongst coaches, assistants and the manager, all working as a team, delivering information to a broad range of ages, experience and attention spans. Mr Raffaella and his coaching team were second to none, Russ Bernall was even more meticulous as the team manager of non-footballing affairs. Jarrod was like a sponge whenever he was around them.

Training in the morning was at St James' Park, the players had been asked to be there for a 10am start. Even without a fine system in place, respect and timekeeping was adhered to by everyone and Jarrod loved the way that he would never be first, even if he was half an hour early. That showed how keen the players were and how much they valued being part of such an important club.

After some very light running and stretching, Mr Raffaella

asked his coaching staff to work the whole squad into a dribbling exercise. Jarrod was mesmerised as the coaching team set up the cones and poles and then took the whole squad through a run-through of the exercise. It was one-on-one dribbling, defenders practising what they did best, while the rest of the players would be the attackers, one serving as a winger and the others racing to get on the end of the cross.

There was a set of players on each wing, about five metres over the half way line, and they would take turns left and right. The defender would start with the ball and roll it to the attacker, who then had to take on his man with a dribble. He could cut inside and shoot if he chose, but the remaining defenders waiting for their turn would be in the D and were allowed to rush out to meet it. The best option would be to take on the man, and that was the scenario that Mr Raffaella was eager to explore. This was a lesson in defending a crazy dribbler and a lesson in how to outfox a defender with pace and skill.

The coaching team shouted encouragement, urging the attackers to take on their man and entertain the non-existent crowd. After three or four goes from both sides, the intensity wasn't there, so two of the coaches acted as extra defenders closing down the attacker from behind and adding to the pressure.

Frustrated shouts from Mr Raffaella turned to praise as David Ponte surprised a defending Jarrod with a step over and raced for the byline, delivering a tempting cross. The on-rushing Sammy launched himself full length to bury a diving header past Max in goal. This was what they wanted, and it soon became a production line. The forward players ran at their defenders at pace. The defenders practised turning and getting their bodies in the right position to block the cross. It was the perfect drill.

The players loved it, Mr Raffaella stopped shouting and leaned back on the advertising hoarding and took it all in. The crosses were not all perfect, but the way the players adapted to the exercise was impressive and the goals kept coming. Ollie Sheen made the save of the session, leaping to his left to fingertip a stinging volley away from Alain Ventoux. It was all very high quality, high tempo, the motivation was clear to see.

The players were instructed to go into the stadium after a slow warm down lap. They made their way down the tunnel and up the stairs to the home changing room. Mr Raffaella had his instructions board in its usual place, crisply cleaned this time with a full set of whiteboard pens of all colours. He went through the team for tomorrow, again sticking with the three defenders, but masking them with another three in front of them. This was either ultra-defensive or he was drawing the formation when they were defending.

He began to get more animated and drew arrows from the two wide players in the defensive six. They were to be the wingers, or wing backs. They would be putting the training from today into practice. The resulting formation was more of a 3-5-2, but a definite emphasis on tight defence when not in possession.

Corners were again for Jarrod and Willem, Sammy taking all the free kicks in dangerous positions, with the instruction to 'mix it up' every third free kick. That suggested a confidence from the manager that they would indeed be doing plenty of attacking, although Jarrod was sure that the players weren't expecting to have that many opportunities against one of the best footballing teams in the world. He certainly wasn't. Young prodigy Ollie Sheen would play the first half with Max replacing him at half time.

Antonio then posted up a number of photos onto the board, held in place by the magnetic counters that normally signified players. These were the people to watch. Javier Santoro, top marksman with his long flowing hair, Nils Kroeser, midfield dynamo and unlikely hard man, and Arjan Moujalli, silky defender and Barça captain. The coaches obviously knew their stuff. A fourth photo was affixed to the board, and Antonio wrote his name underneath – Jay M'Bulaz. This was a new name and there were shrugs and puzzled looks, obviously a new signing and someone else to be wary of.

Jarrod was sure that Antonio had been the coach at Ajax with Kroeser earlier in his career, so these guys definitely would know a great deal about the opposition and about the challenge ahead. Jarrod was sitting next to Andros, and once the session was over, they discussed Barcelona and shared what they collectively knew about tomorrow's friendly foes. Jarrod was trying his best to get as much information as possible, he had a feeling he'd be needing it very soon.

Chapter 42

CLEAN

The players had initially been told to meet back at Little Benton, but Mr Raffaella had changed his mind and the players would continue the day at St James' Park. Some frantic behind-the-scenes organising saw the catering crew from the training ground appear at the stadium with what was effectively a picnic. Everything they had prepared that day already had been packed up and transported.

The groundsmen had commandeered a mini-stage and set it up in the centre circle. The chef and his team laid out the meal on the edge of the stage. There was even a solitary table on the stage with four seats for Mr Raffaella and his coaching team. The rest of the players, coaches and physios made do with sitting on the hallowed turf, some leaning against the edge of the stage to eat their al fresco lunch.

This was truly a sight to behold. Mr Raffaella and his crew were animated in their discussion in Spanish. All that was missing was a bottle or two of Rioja and some classical guitar for ambience. The players were enjoying this moment of relaxation, the sun staying just behind the clouds to make it very pleasant without having to screw up their eyes to avoid the glare.

Lunch was over but the manager was clearly in charge of the next move. Jarrod remarked that it felt like being at a hot and summery wedding venue in a suit, waiting for the father of the bride to take off his jacket so the blokes in the room could take off theirs. The chatter grew and grew, the sun peeked out to beam down on the crowd and it truly felt like a holiday atmosphere.

In the end the catering guys started to clear their equipment onto the two trolleys and this prompted movement from the stage. Mr Raffaella rose from his seat and stood on the edge. All the players instinctively stopped and turned towards him.

"Lads," he said, "I would like you to thank your chef and his team for this exquisite meal."

There was instant applause and cheering, the caterers acknowledging the approval with smiles while continuing to clear away.

"And," he continued, "please help our staff by making sure that you help make this centre circle absolutely spotless when we leave in five minutes. Rendezvous in the boardroom at 1.45pm. No boots allowed."

That was a cracking gesture – all the players made sure that they helped move plates, carry rubbish and load up the trolleys. Andros pushed one trolley away once it was fully laden. Jarrod and a few others went around the centre circle and made sure there was not a scrap of spilled food or a dropped bottle lid, even Antonio was making sure the crumbs from the table were swept into his hand and put in a bin. This was great team building, without the players even realising it.

The players were treated to an hour long tactics session in the boardroom. Normally ten minutes would suffice, but as Antonio explained, there was a lot more to Barcelona than your average

Premier League team. It was all about scenarios. Mr Raffaella drew passages of play on the huge whiteboard, using the big blue counters for the opposition and similarly oversized black and white counters emblazoned with a blue star for the home team. The majority of the time he concentrated on explaining the options that Barcelona would be contemplating when in possession in an advanced position out on both flanks.

All the players listened. There was minimal input from the floor as the manager was in full flow. He was preparing them for an onslaught tomorrow, he was making sure that they were well-equipped to deal with it.

When the session was over, there was a spontaneous round of applause for Antonio and Mr Raffaella, something Jarrod had never seen before. Confidence was clearly being injected into the team and the players were under the spell of the Chilean evangelist before them. But there was more.

The lights went down and a highlights reel began. This was taken from off-the-ball footage of the Barcelona midfield, a bit like when Sky Sports used to have the special channels for seeing the game from a selected player's point of view. The frames froze every now and again, allowing Mr Raffaella to interject with what the player would be thinking. Of course he would have had the benefit of knowing what was coming next, but it made him look and sound like an absolute master of tactics. Jarrod was sold. What a manager.

It was now coming up to 4pm and the players left the boardroom in dribs and drabs, most going back to the change rooms to get back into their civilian clothes. After Jarrod and a few others had their showers, he treated himself to cutting his toenails. It was something that he tended to avoid until his middle toes started to rub up against each other and draw blood, but this time he felt that the occasion and the opposition deserved special treatment. That left him as one of the last players in the changing room, finally donning his socks and finding his shoes that had been relocated three seats up in the rush beforehand.

Stefa bid Jarrod good night with a handshake and Bevil the kit man left with a pile of training gear, whistling as he left. He was replaced almost immediately at the doorway by Iain. He stood there for a moment until Jarrod noticed him, eventually giving Jarrod a shock when he moved in. Jarrod had his hand on his chest as Iain sat down on the seat that was almost directly opposite him. This was dramatic.

"Hello Iain," said Jarrod. "That was some entrance. You're like Count Dracula the way you glide into a room."

Jarrod was subconsciously using the comparison – Iain did look very dark and just a little menacing. Perhaps just really tired.

"Hi Jarrod," chirped Iain, dispelling his unease. "I've got an address for you. You are expected there at 5pm. It's a bit of a drive."

He handed a handwritten note that had an address in Blaydon. Jarrod smiled. It was not even fifteen minutes in the car, hardly a 'bit of a drive'. Iain should get out more!

"Who am I meeting?" asked Jarrod.

"I don't know," said Iain. "I wasn't given that information. What I do know though is that we're all really counting on you this time. Your work so far has been excellent. This one is going to make you and a lot of other people very happy indeed."

Jarrod puffed out his cheeks and stared past Iain before diverting his gaze towards him. Iain did look really tired.

"Are you okay, Iain?" asked Jarrod instinctively. He didn't need to engage with Iain at all but he was showing concern for a colleague.

"Oh yes, Jarrod," said Iain unconvincingly, as if delivering a pre-prepared robotic response, "and we will all be even more so tomorrow night."

Iain put his hand on Jarrod's thigh as if he was going to lean in and say something threatening in his ear, but he was just using it to get up, wincing as he did so. He walked with the limp of someone who had been sitting down for way too long, and disappeared through the door without saying anything further. Jarrod panicked as he looked down and couldn't see the piece of paper, but he remembered he's put it between his legs on the seat. He was already getting frantic.

Chapter 43

HOON

It did turn out to be a bit of a drive. Jarrod was stuck in a ridiculous traffic jam caused by a broken down removal van; the Saturday traffic was proving every bit as bad as the weekday morning peak hour. He began to worry, only slightly, but noticeably and he could feel the sweat start to accumulate on his back against the seat. He took solace that he didn't have to do this every day – teammate James Pelham lived near Hexham and he must be on the road for an hour at least every day after training.

He had a meet planned with the Detective Inspector and Dennis at the Morrisons car park on the way and he was keen to be there early. He swung in to the petrol station, following D.I. Allison's instructions to make it look as though he needed to fill up with petrol. He wasn't far off it, so it wasn't a wasted journey. Jarrod spied the unmarked car over in the shopping centre car park. It didn't look as though there was anyone hanging around or looking shifty. He paid for his petrol and returned to the car.

There was what he would describe as a 'hoon' car right behind his, engine running, ready to let rip with an ear-splitting roar at any moment. The windows were heavily tinted so there was no way of telling who was in there. He felt on edge.

Jarrod eased away from the petrol pump, the car behind

bursting out with a rasping growl and taking his place. He saw someone get out in his rear view mirror as he looked for a gap in the traffic. It looked like one of the Russian physio guys but he couldn't be sure. What a way to keep a low profile. He turned into the traffic and found the circuitous route to the car park. His phone rang and he answered it.

"Go right around," said D.I. Allison, "don't stop where you saw us. We'll meet you in the street next to the church. You'll see it as you drive around. Take the street to the right of the church."

Jarrod didn't answer. He glanced across at the petrol station and the souped up car was no longer there. Whoever it was, if they were at all connected, would be back on the road to the address on the piece of paper that was on Jarrod's dashboard.

Jarrod parked up in the leafy street and quickly got out of the car. He walked to the unmarked police car and got in the back seat on the driver's side. He shook hands with Dennis and gave driver D.I. Allison a pat on the shoulder. There was a third man in the passenger seat - Mick Turner, Chief Superintendent of the Area Command.

"Mick here is in charge of the local police force," said Dennis, making the introduction as the highest ranking officer in the car. Again Jarrod shook hands. It seemed the right thing to do, even though time was against him.

"Dennis will just give you a wire," said D.I. Allison. Jarrod looked at Dennis, who handed him what looked like a stray LED light that had been ripped from a circuit board. "We usually put them on the inside of our shirt button. You'll not be wear … oh wait, yes, you've got a couple of buttons at the top of your t-shirt. Here, we'll just do one of them up and hook this on the inside out of sight."

"It had better be out of sight," said Jarrod nervously.

"It is," said Dennis, "and anyway, these are new. No one knows these yet."

Dennis was a high ranking official these days, but he still knew what he was doing as a foot soldier. He efficiently wired up Jarrod. He prodded a second device into Jarrod's shoe where it lodged under his foot.

"These are super sensitive," said Dennis. "We'll be listening in on each device separately. Don't worry, they don't make any noise, it's all one-way. We don't communicate with you. Just be natural."

"What happens if it gets heavy in there?" asked Jarrod.

"We're listening, we're right nearby," replied Dennis with a smile.

Jarrod got back out of the car and trotted back to his. The microphone in his canvas shoes had lodged down the side, held in place by the thick orthotic insole, so he instantly forgot that one was there. He consciously kept his hands away from his neck, even though he felt like giving himself a good scratch.

The satnav took Jarrod another five minutes out of town and into a newly built estate next to the river. There were rows of detached and semi-detached houses giving a feeling of wealth that belied the rest of the surrounding suburb. He found the address and parked right in front.

Kids were playing in the street on their bikes. This house looked just like any of the others. He walked up to the front door and in the absence of an obvious doorbell, knocked on the middle panel of the door, in between the two thin frosted glass panels. Jarrod could see someone coming to the door. Adrian Barnes appeared. This was the smartarse who had refused to give him a lift back from the last meeting. At least he was friendly enough.

"Good timing," said Mr Barnes, shaking his hand with a smile and invited him inside.

Jarrod walked down the hallway and into the living room. There were two people in there who looked as though they had been in deep conversation for some time. One was the magnificent specimen of Murtaka, Indian heiress and classy businesswoman. The other was a well-dressed man in a pinstripe suit, straight out of the London Stock Exchange. Only thing missing was a bowler hat.

Mr Barnes did the introductions.

"Jarrod Black," he said, turning to Murtaka, "you know Murtaka Chiya."

Jarrod moved closer to offer his hand which she took politely.

"And this is Viktor," said Mr Barnes, offering no surname. "Viktor is a business partner of Ms Chiya, and is very interested to talk with you."

Viktor stood up and shook Jarrod's hand, clasping the hands in his spare hand and giving them both a vigorous shake.

"Big fan of yours," he said to Jarrod. "Loved your work at Gateshead."

"Er … right," said Jarrod uneasily, "how can I be of service to you?"

"My associate Murtaka here has filled you in on our plans," he said, "and to make those plans come to fruition, we're going to need a lot of funds behind us to take this once proud club back to where it should be."

"I get that," said Jarrod.

"And you, Jarrod," continued Viktor, "are the key to unlocking those funds."

Jarrod looked at him, wondering where this was going. Couldn't anyone in the underworld just talk properly? They seemed to use connotations rather than facts, which made it hard to know what they meant sometimes.

"What would you like me to do?" asked Jarrod.

"Jarrod," said Murtaka gently, lending her more soothing feminine tone to the conversation. "Newcastle lose by three clear goals tomorrow and our fundraising is complete."

"Three clear goals? As in 3-0, 4-1 or more?" said Jarrod incredulously.

"Exactly," said Murtaka. "Barcelona are a very good team remember. There's no disgrace in losing to the world's best club side."

She definitely had a point. But three goals? He was just imagining the scene at 2-0 down in the 90th minute, Newcastle doing all the pressing. How would he manufacture that one? He thought for a moment and took a small step backwards, as if he was going to turn and flee. He suddenly became aware of the lump in his shoe. He bent down, sliding his finger down the edge to knock the microphone from under his foot. He stood up with a shrug to himself.

"Can I suggest that you choose some other outcome?" asked Jarrod, keeping to the theme of not talking directly about the subject. "I mean, it doesn't take much to change a game, and I'd hate to be in a position where I simply can't do anything about it."

Viktor advanced towards Jarrod and stood in front of him. Jarrod watched without flinching as he put his hands on top of his shoulders.

"Jarrod," he started, "this is something that we've been planning for some time. Remember, you may not be working on this result on your own. There are many other players and officials who may be working alongside you to achieve this result."

Jarrod hadn't even contemplated that. What if he was one of a team of players or referees or even managers who had been influenced by these people? What if some of his teammates were also in on the plan and were ready to do their utmost to achieve it? Of course that would make the job a lot easier. He was unconvinced though.

"I see," said Jarrod. "So the chances of achieving this goal are high?"

"I wouldn't say high, Jarrod," said Viktor, tightening his hands ever so slightly. "But they will be vastly improved if we have you on board."

"Far out …" started Jarrod, opting to stare around randomly before bowing his head and exhaling heavily. Viktor took his hands off his shoulders. There appeared to be a resignation from Jarrod, whose shoulders sagged noticeably. Murtaka was now standing just behind Viktor.

"We are happy to help you in your troubled times," said Murtaka, referring to the gambling habit that he didn't have.

Again Jarrod thought for a moment. Mr Barnes' mobile pinged with a message, breaking the silence. Jarrod obviously didn't have a choice, he had pushed his resistance as far as he felt acceptable. He was sure that the detectives would have everything they needed, so he lifted his head up and looked Viktor in the eyes.

"A three goal defeat," he said. "I'm in."

Viktor put his hands on his shoulders again, this time on the outside, and patted gently.

"Well done," he said. "A very good decision."

Mr Barnes then stepped in.

"Let me show you out," he said to Jarrod. "Thank you for coming out to see us."

Jarrod was ushered past Viktor and Murtaka, who both smiled politely before sitting back down and continuing their conversation. Mr Barnes opened the door.

"Thank you Jarrod," he said, a degree of sincerity to his voice. Perhaps Jarrod was actually helping these people. Maybe Mr Barnes was simply an employee of these two and was happy to get a result to keep his job. Jarrod turned to him.

"Is this for good or for evil?" he asked.

"This is most definitely for the good of the people of Newcastle," he said, sidestepping the real question. "Good day."

The door closed with a click and Jarrod was left staring at the door as Mr Barnes disappeared along the hallway.

At this point Jarrod was expecting a scene from the movies. The police would appear from the bushes, storm in, kick the door down and arrest everyone. Jarrod would be outside as the villains were marched out past him, scowling.

Unfortunately, Jarrod found himself alone. He got into his car and drove off, back the way he had come. He was shivering with nervous excitement and he would be exhausted that night from the adrenaline.

Chapter 44

SHOE

It was an early start at the hotel. Jarrod had gone to bed super early. The last thing he remembered, after grabbing a quick bite to eat in the hotel restaurant, was ringing Marianne and wishing the family a good journey for tomorrow. They would be back during the day and Jarrod would be able to pick them up at the airport.

He swerved past reception on the way to meet the Detective Inspector to confirm the booking he'd made for the family that night. He was relieved to hear that the second room was next door with an adjoining door. Marianne had insisted on going back to Darlington when they arrived back in the country. Jarrod though had trumped that argument with news of a glamour game against European opposition. The kids were definitely up for prolonging their holiday right up to the last second.

Jarrod walked into the dining room where the staff were still setting up the buffet and tables. Jarrod checked his phone. There was a message. The Detective Inspector was running late but only by five minutes. This was unlike the Detective Inspector and Jarrod's mind swirled with scenarios.

He grabbed one of the newspapers from the bar, the *Sunday Sun*, and walked over to their usual table. He opened it and flicked to the back. There were pages and pages of coverage of today's game. The opponents, the last time they met, interviews with former players of both clubs. This was being treated as a big event, and Jarrod instantly felt nervy. He was engrossed in one of the stories about Shola Ameobi talking through his goal at the Nou Camp and hadn't noticed that the Detective Inspector had arrived and was ordering a coffee.

Jarrod was startled when the he pulled out the seat opposite and sat down. He was red-eyed, as though he was reaching the end of his day as opposed to starting a new one.

"Slept in?" asked Jarrod.

"Oh aye," said D.I. Allison, looking at Jarrod until he straightened up and abandoned his reading. He seemed eager to talk. "We have intelligence on the person who shot Rambouillet."

Jarrod was all ears now.

"What do you know?" asked Jarrod, not expecting a response until the waitress had put their drinks on the table and moved on.

"Can't say much," said D.I. Allison, "but we know that this is all linked. If you could draw a family tree of the people involved, you'd see that the people we're dealing with are all towards the bottom, and there are some very surprising people sitting up in the tree looking down."

Jarrod's skin bristled.

"So, who shot him?" asked Jarrod.

"All in good time," replied D.I. Allison. "Now, have you thought about how you're going to approach tonight's game?"

"It's not going to be easy," said Jarrod, "and I'm hoping that a flat performance rubs off on the team."

"I'm not sure if you'll be able to help yourself Jarrod," said D.I. Allison frankly. And he was right. Jarrod could mull this over in his head, how he would play a few stray passes or not show for a return ball when he normally would, but he knew that he could definitely not lower his standards to such an extent as to give goals away cheaply.

"I wish you good luck," he continued. "We will be with you every step of the way. Say, where are the microphones from yesterday?"

Jarrod looked at him with a querying look.

"You know, the mic in your shoe?" he continued.

"Ah, shit, yes," exclaimed Jarrod, reaching down into his shoe. That one was still there. He'd also put the other one in his wallet, the one that was hanging off the button on his shirt the day before. The one he'd dropped on the floor and only noticed when he stood on it.

"You'd be surprised what these little things can pick up …" said D.I. Allison, holding the one that Jarrod had pulled out of his wallet and handed to him delicately.

"… although this one looks as if it's seen better days."

The once smooth wires were mangled and kinked. D.I. Allison held it by one of the wires and it looked like a week-old daddy long-legs from the window sill.

"Better give them to us so we can deactivate them," he continued. "There's not much gets past these things."

Jarrod eventually clicked to what the Detective Inspector was saying. The microphones didn't appear to have a switch at all and Jarrod ran through all the things that could have been picked up last night. He could picture an operator in a headset listening to him humming to himself in the car, munching away on his dinner, or letting rip in the comfort of his own room. Marianne had been away for two weeks now – it could have been worse. He immediately felt violated, but somehow also mildly amused.

250

"We'll not need these today," he said, tucking them into a small holder which he placed in his pocket.

"What we will need today though," he continued, "is for you to be at the absolute peak of your game. You need to be switched on and alert at all times. You'll see faces, meet people that you've never met, and we need you to take in as much as you can about the day. It could be vital in taking down what appears to be a significant organisation."

Jarrod was sure he was talking about being a witness, but again, the blurred lines of conversation were proving difficult to decipher.

"I'm feeling good about today," said Jarrod finally after finishing a huge mouthful of coleslaw, a peculiar choice from the buffet that took his fancy.

"Well," said D.I. Allison, "you can just be Jarrod Black the footballer today. That's what the fans want to see."

Jarrod smiled. That was as good as any team talk.

Chapter 45

REPORTER

The players were due at the training ground at 11am for media duties, which gave Jarrod plenty of time to rearrange his room and make sense of the wardrobe. He wasn't sure how much longer he'd be at the hotel but he knew that he would have to make a good first impression on Marianne who would be coming into the room all tired after a long journey with the kids. He gathered two weeks' worth of mess into a bag and tidied as best he could. It wasn't long before it looked presentable and there was ample space for the extra baggage coming that night.

Jarrod had been relatively sheltered from media duty since his arrival. He'd given one or two interviews, nothing of real substance, and had been able to relax when the media were around. This morning though, he had been forewarned that he had two fifteen-minute slots after midday, and he had to be prepared for one of them to be an in-depth chat for a feature article.

The scene at Little Benton was what Jarrod would describe as 'frenzied'. There was extra security at the entrance. Jarrod was instructed to leave his keys in the car when he pulled up to reception so the guys could find a parking spot for him. There was a section of the car park roped off with red and white tape, a sign with 'Media' directing the journalists and photographers into that section. He pulled up behind two cars in front of reception, recognising the first one as Rodhri's.

He did as instructed and left the car unlocked and the key on the seat – his was one of those cars that didn't need the key in the ignition, it just had to be near the car. He wasn't sure whether or not the car would lock without him in it though, so he chose to wind down the window and leave it down so there'd be no doubt.

The traditional greeting at the door signalled a little bit of normality, the scene was more or less the usual as he strode through the reception area towards the meeting room at the rear area of the training facility. He could hear the noise as he approached the open door. Everyone was talking loudly, the atmosphere animated. He could sense genuine excitement amongst his teammates, and there was a cheer as he entered the room. It was like stepping onto the field as an eagerly awaited substitute.

It wasn't long before everyone arrived. When Mr Raffaella entered the room, closely followed by Antonio and a team of coaches, a wave of silence enveloped the room. This was going to be a media refresher session. Two of the entourage took a seat on stage at each end of a table. There was a quick introduction by Mr Raffaella of a special guest to the media team, PR specialist Roland Kopf. Roland captured the room from the moment he started speaking. He set the scene.

"Here we are, looking in on an interview with Newcastle's favourite player," he said, not mentioning any player's name, "and the *Times* newspaper, the most respected of all British news sources. Let's see how it goes."

The lights were turned off and only the table was illuminated. A few of the players at the back got up out of their seats in order to see a little clearer. What followed was ten or so questions, each followed by a long answer. As the answers were being delivered, they were interrupted by a spotlight flicking on, with Roland delivering his commentary in the foreground.

It was absolutely fascinating. One of the questions: 'How do you rate your chances of a call up for the national team?" It was well-worded given the mix of nationalities in the room. The answer was one Jarrod would have given. A mix of modesty and hope. The spotlight came straight on.

"No!" he shouted. "If your interviewer is mentioning the national team, it's because you have already been touted for the national team. You need to convince the interviewer and in turn, the people reading in the newspaper that you are absolutely in the scene and that it is inevitable that you will be in the national squad."

Jarrod was loving this. So relevant, so engaging, so unexpected. The interviewer asked the same question again and the player answered with a totally different answer. The confidence of delivery was punchier, the words were all positive, it was a revelation to Jarrod. He had been giving interviews for fifteen years, and perhaps some of this was natural, but to see it broken down and analysed like this was truly eye-opening.

Roland wrapped up the session, all eyes trained on him under the spotlight. The room was stunned. Maybe it was because no one wanted it to end, then everyone burst into applause. The head media guy Warren Marks then stood up and gave the players instructions: where to meet and who they were meeting. He eventually got to Jarrod.

"Jarrod Black, room C4. 12 o'clock with Shabab of *The Athletic*, 12.15 with Caleb from Fox Sports."

Jarrod was intrigued. Shabab was a great interviewer, an Aussie with encyclopaedic knowledge of English football. He had only recently made the move from independent journalist to the new media juggernaut. Caleb seemed to be that one reporter who kept popping up but Jarrod was never in a position to give him enough time for an interview. Might be different this time.

Room C4 was a room off the physio room, and was only given the number C4 for the day. All the players had to find their venue on a hand drawn map in reception. Shabab was already in there when Jarrod arrived with the clock showing 11.59am. It was practice at Newcastle to have a junior player in on the interviews, primarily to give experience, but also to act as a witness if anything went off-topic. The junior players were pre-assigned, and Jarrod was in with Nordic Under-18 midfielder Eli Kristjborgsson, a player who had caught his eye in training.

This first interview went incredibly well. It turned out that Shabab's intricate knowledge of football extended to Spanish football. Towards the end of the allotted 14 minutes, once the two had become more comfortable with each other, it was more of a chat about their respective visits to the Nou Camp and how impressive the stadium was. There was a knock at the door and Shabab quietly gathered together his papers and shook Jarrod's hand. He seemed very pleased to be there and it had been an enjoyable experience for both of them.

The two interviewers exchanged pleasantries at the door before Caleb breezed in, offered his hand to Jarrod and took the hot seat opposite. Jarrod took a moment to stand up and rearrange his tracksuit bottoms that were riding up his legs, allowing himself a moment of composure. Caleb showed Jarrod his mini-recorder and that he was clicking it on. All very well practised.

"Caleb Powell with Jarrod Black of Newcastle United," he spoke into the recorder before placing it on the table. "Jarrod, I'd like to go back to the end of the previous season and your move to Darlington. What were you thinking at the time?"

Jarrod was a little surprised by the forthright nature of the question. Roland wouldn't have led with that question, surely? Why was he questioning his reasons? Jarrod had to think positive.

"Gerry Lincoln is an absolute champion of an owner," started Jarrod, unsure as to where this sentence would take him, "and he introduced me to his vision of the future of Darlington Football Club. I have to say that his vision matches his actions, and look where Darlington are now. I'd not be surprised if we see some more players making the move to what is quickly becoming one of football's success stories."

"Was the Socceroos ever on your radar at that time?" came the next question. Again Jarrod thought for a second, and thought back an hour to Roland's talk.

"Playing for Australia is a huge honour," said Jarrod. "Whilst things didn't work out for me with the Socceroos earlier in my career, this was an absolute shock and I absolutely jumped at the chance to represent my country. It is true to say though that I had no idea it was coming when I signed for Darlington."

"Do you feel as though you've missed out with Socceroos?" asked Caleb, before continuing. "There were some 'nearly moments' with Jerszek captaining the team, Marco Terveris romping down the wing, Taj Hamadi exciting the crowds. You could have been the midfield kingpin we were looking for."

This was getting into murky waters. Jarrod had been in self-exile since a bust up at training, and the mention of that last name caused him to hunch ever so slightly. He noticed and forced himself to relax. This could be the moment when he let rip and cleared the air, finally give his side of the story and pile the blame on golden boy Hamadi for missing out on three World Cup qualifying campaigns.

Having seen ex-England players go for each other on social media in the past and seen no one come out of it with anything positive, he chose to shut down those thoughts.

"It just wasn't to be," said Jarrod, "I've been in England my whole career, in the end it was a combination of concentrating on my club football and being injured at key times that prevented me from continuing with the Socceroos. Definitely making up for lost time now though, eh?"

Caleb smiled at that one.

"Last season was so good with Darlington," he said. "It might be a silly question, but what made you take the opportunity at Newcastle?"

Before Jarrod could answer, Caleb reached down and clicked off the recorder.

"There's something going on, isn't there?" he asked.

"Such as?" enquired Jarrod quizzically.

"It doesn't really add up. A player is shot and you end up being his replacement. It's as if a place was made for you to walk into."

He clicked the record button again and nodded to the device to indicate that it was expecting an answer, as if it was a living being. Jarrod could see himself picking up the recorder, flinging it against the brick wall and stamping on it before storming out. Eli was sitting next to him, not really following. Jarrod glowered at Caleb, who had sat back in his chair.

"As you know," said Jarrod, remembering the tone of his voice the last time he spoke and trying to keep it level, "Newcastle United is part of my heritage."

Jarrod was going for it here. Put the guilt trip on.

"My dad is from Newcastle," he said, "I have an uncle and plenty of family in the area. They all bleed black and white. To be at this advanced stage of my career and to be presented with this unexpected chance to represent the club I have supported through many years of underachievement and disappointment, to be in a position to help the club win and put in 100 per cent for the fans, well, who wouldn't jump at it?"

Stick that in your pipe, reporter boy.

Jarrod reached over and picked up the recorder. He found the play button and pressed it, making sure it was in fact paused.

"Now Caleb," said Jarrod, "Let's get this back on track, shall we? Stick to the script and I promise you that I'll give you my next interview. There may be a lot more to talk about then."

He clicked the play button and put the device back on the table. After a moment he nodded to it and smiled. Caleb was sitting bolt upright now. Eli was looking at him – as far as he knew this was a normal interview going as normally as expected. Jarrod nodded again and looked at the recorder.

"So … so …" started Caleb, "returning to the Socceroos. You played a strong game against Peru two weeks ago, set up the second goal and it looked like you'd been playing in that team for years. What can we expect from the upcoming qualifying phase for the World Cup?"

Jarrod had turned the conversation around to where it should have been – a Socceroos journalist talking about the Socceroos. The rest of the interview went surprisingly well and Jarrod ended by introducing Eli into the conversation to give him a little exposure.

After flirting with a question regarding his chances of playing in the A-League late in his career, the interview was over. Caleb quickly got his things together and left with a handshake without any small talk. Jarrod and Eli followed him out. The sight of Andros appearing from the ladies bathroom adjusting his tracksuit, and being immediately berated by one of the female catering staff for using the ladies facilities, lightened the mood.

Chapter 46

NERVES

There was time for a quick bite to eat at the cafeteria, chef Bruno making sure the usual fajitas were on the menu. Jarrod sat down and shared stories with his teammates. It was clear that Rambouillet was still a hot topic of conversation in the interviews that they had all been in. The news just wouldn't go away, even though the major story was that they were playing against Barcelona.

Jarrod had to excuse himself. The team had the afternoon to themselves, he could have stayed there in conversation for hours. He had to be at the airport to welcome back his family. A text sent an hour prior from Amsterdam Airport suggested that they were on time and arriving in about 45 minutes. Newcastle's proximity to the airport was a big advantage here. He was parking his car up in the horrifyingly expensive short term car park within 30 minutes of leaving the table.

The airport was always a fun place for people watching. He remembered his first time arriving, greeted by his soon-to-be best mate Reggie and embarking on a new life in England. It always gave him a feeling of anticipation. Being on the other side and waiting for someone was always exciting too. He could hear the kids before he could see them. They were laughing and full of joy. He spied them as soon as they came around the corner.

Seb was proudly pushing the trolley for Marianne and Aneka wheeled one of the large suitcases. He didn't think either of his kids would rush to greet him so he decided to run in and shriek himself, scooping up Aneka and grabbing Seb, both of them laughing with surprise and embarrassment in equal measure. A prolonged hug from the kids gave way to a big kiss for Marianne. Seb and Aneka both cooed 'ooooooh' and then burst out laughing.

Oh, it was so good to have his family back. They all looked fit and healthy. Marianne's tan had got noticeably darker and Jarrod's heart thumped with excitement. Jarrod wheeled Marianne's suitcase and walked with his arm around Seb. He had grown an inch in two weeks it seemed. There was so much to talk about, and Jarrod made sure most of it was about them. They loaded up the car, squeezing in the last items at the kids' feet, and headed for the hotel.

Marianne opened the door and peered in, half expecting the place to be a bomb-site, but was pleasantly surprised. The connecting door was open, the blinds were up for a change and the warmth of the room from the sun gave it a holiday feel. The kids quickly scarpered for the second room where there were two queen beds, both racing for the one nearest the window. Jarrod had tickets for them, and some extras for Uncle Craig and his family.

The offer was there to come now with him to the stadium, or to catch a quick sleep and come on later with Uncle Craig in his seven-seater. Marianne called the shots and decided they'd have a snooze and freshen up before heading in. It was never really much fun hanging around an empty stadium for three hours, having already done that too often. Jarrod of course would have made a fuss of them, taken the kids for a tour, introduced them to people and made it an event. He was relieved though that Marianne declined. He knew this was going to be a head-spinning evening.

Jarrod drove into the main gates and quickly into the driveway leading down into the stadium. There was extra security and a surprising number of interested onlookers who were making a whole evening of it. It was before 5pm and already there was a crowd, probably awaiting the arrival of the Barcelona team bus.

The players had been instructed to be on site at 5.15pm. Jarrod liked to be a little bit early, but he was less so today. He parked up behind three other cars, all very expensive latest models, his looking like the poor cousin despite being only a couple of years old. He remembered to drop the key on the driver's seat even before the car park attendant yelled 'keys', and disappeared into the open doorway past the security guard and into a corridor that took him into the Leazes corner of the stadium and out into the sunshine.

The usual two or three lucky people who scored an early entry to meet the players and get their shirts signed had been replaced by a mob of fans and a pack of photographers. Jarrod was accosted first by an eager young fan with his white NUFC training top already covered in illegible signatures. Jarrod made sure he wrote his number under his scrawl so it was obvious who it was.

He was conscious of the constant snapping of the photographers as he moved from shirt to shirt, signing programmes and hats and balls and posing for loads of photos. It was actually quite a soothing few minutes for Jarrod, and his mind was completely off the real agenda. He was now totally switched on to his home debut for his club. He caught up with Stefa and Willem and they all posed for a photo with one of the last of the fans before they walked together into the tunnel and up the steps to the changing room.

As they filed into the changing room, physio Iain came out the other way and hooked his hand through Jarrod's arm and slowly led him the other way. He only let go once they were through a set of double doors.

"Good evening Jarrod," he said, turning to face him, blocking the way back. His smile was fake, withered and shaky.

"Iain," said Jarrod, "you don't seem right."

"Oh, I'm as right as rain," said Iain. "You are the important one today. How are you feeling?"

"I'm a little nervous," said Jarrod, which was completely true and completely understandable given the gravity of the situation he was under. "But I think we're going to be able to pull this off."

Iain patted him on the side and managed a wavering smile.

"You do what you've got to do Jarrod," he said, staring into his eyes. "We're all counting on you. Do *not* let us down."

It seemed that Iain was trying to tell him something by looking into his eyes, or was trying to be menacing, but it was lost of Jarrod.

"Okay, I'll see you later then," said Jarrod flippantly, and walked around him to go through the double doors.

"Yes, you will," said Iain, grabbing his arm to stop him. "Do *not* let us down. Do you understand?"

His grip on his arm tightened and Jarrod moved his face right in front of the physio's.

"Get your hand off me," he scowled, and Iain stepped back releasing his arm, surprised at the un-Jarrod-like retort.

Chapter 47

BRIEF

Jarrod returned to the changing room, entering to whoops and cheers, shaking and slapping hands. He felt ten-feet tall.

Most of the squad was there already and awaiting their briefing. Mr Raffaella would be down soon to give them the final team news. The shuffling from outside indicated that the visiting team had arrived, or at least their kit was being moved into their changing room. Mr Raffaella appeared.

"Gentlemen," he said in perfect English. "Good evening."

Everyone took a second to take a seat or find a spot where they could see the gaffer.

"The away team has arrived. They have given us their team selection. There is one change. Their new signing Jay M'Bulaz will not be starting. They will instead have Enrique Salvio up front with Santoro."

There were whistles and murmurs at that name. Salvio had been a Newcastle player, one of those cut-price signings from obscurity. He had left once he had become established in the first team when the slightest sniff of a big move presented itself. He was not the most popular man with the players nor with the fans as a result.

"Please treat Salvio with the respect that he deserves," said Mr

Raffaella, giving no indication of what that really meant. Did he mean 'chop him and leave him on the floor bleeding' or did he mean 'be professional but let him know you're there'? The interpretation was left to the players. Jarrod saw Rodhri Callaghan look at David Ponte with raised eyebrows.

"Please go and get the food you need to get you through 90 minutes," continued Mr Raffaella, "and be back in here getting ready at 6.15pm."

He left the room and the players started following him out. They made their way to the usual game day cafeteria area, part of the corporate section that would be filled with businessmen in an hour or so. Jarrod was indeed hungry but wouldn't go over the top. He had a knot in his stomach as it was.

Just as they were going through into the cafeteria, a group of guys came past.

"Here he is!" came a recognisable voice. Jarrod spun around, not sure what to expect. It was a group of the Darlo lads, Wes at the front. Wes held his hand up to be grabbed and embraced his teammate.

"Lads!" cried Jarrod in delight. "What are you all doing here?"

He went through each one of them, giving everyone a hug.

"Well, saying as you wouldn't come down and see us after your big money move," said Wes, "we decided to come up and pay you a visit. Gerry's got us a corporate box for the night – the whole club's coming up for the game and it's all on the house!"

"Ha ha, result!" said Jarrod. "Be prepared for a big game."

Jarrod was beaming.

"Hey, get yourself in there," said Wes pointing at the cafeteria. "We've got a fridge full of beers to get through."

At that moment the unmistakable figures of Ivan and Dimitri

walked past, with their number one patient in tow, walking on crutches.

"Davy!" said Nolan, recognising the third of the trio.

The player on crutches put his head down and sped up, pretending not to hear. It was pretty obvious. Jarrod cursed himself for not remembering his name or where he'd met him before.

"Hey, could have sworn that was Davy," said the Darlington player.

Jarrod stopped in his tracks. The rest of the Darlo players were heading off, following Wes.

"Say, Nolan," he said, "that's your mate Davy, isn't it?"

"I thought it was," he replied. "He's not my mate though – I only met him when we were in Dubai. I thought he was mates with Dec and he just seemed to be part of the group out there. That was weird. Makes sense, him being on crutches too, after what happened to him out there. Anyway, catch you later. Good luck."

Nolan patted him on the arm and ran to catch up with the rest of the group. Before Jarrod could turn and walk into the cafeteria, he felt an arm around his neck and a sloppy kiss on his cheek. It was Darlington photographer Caroline. Jarrod gave her a big hug.

Before she could say anything, she spied North East TV celebrities Murat and Andoni and beckoned them in for a photo. Andoni recognised Jarrod and shook his hand. Caroline gave her mobile phone to Sash, the Darlo physio, who got them all in position for a photo, before handing the mobile to a complete stranger and getting in the photo himself. Jarrod quickly excused himself after shaking Sash's hand and getting a 'good luck' from Murat. He had to get some food.

Chapter 48

CAFE

Jarrod caught up with the players as they were getting served at the counter, their trays already getting loaded up with drinks and snacks. He grabbed a ready-made salad from the counter and poured some apple juice from the dispenser. A mini-sized Mars bar completed his dinner of champions.

The players sat at tables of fours and sixes and were full of chatter. That was until some of the Barcelona camp walked in. Heads turned and there were stares. It wasn't the team but some of the officials and some faces Jarrod recognised off TV. They looked supremely confident and professional. They were well dressed and were being led by a lady dressed in Newcastle United corporate attire, speaking Spanish and making them at home.

Jarrod was getting nervous. The players took their cue from Antonio to get up and make their move back to the changing room. They would need to navigate the ten metres of corridor shared with the paying public and he anticipated being stopped again. He wasn't disappointed. This time though it was Jarrod who did the stopping.

He spied Sepp Rolando, the former Boro player and now coach of the juniors at Newcastle, who he had not yet bumped into at St James'. He trotted over and put his arms on his shoulders to turn him around, planting a kiss on each cheek and remembering to do the third.

"Jarrod, *mon gars*!" exclaimed the fit-looking ex-Belgium superstar.

"Great to see you," said Jarrod, making for an immediate exit. "Let's catch up afterwards, eh?"

Jarrod was buzzing. Nervous for his first start at home, excited to be playing against world-class opposition, but at the same time a feeling of unease about what he had to do on the field. He did feel bullet-proof though. The sight of the delightful Murtaka and her associate Viktor coming along the corridor en route to their private box brought home the magnitude of the situation. Jarrod wasn't going to hang around to engage in small talk so darted into the doorway that led through to the changing rooms. Time to get serious.

The players were in various states of undress when he walked in, his shirt number 22 with the name 'Black' above it making it very real. He unloaded his phone, checking for last messages. There was one from Marianne:

JUST ARRIVED, SO MANY PEOPLE!

There were others from well-wishers and another on Signal 7 that read:

CAMERAS EVERYWHERE, WE HAVE YOU COVERED

Jarrod made a point of turning off his mobile phone and slipped off his tracksuit bottoms, hanging them on the hook. He was ready very quickly, his ankle brace was easy to get on for once and he had treated himself to a new set of shin pads, the ankle protectors nice and rigid stayed in place as he got his socks on. A few of the players had come in from a walk out on the pitch. They reported a healthy contingent of away supporters already in the ground and there was some sort of on-field entertainment happening for them in Spanish.

Nelson was doing his rounds, checking all the players, marking off on his list. Jarrod had nothing to report other than being nervous. Nelson couldn't help him with that, but assured him it was a good thing. After all, he suggested, if you're not nervous before your home debut for the club you love, up against Barcelona, then there's something not quite right!

Captain Andros let the rest of the players know that he was heading out onto the field, and that all players would need to be out in ten minutes. Jarrod leapt to his feet and walked over to Andros, out they walked with four or five other players out into the tunnel. Renée was there at the corner before they headed down the tunnel and got them to stop and pose. As soon as they came out of the tunnel there was a round of applause.

There were already quite a few people in the stadium, and the away end high up in the gods was looking quite full. The players did their own quick stretches and started to roll the ball around with gentle easy passes followed by short sprints. The playing surface was absolutely impeccable, a little harder than he was used to further down the football pyramid. Every touch of the ball was an absolute pleasure.

The whole team was out now and the warm-up started. The appearance of the Barcelona players brought a huge cheer from the far end. The home team warm-up took a break for a few seconds as the visiting players went up to their fans and saluted them. It was an amazing sight. Antonio clapped his hands to get the players back in focus.

The stands were filling up, people were streaming in and up the stairways. It was a magnificent structure and looked even more stunning once the seats began to fill up. That was when they were called back in to the changing room for one last run through of the instructions.

They made way for more on-field entertainment, the club having gone to great lengths. On came a band, who started their rendition of the legendary '*Fog on the Tyne*' as Jarrod made his way down the tunnel. Jarrod heard his name and doubled back. It was Aram, the diminutive 'journalist' who he had dealt with a couple of weeks before. Jarrod shook his hand. Aram looked serious and raised his eyebrows with an expectant look. Jarrod took that as a reminder for the expectation of the job tonight.

Chapter 49

SABOTAGE

The players lined up at the top of the tunnel. Their counterparts from Barcelona eventually appeared and they walked halfway down the tunnel to await the refereeing team. A few of the players chatted with their opposition, Jarrod shook hands with a few of the players around him and could only offer a smile. He was so incredibly nervous that he felt he couldn't speak.

With five officials in place, the TV crew signalled to the players to walk out. They were greeted to a thunderous roar as they stepped into the bright lights of a floodlit St James' Park. Apart from a few seats in the directors' box, the whole stadium was full. The players fanned out either side of the refs and took a moment to soak up the applause. The Barcelona fans were fervent. The chants started first from them, then a retort from the home fans that echoed around the stadium. It was amazing.

The formalities done, the teams lined up and they were underway, straight into the game. The first foul came five seconds in, Stefa adjudged to have held his man. The visitors knocked the ball back to the keeper and played a few passes around the defence, lulling the home side out of their compact shape. Mr Raffaella was shouting 'leave it, leave it!' as the lone forward Sammy N'Djame started to lose patience and threatened to race in to close down the defence.

As soon as Salvio got his first touch, boos rang around the stadium and they continued as he danced up the wing and eventually won a corner. Jarrod had not yet contemplated what he could do at this stage to influence the game but made sure he was marking tightly as the corner was swept in. He could do nothing as David Ponte was outmuscled and Santoro powered home the opening goal barely five minutes in.

To their credit, the Newcastle fans weren't phased by this. They started singing and chanting even louder and the players responded to it. Jarrod was in the action, mopping up a couple of loose balls and playing simple passes to get his team moving forward. A long looping cross from Alain Ventoux looked to be heading straight for James Pelham's head before a quick thinking defender headed the ball behind for the home side's first corner.

The crowd roared. Jarrod took the corner and found the head of Andros but the header was tipped over. Jarrod decided to play the second corner short – that had been too close for comfort. He knew that he had to make sure of a defeat here, and the best way would be to get further behind early on to make it look less obvious.

It was a purposely overhit back pass that led to a second Barcelona goal after only eighteen minutes. Jarrod had harried his midfielder into coughing up the ball, and turned to play the ball to Nixon, but made sure he hit it firmly and straight at his feet. The powerful Nigerian player couldn't adjust his feet quickly enough and the ball bounced off his shin and straight to Enrique Salvio who danced into the box amidst the jeering from the crowd and slammed the ball home past Ollie Sheen in the Gallowgate goal.

Jarrod was quick to apologise to his teammate and held his

hands up in remorse before placing them on his head and looking towards the sky. Newcastle down 2-0 at home after twenty minutes. Whilst this was no surprise, it was disappointing all the same. Jarrod felt dirty and cheap. He was sabotaging his own debut. It was truly awful.

Newcastle toiled with no end result until towards the end of the first half when they won a series of corners. Jarrod took three of them from the left, swinging them in with his right foot. On the third, there was a stoppage. The physios were all on the field tending to a clash of heads. One of the photographers moved towards him.

"Hello Jarrod," said the voice, a hint of a French accent. "Yannick Lefevre."

Jarrod shook the hand in front of him. He knew exactly who this was. This was the guy who had been stalking his wife. He noticed straight away that he had a scar along his left cheek and across his nose. The warpaint. That set alarm bells ringing in Jarrod's head.

"You stay away from my family," said Jarrod quietly, knowing that everyone in the Leazes corner would be watching him.

"I mean no harm," said Yannick. "I'm just a reminder that there is a job to be done and you need to make sure it happens. Or else."

"Or else what?" Jarrod's face contorted like he'd just bitten into something unexpectedly sour.

"André Rambouillet is not here to warn you," said Yannick, turning to resume his position behind the advertising hoardings. Jarrod was still staring at him as he got back to his spot. Yannick patted his trouser belt as if to let him know he was armed.

Jarrod's blood was fizzing. He wanted so bad to turn this game around and stick it to these bastards but knew that he couldn't.

Once play was ready to resume, the players were jockeying in the box, Jarrod sent the ball too far, even David racing in at the far post couldn't get on the end of it and the chance was gone.

Half-time came and there was applause. Some of the play had been impressive from both sides. Barcelona were good value for their two goal lead. Jarrod had given a good display, working hard to win a number of key tackles in the centre of the park, but that overhit pass and the corner that was too long were playing on his mind. He sat with his head bowed in the changing room. Mr Raffaella came in and addressed the team.

"The shape is right. The desire is there," he said. "We are playing against the best players in the world. Two goals down is not a disaster. With some patience, we can get this game back. No changes at half-time apart from Max coming on for Ollie, unless Nelson hears otherwise."

Mr Raffaella came over to Jarrod. He put his hand on his leg. Jarrod was expecting some cajoling words.

"Jarrod, you need to go and see Duddy, he's outside now. Be quick."

Jarrod looked up at his boss. He sprung to his feet and bounded for the door. Duddy was there and put his arm around him. He took him through the double doors and to the first door on the right, one of the medical rooms. He opened the door and bundled Jarrod in.

Dennis was there, the Detective Inspector had a headset on. The Chief Superintendent, Mick, was also present.

"Jarrod," said Dennis, "sit quickly."

Jarrod sat down.

"One more goal," said Dennis. "This is massive. If you can hold out for one more goal and make sure it stays at least three, we're moving in. An exorbitant amount of money is involved here. Betting companies around the world are set to pay out big money. We have teams around the UK and Europe ready to make arrests."

"And if I don't?" said Jarrod. "I've just been speaking with your friend Yannick Lefevre. Threatened me when I was taking a corner."

Dennis and Mick looked at each other in shock.

"Lefevre? Are you sure it was him?" asked Dennis. The Detective Inspector had taken off his headphones.

"He introduced himself," said Jarrod. "He's got scars across his nose and cheeks I see."

"Oh shit," said D.I. Allison, "was this when you were taking that last corner when play was stopped?"

"Yes," said Jarrod. "You've got cameras everywhere right?"

"Jarrod," said Dennis, "this changes everything. Get yourself out there and next time there's a corner, let us know where he is. They're all covered up, the photographers, it's hard to know who's who."

"Go," said D.I. Allison, shooing him out the door, "and score us a goal."

Duddy opened the door and Jarrod raced back to the changing room.

Jarrod felt like a weight had been lifted from his shoulders. Although he had not been told directly, he knew that it was game on. Both on and off the field. There was going to be some action here in the second half. He walked into the changing room, just as Mr Raffaella was getting ready to rouse the team for the second half. Jarrod put his hand on his arm as he walked past, as if to stop him from talking. He stood up on the nearest seat he could find, giving himself a stage.

"Lads," he said, full of emotion, "today is my home debut, we're two goals down, I've got my friends and family here, and I'm not going to come back in here losing two-nil."

All eyes were on him now. He'd perhaps overstepped the mark and Andros seemed to be getting a little agitated, looking at Mr Raffaella for intervention.

"Who's in with me?" asked Jarrod. "Who's in for the biggest 45 minutes of our lives?"

The players couldn't believe this. Hector Felipe let out a 'Hell yeah!' and everyone followed. Jarrod banged loudly on the wall to get the noise levels really pumping.

"Mr Raffaella," he said, stepping down from the seat and handing over to his boss, who let the roar die down before addressing his troops.

"Thank you Jarrod," he said. "Said like someone who really knows what it means to wear this shirt." He held aloft a spare shirt.

"Now, fifteen minutes to make something happen," he continued, "and changes will be attacking and will be designed to win the game. Let's go!"

The players all stood up in unison. Again the room filled with noise. Jarrod was getting pats on the back from his teammates. There were hugs and clenched teeth and fists. This team was ready to do business.

Jarrod knew now that he still had some work to do but it was now clear. He passed Aram on the way back out onto the field as the roar went up. He patted him on the back as he ran past.

Chapter 50

GLORY

The Newcastle supporters appeared to have lifted their intensity too. Barcelona had made a couple of changes, their new signing M'Bulaz was on in place of pantomime villain Salvio, who was spared the ignominy of being substituted during play.

From the kick-off Newcastle had a new intensity with Jarrod and Andros patrolling the midfield and they gradually worked their way into control. The first touch for M'Bulaz did give a frightening indication of his outrageous speed, tipping the ball around David Ponte and racing away to the byline. His cross though was fielded by Max Smeltz. He subsequently bowled the ball long and set Newcastle winger Milos Sarovic away down the left on the counter attack.

His trickery took him to the edge of the box, his attempt at a drilled cross ricocheted off the defender's leg and out for a corner. Jarrod was quick to get to it and place the ball on the corner.

"Yannick," he yelled at the group of photographers.

He waited for Yannick to pop his head from behind his camera. Jarrod walked over a couple of metres and pointed at him, looking him in the eyes as he did.

"Watch this mate …" he said and he trotted back over to the ball. He took a look around and lifted the ball perfectly to the near post where Nixon raced in and glanced the ball past the flailing arms of the goalkeeper and into the net.

The Gallowgate rose as one to acclaim the goal, Nixon ran across to Jarrod and they celebrated with the fans. Jarrod turned and could see Yannick being led away by two men and a steward. The crowd were now in full voice. Nixon punched the air as they lined back up for the restart. Jarrod looked over at the directors' box and hoped that Marianne and the kids were safe. There was action in one of the corporate boxes in the main stand towards the Leazes End, it looked as if there were a lot of police officers attending to a scene.

The game continued nevertheless. Newcastle were starting to purr. It wasn't long before Jarrod teased a tackle out of Barça captain Moujalli that resulted in a free kick. Surely not quite close enough for a shot but Sammy stood over it, readying to take it. As the crowd waited with anticipation, the referee blew the whistle, Sammy thumped the ball square for Alain. The wall reacted and a couple of players raced over to block the shot. Alain delicately lifted the ball back over the wall for Sammy who had made the perfect darting run. His control was perfect and he rolled the ball across the goal for Nixon to lash the ball into the net for a crazy equaliser.

St James' Park erupted. The players celebrated in the same corner as the first goal. Newcastle were level. Mr Raffaella was off his feet barking instructions at the players. There was murmuring in the Milburn Stand again and lots of police still in one of the corporate boxes. Things were happening, but Jarrod was concentrating on one thing only and that was winning this game.

There were still over 25 minutes to play. Barcelona began to soak up the pressure and drop deeper still to try and bring the home side out of their own tight defensive formation. Newcastle weren't falling for it though. Young star Marco Vetere was ready to come on. Jarrod hoped it wasn't for him, despite him having taken a heavy knock earlier in the half. He was relieved to see Saro going off. An attacking player for a midfielder. Marco came across and stood next to Jarrod.

"You need to stay on," said Marco. "There's all sorts happening over there and I've heard you're involved. Boss wants you to play the ninety minutes."

"Absolutely no way I'm going off anyway," said Jarrod. "Howay, let's beat these, eh?"

Jarrod and Andros had a little more time on the ball now that they were joined by another midfielder and they started to dictate the pace of the game. Barcelona's cutting edge had gone. They couldn't keep the ball in the Newcastle third, such was the intensity of the defending.

The game could go either way, Jarrod knew that this was not going to be a three goal defeat though. Hopefully the police had done their job and Marianne and the kids were safe. The next break in play for another substitution saw Jarrod scour the stand for where he thought they'd be, eventually seeing the frantic waving hands of Aneka. He waved back. They were all good. He could see a couple of police officers nearby.

Five minutes left on the clock. St James' Park was in full voice. The crowd belted out the *Blaydon Races*, drowning out the Barcelona fans. A feigned back heel from Marco saw him scamper away down the left, pursued by the two Barcelona midfielders he'd just tricked. He checked back, sending them both past him, and played the ball back to Stefa. Jarrod showed for him but Stefa turned instead and gave it to David Ponte who set off galloping down the left wing.

This was a scenario straight from training and Jarrod could see exactly what was happening. He raced upfield at full speed towards the penalty area. David got to the byline and hooked in a delightful cross. Jarrod wasn't sure if he could reach it but launched himself full length at the ball, risking a boot in the face. He connected perfectly. The ball flashed past the goalkeeper's hand and crashed off the underside of the bar. The supporters were off their seats, hands on heads, mouths agape.

A despairing stretch by a defender couldn't make any connection. First on the scene was Nixon who smashed the ball into the unguarded net to complete his hat-trick before racing away into the other corner, eventually swamped by his teammates. It was an incredible scene. Jarrod and David embraced. What a goal! Nixon pointed to the sky and smiled up at the heavens.

Newcastle withstood a heavy onslaught for the final throes of the game, M'Bulaz showed his pace again and flashed a shot that went an inch wide of the target from 30 yards. The game wouldn't be safe until the final whistle and Newcastle did everything they could to make the seconds tick away. St James' Park had never seen a friendly game like this before. The intensity was incredible. The substitutions were indeed made to win the game. The tactics were spot on.

The final whistle was greeted with an enormous roar. Players punched the air. It felt like a Champions League group stage game. Jarrod noticed that he was surrounded by police but they simply followed him as he made his way to the Gallowgate to salute the fans with the rest of the team. Jarrod had tears in his eyes. He was so proud and was so happy.

The players headed for the tunnel, still applauding. The police held Jarrod up for a second, shooing away the reporters and TV cameras. He was the last down the steps, getting even more applause as he went. He had no idea of what was ahead for him when he got to the top of the stairs at the other end of the tunnel. As he turned the corner he glanced back the other way and doubled back to look through an open door.

Ivan and Dimitri were on the floor, face down, with Davy and his crutches, next to what looked like Yannick, handcuffed. There were police everywhere. Aram was sitting in a seat, also in handcuffs. He looked up forlornly at Jarrod. A police officer moved over and closed the door. Jarrod was escorted to the medical room where he had been at half time.

Dennis and Duddy were there. Dennis stood up and showed him back through the door. Duddy was smiling.

"Where's Marianne?" he asked.

"All safe. The family's all safe. Bloody well done, Jarrod," said Dennis. "Now's not the time though. Shit's still going down. Go and celebrate your win with your teammates."

Jarrod flung open the double doors. The referee was there, just about to go in holding a match ball. Jarrod took it off him with a 'thank you' and went through the open door of the changing room. The room was full of chatter. A big roar went up as Jarrod walked in past Mr Raffaella, who grabbed his hand and held it aloft.

He walked straight over to Nixon and gave him the match ball and hugged his teammate. What a night this had been. A couple of the players started throwing water around from their water bottles. There was no champagne but it wouldn't have been out of place. This was a place of celebration. Newcastle United had just beaten Barcelona and they were all about to rightly receive the plaudits. This could be the sort of result that would sow the seeds of progress. Jarrod was absolutely delighted to be part of it.

Chapter 51

BUSTS

"Oh my god!" exclaimed Jarrod. He was sitting on the edge of his seat, watching CCTV footage of the busts around Europe. He was at Scotland Yard. It was like something out of the movies.

After checking in with Marianne and the kids last night to make sure they had a lift to the hotel and that the police were there, he was whisked away with the police via a helicopter to London. The police had him checked in to a secure hotel, seemingly part of the police complex, and collected him the next morning. Jarrod was escorted along a long corridor and into a big room where Dennis, the Detective Inspector, the Northumbria Police Chief Mick and a few other important-looking people in suits were waiting for him. They explained the whole scenario to him.

They had just started running through a map on the big screen showing bets and the time they were being placed. This bounced around Europe, even dipping into the Gambia in Africa, before returning to the major cities of western Europe. The graphic showed the amounts wagered, the odds and the amount set to be won. There were staggering amounts. A single bet in Macedonia went on for eight million pounds, and Riga in Latvia lit up with multiple bets totalling almost seven million.

Once it was established that there was upwards of six hundred million pounds to be returned from these transactions, the graphic stopped in each location with CCTV footage of the busts.

It showed police busting down doors, arresting fleeing individuals, rounding up gangs and placing them in cars. The busts were all synchronised during the second half of the game. There was heavy activity in Paris, an apartment overlooking the river Seine was busted, the police surrounding a couple in their bed, pointing their guns at them.

The most dramatic busts were in the UK. First it showed a raid in Glasgow. The big TV screen showed the police moving in on what looked like a motel, before someone made a dash from the door, sprinting at full speed. His gait was that of Rambouillet's killer, upright and fast, although this time he was dressed in tracksuit and trainers.

He managed to get quite a long way before a police constable fired a taser and he crashed to the floor, convulsing before he hit the ground with a smack. A dozen police officers were on him in a flash.

The footage then moved to Newcastle and specifically to St James' Park. There was footage of the first Newcastle goal, of Jarrod pointing to Yannick before taking the corner, and then of the plain clothed police officers moving in and walking him away in the ensuing goal celebration.

There was footage from inside one of the suites in the Milburn Stand. This must have been where all the police could be seen when the game was going on. The footage showed the moment where the goal went in. Hands went on heads, people looked at each other with hands extended in disbelief. The doors then opened and a huge crew of police officers walked in holding guns and making arrests. Jarrod could see Murtaka being instructed to lie on the floor – there was no sound – and he also saw Viktor and Adrian Barnes being asked to lie on the floor face down. They all complied, there was no resistance.

"So, who shot Rambouillet?" asked Jarrod once the graphic had come to an end.

"Rambouillet was shot by the gentleman you saw taken down by the Metropolitan Police officers with a taser," said D.I. Allison. "No dramatic twist – he was a common-variety hitman. We've matched him with another hit in Prague earlier this year."

Jarrod's skin bristled. He had just been in Prague.

"But who was he working for?" asked Jarrod.

"Well, we've arrested a Mr Jens Lermann," said Dennis, flicking through some papers to find the right spot. "Mr Lermann is a director of one of the biggest companies in the North East. I think you met him recently."

"Yes!" shouted Jarrod. "Oh yes, I remember him. Seemed like a nice fella too."

Jarrod remembered the Scandinavian sounding guy from the Darlington sponsor day. He had kids. He seemed like a normal dad doing normal dad stuff.

"What was his involvement?" asked Jarrod.

"Without going in to too much detail," said Dennis, "he was involved in a relationship with Murtaka. They were hoping to take over Newcastle with the type of takeover bid that couldn't be refused. And yes, when I say relationship, I mean he was shagging your friend Murtaka."

Jarrod gave a disappointed look to Dennis. He didn't need to know that. Dennis smiled, knowing he had taken the sultry Murtaka down a quarter of a peg in Jarrod's estimation. He still had questions though.

"Who's Aram?" asked Jarrod, looking around the room for an answer.

"Ah yes, Aram," said D.I. Allison. "He's …"

He didn't get very far before the door opened. In came another group of police officers, a couple of gentlemen in ill-fitting suits and two familiar faces. It was Mitch Short, Jarrod's Darlington teammate, and Freddie Hughton, ex-Gateshead teammate and now on Sunderland's books.

Jarrod stood up and walked over to his two friends. He got a hug from both of them and some weary smiles.

"You've been in on this, haven't you?" asked Jarrod.

Of course they had, but none of them knew about the other.

"Sounds like we've all been busy," said Mitch. "The offer to play for Rangers was too good to turn down. Sounds like we all had similar offers. I've been so stressed knowing about all this and not being able to do anything about it."

They all sat down and Dennis briefed them all together. Jarrod never did find out about Aram. He might have been a journalist from Armenia as far as he knew. He still had questions about Ivan, Dimitri, Davy and especially Iain and the physio team, but Dennis had practical information to share with them. After talking them through the events of the previous three weeks, he moved on to the present.

"You are all contracted for the rest of the season to your respective clubs," he said. "Thanks to the sterling work of your agent Duddy, you can choose to continue your season in the big time, even if you might not be considered in the first team."

He was looking specifically at Mitch. Jarrod definitely felt part of Newcastle's first team, unless of course Mr Raffaella was part of this whole charade too.

"On the other hand," he continued, "your home clubs are more than happy to welcome you back for the new season. I suggest you have a long discussion with your families and your clubs and decide what's best for you. And, as this is already the top news story all over Europe, be prepared for some media-heavy days."

"One thing we must say though," said one of the suited men, "is thank you. This has been a very important result for us. It rids us of an unwanted blight on the game of football, and ensures the integrity of the game we all love into the future. You have all shown remarkable professionalism in the face of a very unusual and delicate situation."

Jarrod felt an element of pride, but was more interested in knowing all about Mitch and Freddie's stories, about what they'd been asked to do on the field, who they'd met. And why they had been chosen to take part. That would come in time.

"We will definitely need you in the future to provide witness testimony in some high profile court cases," continued the big boss. "For now though, we would like to wish you all the best for the season ahead."

"You all have flights from Heathrow today," said Dennis. "They leave around 1pm, Mitch you will be picked up at the airport and taken to Ibrox for talks. Jarrod and Freddie, D.I. Allison will get you from the airport to wherever you need to be. Go and get your stuff and meet in the lobby in 30 minutes."

The Detective Inspector stood up, as did his team of three. Dennis stood up and shook their hands as they walked out. Jarrod was straight on the phone to Marianne.

"Back about 2.30pm," he estimated. "What's the latest?"

"This is crazy, Jarrod," said Marianne. "It's all over the news, the TV, the papers."

"Did you get back to Darlington?" asked Jarrod.

"No, we're still here in the hotel," said Marianne. "Mental health day – school's out of the question, and we've all just been glued to the TV."

"Okay," said Jarrod, finally grasping the enormity, "I'll be there this afternoon."

Jarrod had so many people he wanted to talk to. He wanted to confront Iain and find out exactly what his role was. He wanted to know more about Aram and threw his hands up when he realised he hadn't asked the question again when they had been interrupted. He needed to know the full story behind the face paint and more about this Yannick character. He made a mental note to ask Andros about why he took the penalty at Everton last season. So many loose ends to tie up, but he began by making the call to Caleb, the Fox Sports reporter. He felt a duty and he was a man of his word.

"Jarrod, is everything okay?" asked Caleb answering the phone in an instant. That showed a level of empathy and camaraderie that he recognised from a fellow Australian.

"Hello Caleb, yes, all good," came the calm response. "You can maybe appreciate now why I was a little on edge yesterday."

"I must apologise" he said. "I felt that everyone was ignoring a big, breaking story. Do you have time to talk now? I'm still in Newcastle."

"I'm heading there now," said Jarrod looking at his watch. "I've not got long. Meet me at the airport at 2pm and you can drop me at St James'. I'm on a tight schedule."

"Done."

Chapter 52

JIGSAW

D.I. Allison was reluctant to let Jarrod leave him once they arrived at Newcastle airport and made their way to the car park. Caleb was there as planned, in the taxi bay, risking the ire of the drivers. Jarrod gave Freddie a quick hug, and gave Marcus a much longer one. They had become friends, or so he hoped, through this crazy rollercoaster ride. The D.I. also had concerns about letting him out of his sight until he had been delivered to St James' Park.

"Thank you for everything," said Jarrod, almost with a tear in his eye. A toot from Caleb, who was just about to get moved on by the taxi rank steward, made the exit a lot quicker. Jarrod ran across to diffuse the situation, jumping in the passenger seat. Caleb was driving before he fully closed the door and offered his hand to Jarrod once he finished buckling up.

"Oh my god!" said Caleb. "This is some story, you know. I don't know if you're keeping up with it, but there's been twists and turns all morning. That Viktor Andreyev looks as though he's done for."

"Of course!" exclaimed Jarrod, realising that Andreyev had been the operation behind the parties, and that he was the Viktor he had met on the Saturday afternoon.

"Of course what?" asked Caleb.

Jarrod wasn't quite sure what he was meant to divulge at this point. It was a complex story that would take much longer than a drive between the airport and St James' Park. He decided to save it for another time.

"Still piecing things together," Jarrod said by way of response while his mind whirred. "Anyway, ask away. Unless you're planning on taking some wrong turns, I reckon you've got twenty minutes tops to ask as many questions as you can."

"Yannick Lefevre," said Caleb. "Rambouillet's so-called friend. Was he the killer?"

"No, no," said Jarrod. "The killer was a hit man. Yannick was definitely involved though and must have organised the whole thing. There were some details along the way that, looking back now, do suggest that he was the mastermind."

Jarrod was referring to the face paint and the fact that Yannick had scars across his face and nose. It just seemed like a vanity thing or a way of making everyone feel like he did. Jarrod couldn't quite understand it himself.

"Anyway," continued Jarrod, "let's not dwell on these non-footballing matters. I'll give you a quick rundown on how I came to play for Newcastle United and then you can ask me about the game."

Jarrod took Caleb through the transfer process, forgetting the details like meeting the police at the Arena and the regular meetings with D.I. Allison. He spun the story that Mr Raffaella had been tracking him for years. To be fair that was true. He concluded at the point where he was unveiled as a Newcastle player. Caleb knew the rest.

"I knew there was something going on," said Caleb,

concentrating on the road. "It was you that took down the betting syndicate."

"That was the police," said Jarrod. "I was there merely to pass on anything unusual at the club. A very small piece in a very complex jigsaw."

"You've done well to come out of this alive," said the reporter.

Jarrod didn't want to think about it.

"What a game last night though, eh?" said Jarrod enthusiastically.

They chatted the rest of the way about the game and how the masterful tactics of manager Benito Raffaella had changed the game in the second half. Jarrod was happy with the way Caleb was interpreting the events. There was some confirming of facts about the Socceroos and some loose ends that Caleb tied up about his move from Gateshead to Darlington last year. As they passed the BBC on the way down to Barrack Road and the stadium Caleb asked the question he asked the day before.

"So will we be seeing you in the A-League before the end of your career?"

That was an interesting one. He hadn't lived in Australia for nearly 20 years. His family were not Australian and, although they had enjoyed many trips there, their home was definitely in England.

"We'll see," said Jarrod nonchalantly. "There's plenty of options open to me at the moment, but we'll see."

Jarrod held out his hand and Caleb took it for a warm handshake. Jarrod quickly jumped out and jogged over to the main reception. He was ready to find out his future.

Chapter 53

RETURN

Newcastle United cleared out their physio team immediately. Iain and his assistants, Ivan and Dimitri, were nowhere to be seen when Jarrod returned to Little Benton on the Tuesday. The promise of a year's loan was not technically correct as Jarrod found out. As he had suspected after talking with Duddy, the agreement was officially a month-to-month contract.

Duddy was sure that the club would honour the terms as discussed at Scotland Yard, but he couldn't give a guarantee. Mr Raffaella had been busy in the transfer market, bringing in two world class midfielders. These two long term targets had been pushed quickly over the line the morning after Sunday's magnificent win over Barcelona in front of a worldwide TV audience. The result of the game was as big a story as the arrests and scandal that followed. Mr Raffaella welcomed Jarrod into his office and explained the lay of the land to Jarrod.

Of course he wanted Jarrod to stay. He had been fantastic in the first part of pre-season. He also said that the quality he had brought in was for the long run, and he couldn't be sure that Jarrod would figure in the first team as a result. Effectively Jarrod was being given an honest appraisal of his situation by a straight-talking manager who simply wanted the best for his player. That was enough for Jarrod to make up his mind.

The telephone call to Pauline and June at Darlington was one of pure joy. The wheels were put in motion so quickly that he was saying goodbye to the staff and players at the Newcastle training ground by lunchtime, and he had checked out of his hotel by two. He was home in Darlington just as the kids returned with Marianne from their first day back at school and he enjoyed an hour catching up with his favourite three people in the world.

A meeting at the Arena with Gerry, Pauline and June just after 5pm saw him officially registered as a returning loan player, and after a quick dash back to the house to fetch his gear, he was in the changing room getting ready ahead of a pre-season friendly with Peterborough. He was glad to have had no time to read the socials, the papers or his text messages – they were awash with rumour about his availability and future destinations. Caleb had told him earlier that day of some big A-League interest. There were Premier League teams circling too.

"Tonight we welcome back our club captain Jarrod Black," said Gary as the first item in his pre-game preamble. There was a cheer. "As a result of abandoning us for those upstarts at St James' Park, Jarrod will start on the bench tonight as he begins to win back our trust and tries to break back into our first team."

The changing room burst with laughter. That was exactly how Jarrod felt – he didn't want to barge in to a guaranteed place in the team, and Gary played it to perfection. Jarrod got changed surrounded by three or four new faces and he quickly became acquainted.

The two loan players from Newcastle were set to be with them for the season, and Gerry had brought in some fresh talent from last season's Championship. There was also a well-known older player from the Dutch Eredivisie. Darlington had definitely not stood still while Jarrod had been away. They were continuing to aim high. Gary had been signed up for another three years, and their first two pre-season results had seen them knock over higher level opponents in some style.

Jarrod was home. It felt right. He was already looking forward to the end of season party.

ACKNOWLEDGEMENTS

Fair Play Publishing have done it again. Thanks to Bonita and her team, we have another Unashamed Football Novel to add to the series. It has been a testing time, and I applaud her decision to go ahead with a book release during the Covid-19 pandemic.

Thank you to my sources in Newcastle - you know who you are - for giving me inspiration during the writing process, Jacqui too for setting me straight with some facts about the Toon. I've absolutely loved being taken back to the streets of Newcastle by this story, and I know how much I miss it.

To everyone who has taken the time to read the first two books in the series, I salute you. There have been photos from all over the world from eager readers. I really love it that you have all come along on this fantastic journey. Keep giving feedback and writing reviews online to help spread the word. That will provide the incentive to keep on writing. Lots of love to you all!

And finally to the Boolas Spreaker Clerb - Steve, Barry and Jules - I look forward to getting back to late night banter in front of the Premier League. It's been too long.

Other really good football books
from Fair Play Publishing

The Time of
My Football Life
by David Picken

Surfing for England
Our Lost Socceroos
by Jason Goldsmith

Encyclopedia of Matildas
by Andrew Howe
and Greg Werner

Encyclopedia of Socceroos
by Andrew Howe

'If I Started to Cry,
I Wouldn't Stop'
by Matthew Hall

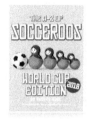

The A-Z of Socceroos -
World Cup Edition 2018
by Andrew Howe (with Ray
Gatt and Bonita Mersiades)

Playing for Australia
The First Socceroos,
Asia and the World Game
by Trevor Thompson

The World Cup Chronicles
31 Days that Rocked Brazil
by Jorge Knijnik

Chronicles of Soccer
in Australia - The
Foundation Years 1859 to
1949 by Peter Kunz

Support Your Local League,
A South-East Asian
Football Odyssey by
Antony Sutton

The Aboriginal Soccer Tribe
by John Maynard

Achieving the Impossible
- the Remarkable Story
of How Greece Won
EURO 2004
by George Tsitsonis

Whatever It Takes - The
Inside Story of the FIFA
Way by Bonita Mersiades
(Powderhouse Press)

Introducing
Jarrod Black
by Texi Smith
(Popcorn Press)

Jarrod Black
Hospital Pass
by Texi Smith
(Popcorn Press)

The Australian Youth
Footballer Regulatory Guide
by Peter Paleologos
(Popcorn Press)

www.fairplaypublishing.com.au/shop

Lightning Source UK Ltd.
Milton Keynes UK
UKHW020039060620
364498UK00002B/63